LIFE CHANGING YARD SALE

DEALS TO DIE FOR

LAZARUS SPIRAL I

T. KULP

ISBN: 978-1-956612-22-6 (Paperback)
ISBN: 978-1-956612-21-9 (eBook)

Making Adventure Publishing
16944 York Rd, Suite 62
Monkton, MD 21111

To Mom & Dad,
thank you for all
the evil toys.

*Most of the evil in this world is done
by people with good intentions.*

T.S. Eliot

AUTHOR'S NOTE

On the way home from Dunkin' Donuts, my wife spotted a sign and laughed. She said, "That's going in a story." It said "Life Changing Yard Sale," with an arrow pointing down the road. The sign was neon green poster paper written in thick black marker.

What did it mean? Life changing? Growing up in a small town, I had seen many yard sales, but none of them rose to the status of "life-changing."

That day was rainy, terrible weather for a yard sale. My mind spun with ideas of why the person had to have the yard sale today. A few stories sprung up but nothing really caught me, and so I let the idea marinate.

A few months later, I was teaching a class on using Artificial Intelligence for story ideation and demoed my "Idea Store" method for building story concepts. The title that I landed on using a random book title generator was 2938: Beta. I was hooked! As I started writing 2938, the idea of the yard sale crept in as the initial setting. From there, more ideas, more toys started popping up in my mind. A collection of stories about haunted toys was born, all from one "Life Changing Yard Sale."

I hope you enjoy this collection and have as much fun reading the stories as I had writing them.

And if you're wondering, no, I don't usually stop at yard sales. After exploring this world, I don't know that I ever will.

Enjoy,

Tim

06/02/2023

29

ONE

Lucy shuffled through the antique game cartridges like a bulldozer in a mass grave. She didn't have time to care for the discarded. She needed the game that would save her stream: *Ninja Gaiden* for the Nintendo Entertainment System.

This was her third yard sale today, searching for a game to reengage her viewers, but she struck out everywhere. There were lots of old games, but they were all the popular games. She needed something more obscure, something to show her gaming skills. Engagement was key to stop bleeding subscribers, and very difficult retro games always led to a hot stream.

While she struck out at the other two yard sales, this one's sign promised big things. A pollen-yellow sign with jagged black letters said, "Life Changing Yard Sale." She didn't expect her life to be changed, she just hoped to save her live stream. Unfortunately, the Life Changing Yard Sale didn't have *Ninja Gaiden* or any other obscure, difficult retro games.

Lucy wondered, why not just call it a *Moving Sale*, or an *I Got Divorced Sale*, or even an *I died and My Family Doesn't Want My Stuff Sale*? "Life Changing" is dramatic, even by her sixteen-year-old, public high school standards.

Regardless of the drama, the sign worked. More people joined the crowded front lawn of the small ranch-style house. Chaos reigned over the scattered mismatched blankets. Old ladies bickered and swarmed over them, arguing who saw what first. Junk of all kinds was thrown over the bunched-up blankets except one: a burgundy patchwork quilt covered with well-organized toys. On this blanket, a gray rubber container overflowed with video games.

Lucy sighed as she checked the last game cartridge in the bin. She hadn't heard of it, but the cute turtle on the cover told her it wasn't what she needed tonight. She dropped it back into the bin. A plastic crack came from under the other games. Her hopes sparked. Did she miss the treasure she needed for tonight's live stream? Lucy shoved the games aside. At the bottom she found something that didn't belong with the video games.

A boxy VHS tape gleamed in the midday sun, pristine and bright white; not black like most VHS tapes. No yellowed stain from age or smoking or coffee on it, just a smeared thumb print near the black marker title. Lucy examined a black or deep crimson smear on the case, unsure of the color, but certain it was a thumbprint. The title on the tape was handwritten and scrawled with the same care as for the video games in the bin.

"Wow! I can't believe you found that." Her mom, Trudy, helped dig through the bins. "Is that an original?" She laughed.

"What is it?" Lucy waved the VHS tape like an ancient artifact.

"It's a game. Well, it was a game." Trudy took the tape. "Yeah, *Captain Light and the World of Darkness*." She read the marker title, keeping her own thumb clear of the smear. "This came out when I was a kid. You played it on your VCR long before the Nintendo."

Other shoppers moved around them. One old lady bumped Lucy out of the way so she could explore the game bins. Probably looking for potential eBay sales. None of these games were worth anything, but rude old biddies never cared about any of that. They just wanted the bargain.

Lucy searched again for whoever ran the yard sale. No one checked on the customers as they gathered armloads of junk, from lamps to velvet paintings. At the edge of the sale, there was a table with a money jar on it. Lucy watched the house to see if anyone came out. Maybe they just went in for a drink and were on their way back out? But that didn't feel quite right. Lucy had been here for over an hour. No sign of anyone. A few people shoved money in the jar as they left, but most just left. Rude.

Trudy dug through a bin beside the games and pulled out a plastic spaceship that looked like a scorpion. It had a red body, boney red legs that curled around your forearm, and a handle that dropped from under the cockpit with a yellow trigger. Lucy examined the toy to see how it worked. She found an empty battery compartment and an infrared emitter like a TV remote.

"Was this one of those light gun games?" Lucy asked as she tried the ship on her wrist. She gave the trigger a few squeezes. She felt the spring's tight resistance. Turning the ship over, the number 29 was written in the same handwriting as on the white tape. The handwriting on the ship and tape were jagged and messy, while the yard sale sign was crisp, almost calligraphic. She stared at the yard sale sign for a moment longer. Whoever wrote that didn't write this.

"What's 29?"

"I don't know." Trudy looked for more treasures. "But that game didn't stay on the shelves long. It got wrapped up in the whole Satanic Panic crap from the 80s. Disappeared fast. I wonder if there's anything more around. You need something great for tonight?" Trudy waved the tape. "This is something different. It's retro. It's unusual, like, I'm betting your viewers don't know it. And when you show them a VCR, it's going to blow their minds." Trudy's eyes popped open as her hands contained the imaginary explosion from her brain.

"Yeah, that might be cool. Do we have a…" Lucy searched for what her mom said. "One of those VCR things?"

"Yep. Your dad has one in the basement. He loves all that old tech stuff."

"You know where?" Lucy thought about the junk piles in the basement, aka her dad's treasures. With him away on business, Lucy didn't know if anyone else could understood the chaos of his organizational system.

"I'll find it. Want to get it?"

Lucy smiled. It's not *Ninja Gaiden*, but it might be what she needed to hook more viewers in her live stream. "Yeah, I can't find a price."

"Probably fell off." Trudy shuffled through the game box again, now competing with the rude old lady. "These look like they're about five bucks each, so we'll leave ten."

Lucy noticed a small figure inside the scorpion ship. She popped open the frost-blue plastic cockpit. The sour tang of spoiled milk hit her nose, knotting her stomach. Thick spit lumped in her throat as she pulled the cockpit open to see the figure inside. The revulsion at what she saw squeezed a faint whine from her gasping chest.

She wasn't sure if the face had melted or was chewed by an overly anxious dog, but it was mutilated in streaks of slashed plastic. One eye bulged wide, painted infected pus-yellow with a red dot in the center, while the other was proportionate but black. The mouth curled in a knowing smile. His clothes were molded plastic, high tech as if robotic, but the paint had chipped away long ago. A thick grease covered the figure. Lucy shivered at the idea of touching it and wondered if whatever that oily gunk was was what smelled so bad. She shut the cockpit with a thunderous click that silenced the yard sale around her.

"We better get home. If I'm going to do this, I'll need setup time for the stream tonight."

"Sounds good. I'll just put this," Trudy held up the ten-dollar bill, "in the jar over there."

They pushed through the other shoppers and left the Life Changing Yard Sale feeling their lives were no different from when they arrived.

TWO

Nadia and Sam were waiting for Lucy when her mom pulled into the driveway.

Sam leaned his slight frame against the railing of Lucy's porch. Of the three friends, Sam was the lankiest, with long arms and legs that still tripped him up in his clumsiness. His skinny jeans and track jacket only emphasized Trudy's urge to feed him.

Nadia slowly swung in the gliding rocker. Her long black hair comfortably settled over her shoulders. She was short but ferocious, having chased Sam out of that rocker many times in the past. Nadia loved swinging to calm her anxiety. A constant fear of the world and all the horrible things that could happen were managed with hot tea, swinging, and, when all else failed, medication.

They were Lucy's production crew. Sam did the video production to build his portfolio for art school after senior year. Nadia did the production setup as practice for her future interior design career. Lucy was the gamer and online personality, which wasn't anything she was interested in for the future, but was a fun way to spend time with her besties. But losing subscribers wasn't fun. It was a reminder that Lucy was the weak link, and she never wanted her friends to fail because she couldn't cut it.

Sam and Nadia looked hopefully at Lucy, waiting to see a treasure that would save their stream. Instead, Trudy hurried inside to find the VCR and said, "Drinks in the fridge," as she passed.

"Okay, so check this out." Lucy held up the VHS tape. "This is a video game." She held up the scorpion ship. "This is the controller. You play it on a VCR."

Neither Nadia nor Sam reacted immediately; they only screwed up their faces wondering what Lucy was thinking. How would you stream this?

"Dino-tech?" Sam laughed. "Our plan to save our subscribers is Dino-tech?"

Nadia rolled her eyes. "It's not that old. Only like almost three times as old as we are." She laughed, and the others joined in. Forty years old is ancient when you're sixteen. Trudy wouldn't have laughed.

But the laughing stopped quickly as the three got down to business. They went straight to Lucy's room and prepared for the evening's stream. Her room was too small to keep up the cameras, lighting, and backdrop she used.

Sam set up the camera. Nadia took the spaceship controller from Lucy and set it on her desk as part of her backdrop.

"Here, the ship will be in your intro shot." Nadia placed the red scorpion ship on the edge of Lucy's computer desk. "Do you know where—" Nadia turned and hit the ship with her hip. It fell to the floor with a plastic snap, sending the figure tumbling out of the cockpit. "OMG! I'm so sorry!" She quickly swooped down to pick up the ship and its pilot but recoiled at the pilot's gnarled body and hideous features. The appearance of the figure fused into a sense of loathing that Nadia never knew a toy could deserve. "Uh… What happened to that thing?" She backed away from it, startling when her butt hit the desk.

"Yeah, just ugly. Guess some dog got it or a kid tried to blow it up or something." Lucy shrugged.

Sam picked up the toy without looking at it and set the figure on Lucy's desk. Unconsciously, he wiped his hands quickly on his jeans, trying to scrape away the oily feeling left behind by the action figure.

They kept setting up as Trudy came in with a black rectangular box. She grunted as she set it down on Lucy's desk. "This," she sighed, "is a TV-VCR combo. You just put the tape in there, hit this button, and it will play."

"How's it hook up to my computer?" Lucy looked at the connection ports on the back of the VCR. Three plugs stuck out: yellow, white, and red. She'd never seen an HDMI cable like that before.

"It doesn't." Trudy chuckled. "Believe it or not, once upon a time, not everything hooked up to a computer."

"Just need an adapter for your video card," Sam chimed in as he inspected the ancient device. "Probably can pick one up from—"

"We don't have time for all that. Stream's live in an hour. We've gotta make sure all this works before then, or I've gotta cancel for tonight," Lucy said. Missing a stream could be recovered. Having a bad stream was death.

"Okay, well, how about I setup the DSLR camera to record the screen and we'll stream your intro from my phone?" Sam offered.

"Sounds good," Lucy confirmed. "Can you set up the camera while we do a tech check?"

Nadia examined the tape. "How much data goes on this?"

Trudy laughed as she walked out of the room.

"Look, it can't be that hard. We're techies and smart. We can figure this out," Lucy said. Much later, she'd remember these events and hear the hubris of someone who doesn't know how badly things could go wrong. As if to further damn herself, she said, "Besides, it's just a toy."

Sam set up the tripod, set up the camera, and was eyeing the viewfinder. "Can you put in the tape? I want to see what kind of distortion we get."

"Sure." Nadia pushed in the tape and turned to help Lucy get her computer stream prepared. They jumped at the hiss of static that erupted from the TV-VCR. Nadia screamed. Both their eyes jumped to the TV screen. Both their jaws fell open at the view.

The camera on the screen was panning around a destroyed wasteland. Buildings in the background were skeletal hulks, gutted and crumbling. The sky was gray, and Lucy assumed, at first, that the video was black and white. She squinted at the ground as the camera panned across the landscape. What she thought was sand looked more like glass after the static cleared and the camera slowed down. The glass dunes rolled and coiled in razor waves, wrapping along the horizon in an ocean of desolation.

"Is the ground made of glass?" Lucy wondered out loud, in a dreamy trance.

"What is this?" Nadia held her stomach, the butterflies inside ready to evacuate through her mouth. The pilot was still the most horrible thing she'd ever seen, but this landscape, this world on the TV, was a close second. "That's amazing production quality. The set design is so," she coughed dryly, trying to bring spit back into her mouth, "so real."

"Sam, how's the shot?" Lucy shook her head, pulling her attention away from the TV screen. "Sam?" She looked back at the camera. Sam was on the floor spasming, with a thick white foam spurting from his mouth. His eyes were open, staring into nothing but screaming for help. Every muscle in his body fired in a coiling, writhing mass, jerking him up and down like a teetering ship on a stormy current.

"Sam!" Lucy jumped out of her chair and rushed to him. Nadia followed. Neither watched the TV screen as the view changed to black static. Flickering faces emerged from the darkness. Two teenage girls appeared, pressing their faces close to the camera. They called for help, but no sound was heard over the screaming in the room.

"Mom!" Lucy shouted. "Mom! Help!"

Static crackled through Lucy's bedroom in a constant popping drone. Nadia grabbed her ears and clenched her eyes shut. She screamed for help too, but not just for Sam. She wanted the overload to stop—the static, the screaming, Sam's gurgling, the rotten milk stink filling the room, the floor shaking from his seizures. Groping behind her, she found the power cord to the TV and ripped it out of the wall. The static stopped just as Trudy ran into the room and told Lucy to call 911.

Nadia rocked on her knees, squeezing her ears to keep the noises out, but it didn't help. She could still hear Sam choking on the foam bubbling out of his mouth. She could still hear Trudy screaming at the 911 operator. And she could feel Lucy holding on to her tight, rocking with her as they watched their bestie die.

THREE

"Is he okay?" Lucy rushed to Sam's parents as they came out of the emergency room.

The EMTs were able to get Sam to the hospital before it was too late. Of the three EMTs who arrived, two turned vampire white when they took Sam's vitals. The third vomited in the bathroom after seeing his twisted body and smelling the nose-seering stench of whatever was leaking from Sam's mouth. Trudy followed the ambulance with Lucy and Nadia, arriving at the hospital just a few moments after Sam's parents. Sam was taken to the Emergency Room and his parents were swept into another room to talk with doctors.

The hospital waiting room was full of people coughing, kids crying, and a surly old man shouting how he was fine no matter what the stupid heart machine said. Green chairs were meant to calm the patients in waiting, but that never happened. Sea foam walls were the same, but when you're waiting for bad news—and healthcare news is always bad—nothing is all that calming.

"He's awake. The doctors want to keep him here overnight." Sam's mom tried to trap the tears in her eyes, but they broke free and streamed long black mascara streaks down her cheeks.

Lucy wrapped her in a hug. "Sam's tough. He'll get through this."

Nadia joined the hug. "Yeah, Sam's too stubborn to be sick." They laughed.

"Did they say what happened?" Lucy asked as they all let go of the hug.

"Seizure," Sam's mom said. Her face twisted in the same expression of doubt the old man having a heart attack had on his face. She doubted the doctors like the man in the waiting room doubted the heart machine.

"Has he ever had—" Nadia started, but Sam's mom cut her off.

"Never."

Lucy and Nadia exchanged glances, both wondering what was on that tape. Why did it cause Sam to seize? They'd seen enough horror movies, read enough Creepy Pasta to recognize when the monster appears. Here, the tape was the monster, but nothing came out of it, no monster leaked from the TV and claimed their souls. Instead, it did something to Sam, made him seize, but why only him? As best friends do, the girls were thinking the same thing at the same time: Why Sam and not them? All three saw the tape. But only Sam was here.

"Can we see him?" Nadia asked hesitantly, but Sam's mom nodded quickly.

"Seeing you two would do him good. He's…he's down."

Sam's mom took Lucy and Nadia back through the ER doors, away from the coughing, crying, pale greens to a world of buzzing alarms, quiet conversations, and light blue curtains. An antiseptic smell permeated the air, making Lucy wonder how many showers it took for the nurses to scrub off the hospital stink.

Sam was behind the third blue curtain. Nadia peeked around each curtain as they went, always curious, always listening in on conversations. A man was asking his daughter about the other driver. Next curtain was about all the ice cream someone could eat. Behind Sam's curtain, he was mumbling something about getting free.

Sam's mom cleared her throat, announcing their arrival as she grabbed the blue curtain.

Sam answered, "Come in." He coughed hard, scraping his lungs clean, and then swallowed hard.

Nadia stepped in first with a happy, *everything will be alright* smile.

"Hey, guys!" Sam smiled and pointed to his pale blue medical robe. "Don't look behind me. You'll catch a full moon."

Sam's mom blushed and swatted at the air between her and him. "Now stop that fresh talk. I'll get a coffee while you three chat." She turned, shot Lucy a worried smile. Lucy heard the mumbling as they approached and was certain Sam's mom did too. Do seizures make you talk to yourself? Lucy wan't sure.

"How are the numbers?" Sam asked.

Lucy waved away the question. The numbers didn't matter to her. Never really did. Their stream was about spending time together, and she'd thought Sam was a goner. She didn't care if they ever did another stream, as long as Sam got better.

"Forget all that. What happened?" Lucy asked.

Sam shrugged. "Not sure. Was looking through the camera, then I woke up in the ambulance." The tip of his nose turned red as he finished his sentence. Nadia and Lucy knew Sam better than his parents. He told them secrets he wasn't ready to share with anyone else, and they both knew that the red nose meant he was lying.

"You're Pinocchio-ing." Nadia called him out. Sam's hand jumped to his nose, and he quickly shook his head.

"Serious, I don't remember." Sam looked at something past Lucy. He shook his head, denying someone behind them. Nadia turned, but there was no one there.

"Do you remember seeing the wasteland on the video?" Lucy probed carefully. "Maybe something flickered there, like when you get the warning about video games with strobing lights?"

"I don't remember." Sam dismissed the conversation and leaned back. "Are you guys…" He trailed off and again looked past them. His eyes fixed on something no one else saw. His pupils inflated, shrinking the brown of his eyes into a golden sliver.

"What's there?" Lucy looked back. There was a clock on the far wall, but that's not what Sam saw. His eyes were fixed far beyond anything in this world.

"I'm going to be sick." Sam covered his mouth, but not in time. The vomit sprayed out between his fingers, catching Nadia on the cheek. She jumped back and squealed. Lucy didn't move. She watched Sam's eyes as they dilated to complete black, blood vessels popping as every muscle in his body flexed, locked, flicked, and rocked him in the hospital bed. Sam's alarms blared in deafening panic. A medical team arrived quickly. Nurses rushed past Lucy and Nadia, who was still wiping chunks of Sam's dinner from her face. One nurse told them to step out and showed them the door. Sam's mom was at the door when they arrived.

"I don't know what happened," Lucy said through tears. "He was fine and then he wasn't." But Lucy didn't think Sam was fine. Nothing about him in the hospital seemed fine. Why did he lie about what he remembered? What was he looking at?

Sam wasn't himself, and Lucy knew the white tape was Sam's real problem. Not seizures. Not anything a hospital could help. She didn't know who *could* help, but a thorn in her mind suggested the tape could have the answers. The tape started this. The tape could end it.

FOUR

Nadia's parents were at her brother's play, *Legally Blonde*, when the craziness occurred at Lucy's. Nadia didn't call them; she didn't want to take away from her brother's opening night as "Guy in Background." Small part, big excitement in her family.

Trudy drove the girls home from the hospital. Everyone was too trapped in their thoughts to talk.

Trudy thanked God her daughter wasn't in Sam's place. She felt bad for Sam's mom, but couldn't help the deep gratitude that bubbled in her that Lucy was safe.

Nadia remembered how sick Sam looked. To her, he was slimy with sweat, with puffy cheeks and bulging, bruise-circled eyes. He looked worse than when he left Lucy's room on the stretcher. And the smell. No amount of antiseptic covered up the eye-watering stench.

Lucy was thinking about his eyes. How big they grew in the end and how, in the deep black of those pupils, she swore she saw static. Static like the buzzing from the white tape. She dismissed the idea quickly, finding a million things the reflection might have been. The neon lights above, the beeping machines around him, the sanitizing gel dispenser near the entrance. A million could-bes flew through her mind with only one idea anchoring into her gut and twisting to a stop: the TV static.

"You want to stay over until your parents get home, sweetie?" Trudy broke the silence and brought everyone back to the car as they parked at Lucy's house.

"Yeah, I'll get some stuff. I know my mom and dad will be back late. I'll just message them," Nadia said as she got out of the car.

Lucy got out quickly. "Want me to come with you?"

Nadia shook her head and looked at her house. The porch light was on. She held up her watch and said, "Hey, Siri, turn on the lights in the house." And the house came alive with a warm glow. She smiled and sighed, thankful for the safety of modern technology.

Nadia crossed her lawn. The keys rattled in her pocket as she pulled them out. A light wind blew, bringing sounds that should accompany a wind, like rustling leaves and creaking branches. No need to turn and see what made the noise. It was the wind, she was certain, but to calm herself she took a deep breath, like her therapist taught her, and walked inside.

Her house was the same as all the other houses on the street. They were cookie-cutter designs with the only defining features found in small things like trim, a bay window, an extra half-bathroom. Things most wouldn't notice unless you lived on the street. Lucy and Nadia's houses were clones.

In the warm light, Nadia hustled upstairs and grabbed her bag, which was always ready to bolt to Lucy's house. They joked it was a "bolt bag" for escaping suburban life, as Nadia kept it equipped with clothes, sleeping bag, and flashlights. Standard needs for any sleepover.

She stepped quickly downstairs and stopped in the kitchen for her anxiety medicine. After a day like today, she knew she'd need some extra help to get to sleep. She grabbed the bottle and headed for the door.

"Hey, Siri, turn off all the lights except the porch," Nadia called out.

"On it," Siri responded in her cheery voice, and a moment later, all the warm light drained away into the dark murk of a moonless spring night.

Nadia left out the front door and circled around to her back yard, which connected with Lucy's back yard. A white picket privacy fence stretched between Lucy and Nadia's yards. Nadia opened the gate to go through the fence. The wind picked up again in a gusting cool breeze. More creaking branches, some cracked now. Probably falling from the trees. She shook her head but suddenly felt just how dark the night was without a moon, without the backyard lights on.

"Siri, turn on the backyard lights."

No answer.

Nadia kept walking, knowing where to go. She'd walked this path countless times in darker nights than this, but she never remembered a night so…oppressive.

She realized her mistake and asked again, "Hey, Siri," emphasizing the *hey* to wake Siri. Nadia repeated the command as the fence gate hinges whined open.

That made her stop. Probably the wind, but worth a look.

No one was there.

"On it," Siri responded, but the lights didn't come on. Nadia stood, watching the gate swing in the night. "The request is taking longer than expected." Siri confided, almost ashamed.

The lights didn't come on. Nadia wasn't waiting anymore. She walked faster toward Lucy's house. Then, slowly, the lights came on as a loud rustling came from the line of trees at the edge of her back yard. They were still shaking as she looked at them, but the lights didn't reach that far. *Only the wind.* She laughed at how the characters in horror movies kept explaining away weird things until a knife was sticking out of their throat. The killers never used reasonably sized knives. They used bushwhacking, deep-forest survival knives found in butcher shops and jungle expeditions.

Imagining the knife sizes made Nadia walk faster. As the knife grew in her mind, her pace quickened until she saw a machete and started running. The knife was only in her mind, but she knew, if she turned, there'd be a real one right behind her, and a moment's pause would end up with that knife through her chest.

"Hey! Hey!" Nadia slammed on the door with her palm. "Hey, Lucy! Hey!" She glanced over her shoulder. The trees shook in a wave now, that wave coming toward her quickly. *It's just the flow of the wind.* "Hey!" she screamed. Panic bled into pleading as she hit the door harder and harder, faster and louder.

Lucy appeared in the door's window and ran to let her in, but Nadia kept pounding. When Lucy opened the door, Nadia pushed through, knocking her back. Nadia panted, on the edge of hyperventilation. Lucy shut the door quickly.

"What's wrong!?" Lucy looked out the window but only saw a windy night.

"I don't know." Nadia gasped, her chest heaving from not breathing. She realized she'd stopped breathing when the gate opened and hadn't taken in air since. "I don't know. Probably just spooked."

"You ladies okay?" Trudy called from the kitchen. "I've made some tea to help calm us all down."

Nadia looked back outside. The wind roared on, but no sign of a stalker. No killer. No unreasonable knife glimmering in the moonless night. She pulled her anxiety pills out of her bag, rattled them, and thought, *Yeah, good call.*

"Hey, Siri, turn off the lights except for the porch," Nadia said into her watch, and stared outside with Lucy. The lights faded away. The wind howled on.

Waiting another moment, Lucy and Nadia left the back door for their tea and went upstairs to Lucy's room.

Everything was still set up the way it was when Sam was taken out by the paramedics. The TV-VCR combo was turned off. The camera tripod Sam set up was knocked over. Lucy picked it up and put it to the side as she walked in.

"Was it the tape?" Nadia said, finally able to ask the question she couldn't get out until now.

Lucy shrugged.

"I mean, video games with flashing lights can give people seizures. And, like, looking through the camera, he saw some kind of distortion that triggered it?" Nadia looked at the camera. The black DSLR felt cold as her thumb hovered over the play button. She wondered what Sam saw, but a voice in her mind told her to put it down. Do not proceed. She listened. "Where did you get it again?"

"A yard sale," Lucy answered, but then gasped. "A life-changing yard sale."

"What?" Nadia chuckled at that. "For real?"

"Yeah, it was called a Life Changing Yard Sale." Lucy plugged in the TV-VCR, then ejected the tape. Her finger traced the thumbprint smear. It was dark red after all. Perhaps the blood of the previous owner.

"Who sold it to you?"

"There wasn't anyone there." Lucy remembered the full jar of bills. "An estate sale or something."

"Think we should go back?"

"Probably."

The girls sat on Lucy's bed and stared at the white tape now sitting between them. Neither wanted to touch it. They just looked at it, waiting for it to do something. The tape did what it was best at doing: it silently waited for what always came next. Curiosity.

"I'm going to turn in." Nadia pulled out her sleeping bag.

"Good call," Lucy agreed, and looked around her floor. She picked up the tape with a shirt to avoid touching it and quietly placed it on her desk by the VCR. Shivering, she threw the shirt into her laundry bin and quickly wiped her hands on an old towel.

Lucy crawled into bed. Nadia crawled into her sleeping bag. The two girls closed their eyes and tried to sleep. One of them was successful.

FIVE

One of them, to her surprise, fell asleep quickly, but the other did not. Lucy laid awake with her eyes closed until she heard Nadia's breathing slow to the even pulse of sleep. She opened her eyes. They locked onto the tape. Beside the tape was the red scorpion ship. She glanced at Nadia, not wanting to disturb her, and got out of bed.

She tiptoed over to the ship and picked it up. *It's just a toy,* she admonished herself for being afraid of something made of plastic. Cheap plastic at that. Her finger traced the crack on the ship.

Like many gaming streamers, Lucy had a stream deck that allowed her to control components of her computer and the lighting in her room. She reached over to the stream deck, a little rectangle of buttons on her desk, and pressed the button for her wall lights. The hexagons of light on her wall lit up slowly in a faint purple hue. A honeycomb of purple so dim that only the edges of objects could be seen. Edges, and the white tape. It stood out in the dark like an item in a video game, glowing, inviting the player to pick it up, examine it, use it. Many of her games have power-ups like this. They shimmered in the darkest lights, like this white tape. She was drawn to them in the games like she was drawn to this white tape. Lucy picked it up, but it didn't automatically go into her inventory as it would in a game. In the real world, it stayed in her hand. If she was going to use it, she had to do it now or put it down.

Without thinking, she slid the tape into the VCR and pressed the TV's power button. Static hissed as it came to life with black and white snow streaking across the screen. A haunting green light was cast throughout the room, covering Nadia's face with a sickly pallor that reminded Lucy of Sam's face in the hospital. Nadia stirred from the light, but rolled over and returned to her even breathing.

Lucy pressed mute. Her finger darted to the play button but didn't press it. Chaotic light strobed throughout her room from the TV's static.

"It's just a toy," she whispered, and looked at the action figure sitting beside the scorpion ship. Its melted face and yellow eye looked into her room. The way the figure was positioned for the stream, it looked like it was staring at Nadia. One yellow eye, one black eye, watched her sleep. Lucy shivered and turned the figure around, instantly wiping away the feeling of the scarred and twisted plastic body. "Oh, this is stupid." She pressed play.

Static vanished, but it wasn't the strange alien world. This time, the video was a window. Someone was watching TV inside the window. The camera was far away from the window and at a strange, tilted angle. Lucy leaned in to inspect the scene closer. The person in the window leaned closer to the TV too. She jumped back, and the person on the TV jumped back. The room was dark on the TV with only the edges of things showing. Lucy didn't understand yet, but her heart did, and it pounded in her chest.

On the screen, a girl watched TV as the camera swayed gently. Lucy pressed her face into the TV to see the girl. The moment she did, the light from the TV illuminated the girl's face and Lucy screamed. On instinct, her finger smashed into the eject button and the tape spit out with a whirring, grinding sound.

Nadia sprung up from sleep fully awake. No drowsiness slowed her as she jumped up and screamed, "What's wrong?! What happened?!"

Lucy pointed to the TV. "It—" She looked at the window beside her bed. The trees in her back yard swayed with the wind outside. Lucy pulled her curtains closed and rushed back over to her streaming deck. She slammed her finger into the button that set her lights to full brightness. Her room lit up, chasing all shadows away.

"What happened?!" Nadia looked around the room. The tape hung from the VCR slot like a tongue licking hungry, predator lips. "Did you play the tape?"

"It was me," Lucy said, as she checked the curtains again to make sure they were fully closed. "It was me. On the tape. It was watching me!"

"Wait. What?" Nadia reached for the tape to push it in.

"No!" Lucy grabbed her wrist.

Nadia winced, the pain buckling her knees. "Ow!"

"Don't touch it." Lucy let go and flapped her hands as she quickly paced her room. Nadia's sleeping bag got caught in her feet and she almost tripped, but Nadia caught her. "I couldn't sleep," Lucy said. "I thought I'd check it out. It's just a—" She left the lie incomplete as she glanced at the scorpion ship.

"Do you want to get your mom?" Nadia asked. She reached for Lucy but kept her distance. Nadia knew when someone was too anxious to think. She'd felt that way many times and saw the signs. Panting. Self stimulation. Pacing. Lucy nodded, and they left her room, lights on, bright as the morning, to find Trudy.

Trudy was in bed, but not asleep. She was sitting up, reading her latest book, *Billionaire Baby Bundle*. She knew all about the billionaire's love child and that the protagonist was head-over-heels for him, but Trudy couldn't put the book down. It was the predictability she enjoyed, and the ability to smile at the happily ever after.

Lucy and Nadia came in, arms full of bedding. They were panting and sweaty.

"You guys okay?" Trudy rested the book on her stomach.

"I got really freaked out." Lucy glanced over her shoulder. "This might be weird, but do you mind if we hang out here for a bit?"

Nadia smiled and nodded.

Trudy shrugged. "Sure. Is there something wrong?" She didn't get up, but moved her book to the nightstand, assuming tonight's reading was over.

"We're worried about Sam," Nadia said before Lucy could answer. "And that game, the video, kind of freaked us out."

Trudy nodded and patted the bed. "Yeah, supposedly that game freaked a lot of people out."

Lucy and Nadia sat down on her bed. Nadia tossed her sleeping bag on the floor and dropped her bolt bag beside it. The bag rattled with her anxiety medication, which reminded Nadia that she had it and she should use it or be where Lucy was a few moments ago.

"Back when I was a kid, that game was legendary. Mostly 'cause no one could get a copy. The company that made it pulled it off the shelves after the story about those kids was in the paper."

"What kids?" Lucy didn't want to ask, but did. Nadia didn't want to listen, but did.

"Back then, everything was satanic. Heavy metal was satanic. Games like *Dungeons & Dragons* were doorways to hell. If you listened to Ozzy Osbourne while playing *D&D*, you might as well get ready to burn forever." Trudy chuckled at the absurdity. "Well, *Captain Light* got wrapped up in all that when some kids died. The newspaper said the kids were playing the game and thought it was real. I don't think that's what happened, but it was an easy thing to blame and get an insanity plea." Trudy waved away the thought and shook her head. She squinted like she was concentrating on remembering more, but nothing else came to her. "The point is, people don't need a game to make them do bad things. We can do evil crap all on our own. That tape in there is a collector's item. Probably could sell it on eBay for a pretty good profit."

"So, someone died?" Lucy asked.

Trudy shrugged. "I don't know. News like that isn't always accurate, and I didn't read the articles myself, so who knows? We didn't have Tweeter back then to keep up on all this stuff."

"Twitter, Mom." Lucy sighed and found her way back to calm through her mom's lack of internet knowledge.

"Yeah, that too." Trudy climbed out of bed and pulled open her closet. "Why don't you ladies camp in here tonight? I'll set up a bed for you, Lucy. Nadia, you can use your sleeping bag."

"That sounds good, Mrs. Nelson." Nadia agreed quickly, "Do you have any water up here so I can take my meds? I think I need them after all the stuff today." She smiled, abashed.

"No problem, sweetie." Trudy went into the master bathroom, came out with a cup of water as Lucy was settling into her makeshift bed. "If you need anything, let me know. Want a movie or something?"

"No!" Lucy jumped. "Just bed."

And with that, they all laid down. Trudy tapped her phone to enable the home security system. A quiet beep confirmed all the locks in the house were tight, all the cameras activated. Lucy sighed with relief. Any intruders would have their ears melted by the blistering sirens. Police would be here so quickly, it'd make any would-be killer's head spin. Safety and security brought to her by modern technology.

Nadia gulped down two of her pills, the max her doctor recommended for very stressful times. *If this doesn't count, I don't know what does.* As she laid down, she could see Lucy's room. The lights were still on. She pushed Trudy's door half-closed to block the view. Seconds later, she fell asleep. Even a blood-curdling scream from her best friend wouldn't wake Nadia up in time to save Lucy while sleeping this deeply.

SIX

Lucy was always a light sleeper, even when exhausted. The low garble of static was enough to wake her up. At first it sounded very far away, but as her senses rejoined the waking world, she noticed the constant fuzzy hiss coming from her room. Faint fizzy TV static lit up the hallway.

Didn't I leave my light on? She didn't remember. The only light behind her partially closed door was the pale green static flicker. It buzzed and hissed a quiet whisper into the few feet from Lucy's room to Trudy's.

"Nadia." Lucy reached over and tapped her, but she didn't move. "Nadia." Lucy tapped harder. Nadia didn't even hitch a breath. Her anxiety medicine was doing its job. She was dead to the world. "Mom." Lucy sat up and looked at Trudy, but she was out too.

Don't be stupid. You left the TV on. Just go turn it off. The bedroom door was only a little open. If she closed the door, would that keep the sound out enough for her to go to sleep? She didn't think so. And she needed sleep. Her mind was a fog, and the daze of the day begged her to sleep, but with that constant hissing, she couldn't do it. Lucy tried her mom one more time. She didn't budge. *Fine. Yeah. Just the TV.*

She walked quickly down the hallway, thinking of horror movies. The final girl always creeps around, but not this time. *I'm not in a horror movie. I'm not acting like it.* She strode into her room, almost stomping her feet to announce her arrival. Family photos rattled on the wall as she passed.

"Can't believe I left the TV on," she said, with no attempt at quieting her voice. "Guess I'll go turn it off." And that's when she remembered her mom turned on the security system. If anyone came in her window—any window—or door, they would have heard it. Her dad was always traveling for work and always worried about Lucy and Trudy. He had the security system installed and verified by two independent consultants. He even paid someone to test the system by trying to break in, and the system worked. *See, I told you, it's just the TV.*

Lucy chuckled when she got to her room, shaking her head. She walked in before she noticed the man sitting in front of the TV. He was captivated by the static on the screen, pressing his face so close he saw each individual point of interference. The flickering static cast a sinister, dim glow around him, like a toxic halo.

He wore a filthy gown or dress that opened in the back, exposing sagging folds of skin. Both hands cradled the red spaceship toy, with one thumb gently tracing the crack in the plastic where Nadia had dropped it. The four fingers of that hand were fused together, giving it the appearance of a fleshy claw. It reminded her of the claw machines at the arcade, but this one didn't pull prizes out of a pit—it pulled your guts out of your stomach. His face was too close to the TV to see him, but the sagging skin drooled off his skull like melting wax.

A tunnel of static was on the screen, like those infinity mirrors

Lucy saw online. A mirror reflecting a mirror, creating an image that goes on forever. The white tape was in the VCR. It was playing. The tape showed what the kneeling man saw, static into infinity. Was he staring at the static? Into the tunnel? At something in the depths of the tunnel?

Lucy thought to scream, to call for her mom, but couldn't. If she moved, he'd notice her. He'd hear her. But she was too late, too loud, too eager to deny a monster was in her house.

He stood to face her. His skin was out of sync with his body, dragged along as he shambled. His enormous yellow eye rolled to her before his head turned. The other eye was hidden in the flickering shadows. His face sagged as if burned or chewed off, or both. Lucy thought that face looked familiar. Not only like the action figure, but the mutilation of someone she knew long ago—in a life where things like this man did not exist.

The TV screen changed. It was now a picture of her standing, staring at the camera, frozen in fear and wonder and curiosity. She didn't move as the camera on the TV got closer, as the man in her room stepped closer. Lucy pushed off the doorframe but couldn't move. Couldn't scream. Couldn't breathe. He held her without touching her. His bulging yellow eye paralyzed her. Lucy waited for the eye to pop as it pulsed with the man's wheezing breath.

He lurched closer. The TV screen zoomed in on Lucy's wide eyes, her silent, screaming mouth. He pushed his face into hers. The stench of spoiled milk swirled around her, curdled and clumping like his skin. His bulbous yellow eye grazed her eyelashes, but she couldn't pull away. She didn't blink as tears rolled down her cheeks. He licked her tears with his long, viscous black tongue.

Nausea clamped her stomach, the pain doubling her over, finally freeing her scream. A shrieking mix of gratitude and agony exploded from Lucy's throat.

The man chuckled, a wet, gargling laugh. "Almost." He faded to static, hissing and snarling, then imploded into a single white line, finally popped out of existence.

Lucy fell to the floor, still screaming as her mom rushed to her.

"Lucy! Lucy! What happened!?" Trudy grabbed her, squeezed her in a hug. Lucy didn't fight. She only sobbed a mess of tears, drool, and snot as she scraped away the thick mucus left behind by the man's tongue.

SEVEN

Sleep was over for the night. Lucy told her mom what had happened. They called the police. Trudy checked the security camera footage around the house as they worked on waking up Nadia. Lucy didn't have a camera in her room, but there was one outside her window pointed at the back yard. The cameras saw nothing.

Nadia was stuck in her chemically induced calm. She saw the panic and tried to respond, but her anxiety medication did its job too well. Lucy held onto her and cried, still scrubbing at her red cheek with her sleeve.

Officer Littleton arrived quickly. He was what you'd expect in a small-town cop: polite, nervous, and by the book. Littleton reviewed the security footage and examined Lucy's room where the incident was reported to have occurred. There were scratch marks around the TV-VCR, but they could have been from sliding it onto the desk, Littleton noted, and Lucy agreed. Nadia was just coming out of her haze when Littleton was reviewing Lucy's room with Trudy and Lucy.

"The suspect came through this window?" Littleton tried the window. It was locked. He noticed it was locked from the inside in two places. Both needed to be unlocked at the same time to open the window. "This is an impressive security setup."

"I don't know how he got in," Trudy said, impatience growing. "Lucy said he was here, he was here. She doesn't make stuff like this up."

"I'm not saying she did." Littleton's voice downshifted from his cop tone to a comforting, *we're all in this together* tone. "I think y'all've had a stressful day." He pointed to Nadia. "Isn't that so, ma'am?"

Nadia shrugged a non-committal agreement.

"Night terrors happen when people are strained or stressed. I don't doubt Ms. Lucy experienced something terrifying, but the evidence suggests no one was here."

Lucy didn't roll her eyes, didn't sigh or huff. She nodded. It made sense to her. More sense than an action figure coming to life in her room. The red scorpion ship was on the floor in front of the TV, but maybe she knocked it down there when she got scared earlier in the night. Maybe the ship was already on the floor from when Sam's seizure shocked all of them. Evidence pointed to a night terror, and Lucy wanted to believe that was all that was happening here.

"Well, then we're done here, Officer Little." Trudy huffed.

"Littleton, ma'am," he corrected. "And I'm happy to stick around and keep an eye on things if that'll help you feel safe."

Trudy cocked her head and scoffed. "No. We'll be fine. You can go be unhelpful somewhere else."

"Ma'am, I'm doing—"

"You weren't here!" Trudy snapped. "You didn't hear her! It wasn't a nightmare! I've never heard her that scared and I never want to again. So if you're not going to help us, get out. We have work to do."

Nadia and Lucy shrank back away from Trudy. Lucy couldn't remember ever seeing her mom this mad. The two girls watched in awe as Trudy took Littleton to the door, opened it, and practically shoved him out.

"Nightmare." Trudy scoffed. She took a deep breath, slowly counted from five to one, composed herself to the smile she always wore, and turned to the girls. "Coffee or tea?"

"It's 4am." Nadia pointed to the clock in the kitchen. After the screaming and panic, Trudy turned on all the lights in the house and grumbled how she needed one of those Siri things like Nadia had. Lucy was certain they'd have one as soon as Dad got home.

"Perfect time to get the day started. We're taking that stuff back to the yard sale as soon as it opens." Trudy hammered her fist on the kitchen counter with every syllable.

"The Life Changing Yard Sale?" Nadia chuckled.

Lucy didn't laugh. She got her laptop from the living room and flopped on the couch.

"Research?" Nadia asked.

Lucy nodded and pointed to her mom's laptop on the desk.

"It's not the tape. It's not just the tape," Lucy said, and wiped at her cheek again.

Nadia grabbed Trudy's computer, sat beside Lucy, and started searching. Years ago, Trudy didn't have the internet to learn what happened with those kids, but Lucy and Nadia did. Together, they would unearth the game's dark past.

"Maybe," Nadia paused, put her hand over Lucy's keyboard,

"maybe we just get rid of the stuff and be done?" She knew if they dug deeper, they'd find more skeletons. "I mean, the guy wanted the tape, right? We just get rid of it and be done? He goes away?" Could they walk away and stop the skeletons?

Lucy shook her head, typed *Captain Light and the World of Darkness* into the search bar. As she pressed enter, she sealed her fate. In the next 48 hours, she'd look back at this moment as the point when she could have stopped. She could have escaped the horrors to come, but chose curiosity, anger, and the deep need to know over her and Nadia's safety.

EIGHT

Lucy had her laptop out on the kitchen counter as the sun came up. Golden light streamed into the kitchen through the bay window. A hard glare blinded her, so she moved back into the living room with Nadia. Coffee brewed in the kitchen. The smell kept Lucy going. Her sleepless night was catching up to her now as the words on her screen blurred and her thoughts muddled.

"Find anything good?" Lucy said, and flopped on the couch.

"Yeah." Nadia kept her eyes on her laptop screen. She was researching the kids Trudy mentioned while Lucy learned about the game.

"What'd you find?" Lucy had her own news but wanted Nadia to start. She was hoping for something sane to counter her findings, something mundane to explain all this away.

"No." Nadia shook her head and slowly leaned back from her laptop screen. "No, you better start. This is just…" She trailed off and kept shaking her head. A shiver rippled over her like a dog shaking off rain.

"Okay, well, it looks like the game was released in 1987. There was only one tape produced, but apparently a second was in production when the company was sued and shut down." Lucy flipped open her laptop and went to her notes to keep everything straight in her tired mind. "The show was about this band of rebels, led by Captain Light. They were trying to rid the world of King Dark and his army."

Nadia shifted in her seat at the name. Lucy paused. "You okay?"

"Yeah, just keep going." Nadia waved for her to continue. Sweat beaded on her brow and slipped down around her eyes.

"The show was supposedly set in the present 80s, and a bunch of scientists opened an experimental doorway into another dimension. That was the door to King Dark's realm, and before they could close it, King Dark came through." Lucy looked up from her notes, saw Nadia shivering. "This is just the story of the show," Lucy said quickly, but it didn't comfort either of them.

"What does it say about the army?" Nadia asked, to Lucy's surprise. They hadn't talked about what either had found out yet, and so the mention of the army was a shock.

"Yeah, that's what Captain Light was fighting against. In the show, King Dark could take over a person's body and mind. Like an infection, a virus. In the show, most of the world's population is controlled by King Dark and hunting out the rest of humanity."

"Why? Why was this guy taking over people's minds?" Nadia's voice was too eager for Lucy. But she had an answer this time. King Dark's motivation was in the storyline.

"He, King Dark, wanted to escape his dimension and take over other dimensions with his army. The dimension he came from—it sounds like the place we saw on the white tape—had already been conquered and destroyed."

Nadia whimpered; her legs bounced nervously as she bit her lip. Dots were connecting in her mind to make a horrid picture. She couldn't quite see it all yet, but the forms that were emerging turned her stomach.

"Can I stop you there?" Nadia squeaked out. "'Cause I think things are making more sense now and I hope they're not."

Lucy nodded and closed her laptop to listen without distraction.

"There's some really screwed up people online." Nadia gulped hard. The sound ended in a deep click, like a switch was flipped within her. Lucy saw Nadia's face harden and turn to the emotionless, *just the facts* face Nadia often used to talk about stressful things. It was like she unhooked her feelings for a moment so they wouldn't get in the way.

"Okay, I didn't dig into the show, but looked for information on the toys. And there's a whole lotta people very interested in these toys. There's a ton of subreddits about this." Nadia paused. "I mean JUST this toy. Not the show, the one toy of the red ship and the pilot guy, King Dark. The ship's called the," Nadia points to her screen, "Scorpion Cruiser, Beta Class. And it was the ship used by King Dark. People are obsessed with it." She again pointed to her notes. "And they're insistent that the ship must be 'intact and contain King Dark.' Someone asked about the ship without Dark and people responded with laughing emojis. No one talked about the price. They always offered trade. And the trade was always some other toy."

Lucy felt the chill that had been building in Nadia. Toys were fun things. Children's things. Not commodities for grown men to be trading, discussing, obsessing over online.

"What about the news thing Mom was talking about?" Lucy pivoted quickly to escape the idea of creepy toy people talking about what's in her room right now.

"Yeah, I found that too. It's real. There was a kid in Summerdale, Indiana, who killed his friend while playing *Captain Light*. The kid beat his friend to death with the Captain Light ship. He said he killed his friend because the game told him to." Nadia shook her head again, this time in doubt rather than disbelief. "When he was arrested, he kept screaming that he was doing what needed to be done. The police report said the kid had a Captain Light ship in his hand, and the other kid, the kid who was killed, had King Dark's Scorpion Cruiser on his arm."

Nadia paused there for a moment to gather a long breath, readying herself to deliver the *coup de gras*, the most damning news she had discovered so far.

"And, ready for this?" Nadia didn't smile as you'd expect. She kept her dead, even face. Her monotone explanation, *just the facts* voice. "There was an investigative report on the whole thing a few years later. The Captain Light toys were confiscated by the police when they arrested the murderer, but the evidence disappeared before the trial. The toys were missing. And because of that, the murderer didn't get the chair. He got life in an insane asylum."

"What!?" Lucy jumped up. "You're telling me—"

"I'm telling you we need to find out where that ship upstairs came from."

Lucy's mind processed the connections Nadia had already formed, but one question came up from the swirling nadir within her. *Was there anything about the number? 29?*

Nadia's emotions were back now, her fear, confusion, and concern peeking through.

Lucy stuck on the number, thinking it didn't belong on the original toy. It must have been added after.

Trudy's phone rang on the kitchen counter, making Lucy and Nadia jump. They never thought "Celebrate" by Cool and the Gang would terrify them so much, but any loud noise in such tense silence would do the trick. Trudy hurried to her phone and answered.

"Hello?"

Lucy and Nadia listened carefully, feeling the gravitational draw of Trudy's darkening mood.

"What?"

"No. I…" Trudy looked at Lucy questioningly. "No. I haven't seen him. I'll let you know if anything comes up. How are you doing?" Trudy turned from the girls and lowered her voice as the conversation continued.

Lucy and Nadia didn't move. They forgot to breathe, waiting for whatever news Trudy was getting.

Trudy hung up and came to them.

"Nadia, can you call your mom and let her know you're okay?" Trudy said with calm plastered on her face. It was cracking plaster, snapping under the pressure of a sleepless night and stressful morning.

"Yes, I'll call her now." Nadia pulled her phone out of her pocket and stepped into the kitchen.

"What's wrong?" Lucy asked.

"That was Sam's mom. He's disappeared from the hospital."

The living room's air clawed at Lucy's lungs, leaving her gasping as Sam's voice invaded her mind. *Don't look behind me. My gown is an open back.* Was that Sam in her room last night? His familiar face, the open back gown? The face was too melted, too mutilated to tell, and that one yellow eye, all she could see, was pressed into her face.

"Lucy, you alright?" Trudy reached for her but didn't touch, didn't want to jolt her if the memories of last night had her. Trudy's mom's intuition sensed a link between Sam's disappearance and Lucy's visitor. She didn't believe in ghosts and monsters, wouldn't have connected the toy to the situation like Lucy had, but Trudy knew when something was wrong. And now, her mom-sense wasn't just tingling, it was screaming a ten-alarm fire.

"Can we go back to that yard sale?" Lucy asked. She glanced up to her room, the door visible past the second-floor railing. "I want to take that game back. I don't want it here. It's freaking me out too much."

"Of course," Trudy agreed. "We probably can't get our money back, but we can get rid of it if that's what you need."

Lucy nodded.

Nadia returned. "I told her I was with you. She said that's fine but to call her when I get ready to come home." Nadia didn't think that would be soon. She'd heard Lucy's request to go to the yard sale and wanted to see where the game came from. Who would have such a thing? Was it the game from the murder?

The three stood there, looking up at Lucy's room.

Trudy cleared her throat. "I'll get the game."

Lucy and Nadia let out a sigh of relief as Trudy walked upstairs quickly.

"Get ready to go, ladies. Let's get this thing out of here."

NINE

To no one's surprise, the yard sale was closed when they returned. The blankets and bins had been cleared away. All that remained was the trampled overgrown grass and tire marks from people parking in the yard.

"Guess it was one day only," Trudy said. "Life changing for one day." She chuckled, but the girls didn't laugh.

Lucy picked up the grocery bag with her return in it. The gray plastic bag crinkled as the tape, ship, and figure shifted around inside.

The three studied the front yard from the car. It was overgrown, needed a mowing for a few weeks now by the looks of it. There was a bird feeder, empty, hanging from a hook near the front door. The house's aluminum siding was a worn-out green color. Lucy couldn't tell if it was meant to look like that or sun-bleached. All the windows were blocked by curtains. The front door was a dark wood with an ornate frosted-glass oval in the center. They stayed in the car until Lucy gasped.

An idea popped into her head and she looked for the house's mailbox. Lucy opened her door and got out of the car, walking toward the driveway where the black mailbox stood, front open and dangling down like a broken jaw.

"What house number is this?" Lucy said.

Nadia followed her. Trudy was the last one out of the car.

Old mail burst out of the mailbox's mouth from too many stuffings.

"You from the real estate company?" An old lady stood a safe distance away in the neighboring yard. She was stout, wearing a sunshine yellow dress under her floral gardening apron. Her yard was well manicured, with flowers and fountains direct from a home and garden magazine. It looked cheery compared to the ragged house of the Life Changing Yard Sale.

Lucy reached the mailbox and read the number. *1211*. She sighed, disappointed.

"No," Trudy answered the old lady. "Just here to return something from the yard sale."

The old lady coughed out a laugh. "Return? I'm guessing all sales were final." She chuckled through her smoker's cough.

"They moved?" Lucy asked.

"They died." The old lady shrugged and waved away the idea like it couldn't happen to her. Between her heavy breathing and creaking bones, Lucy thought death loomed closer than the old lady realized.

"So, yesterday was an estate sale?" Trudy asked.

"Yeah, I guess. Real estate company wanted to empty the house out, but no one wanted most of that crap."

"Did you know them?" Nadia asked and pointed to the dead people's house.

"Them? You mean him." The old lady trimmed a manicured bush with tiny scissors. She examined each branch carefully before snipping with a smile, as if gardening freely for the first time. "Didn't talk much. Quiet. Always took care of his yard. Guess not now."

"How'd he die?" Nadia glanced at the bag Lucy was holding.

"Dunno. Ambulance came and got him. He was dead when they pulled him out. Quite the scene. Screaming and shouting when the paramedics first went in. Came out all pale and trembling. Neil was all covered up when they wheeled him out."

"Neil? The owner?" Trudy asked.

The old lady nodded. "Kept mostly to himself. Got shipments every once in a while. Shipped a lot of stuff out of his house too. Did something with eBay or one of those internet places, I guess." There was something else she wanted to say but didn't. A memory flashed across her eyes but she shrugged it away.

"Toys?" Lucy asked and pulled the grocery bag around, holding it out.

The old lady moved on to another bush. "Maybe. Like I said, didn't talk much. Real estate people don't want nothing to do with that house though, I'll tell you that. Every time someone comes by from the real estate company, they only come by once. Go in. Leave. Don't come back. Guess they're just going to bulldoze the lot. Probably mold. Mold gets everywhere 'round here."

Lucy's eyes drifted to the pale green house. *What's inside?* Her curiosity grew. Nadia was thinking the same thing. Neither girl considered dropping the bag on the porch and walking away. They wondered what's behind the door. What's deeper? They didn't want answers; they needed them. The need of a junkie who smells their junk, the need to explore the unknown and come out knowing. Both wondered what they'd find when they came back later that afternoon. Friends like Lucy and Nadia knew each other's thoughts when it came to mischief and danger.

TEN

Trudy's exhaustion made the road fuzzy as she drove. Everything around her moved too fast, and she moved too slow. When she pulled into her driveway, a loud, appreciative sigh escaped her.

"I need to get some sleep, ladies," Trudy said when they walked in. Morning had almost become afternoon, but Trudy's curtains were dark and thick. The midday sun wouldn't be able to break through. She kissed Lucy and left the girls to get their own rest.

They had other plans.

Lucy and Nadia got drinks in the kitchen. Their second wind blew in on the drive home. Youth has so many winds, where parents only have the one. The girls drank orange juice around the kitchen island counter and considered the shopping bag sitting between them.

"Now what?" Nadia asked.

"We go back to that house and see what's inside," Lucy said.

"Agreed," Nadia said.

Lucy pulled out her phone. "Uber?"

Nadia nodded.

Ten minutes later, they were in a blue Toyota Camry with Dina, a five-star driver who loved gospel music. Dina kept water bottles in a cooler on her backseat for her riders. She said they could listen to any gospel station they would like, but of the two, one was mostly static. Both girls declined that station immediately.

The drive to 1211 Gordon Avenue was quick. Nadia thought Dina's constant chatter made the ride feel faster. She had a gift for gab and reminded Nadia of Trudy. Lucy's anticipation and wonder made the drive go by quickly. She imagined what they'd find inside. It made her smile, unsure why. What turned all those real estate people out? What happened? She wanted to know.

"You ladies want me to wait?" Dina asked as she eyed the sickly green house.

"No thank you, Ms. Dina," Lucy answered. "We have a friend meeting us here, and we met the neighbor earlier today."

Dina left. They watched her turn off Gordon Avenue. After checking for the old lady neighbor, they went around the back of the house. Lucy lifted the welcome mat and found a house key.

"How'd you know that was there?" Nadia pointed to the mat.

"Lots of people do that."

"Do you?"

"Hell no." Lucy laughed. "Dad would kill me." She unlocked the back door and opened it quickly. It didn't creak or squeak as Lucy flung it open. She acted like it was her house and nodded for Nadia to do the same. *No one's going to suspect anything if we look like we belong here.* Again, she thought of horror movies and the timidity of the final girl. She would not be that. Would not do that.

The back door opened into a small hallway. The house was clean. Lucy expected cobwebs, dust, moldy smells—the old lady next door said mold grew easily here. But none of that was present. The hallway was clean. Walls painted off-white. Floor black-and-white checkered tile. There were no pictures on the walls in the hallway, but the paint looked like it had been recently redone. It was glossy and without the smears and stains you expect in a used hallway.

An opening to the right led to the kitchen. It was clean. No dishes in the sink. No foul smells. No cleaner smell either. It didn't look empty or abandoned, and that made her call out.

"Hello?"

Nadia elbowed her hard in the ribs. Lucy gasped at the impact.

"Sorry." Nadia grabbed Lucy's elbow. "Sorry. Just startled me. Besides, we're breaking and entering. Let's keep it down," she whispered.

Lucy nodded and kept moving forward into the living room. The front door of the house was on the right-hand wall, along with a large window. Another door was in front of her, probably out to the garage based on the outside of the house. Curtains kept most of the light out of the room, but a sliver of daylight broke through at the edges. More light came through the frosted-glass oval on the front door. There was nothing remarkable about the living room. A blue fabric couch. A brown leather recliner. A reasonably sized TV hung on the wall in front of the couch and recliner. There was a staircase going up and another hallway across from the front door.

Lucy was drawn to the large bookshelf that framed the TV. Nadia wandered off.

There were hundreds of books here with all kinds of titles. It seemed like Neil was a reader. Romance books, horror books, sociology books, psychology, all kinds of science and everything in between were on the shelves. She noticed stacks of books beside the couch. A pile of books on the end table beside the recliner. Even books piled up on the books on the bookshelf. But there were a few books on the bottom shelf that really stood out. They were ruby red leather-bound books with numbers stamped into the spine. She ran her finger over the first few and felt the deep numeric indents on the spines.

She knelt and pulled a book off the shelf. Holding it into the beam of light cast by the door's oval, she read, "2-10". Lucy pulled the next one from the shelf. "11-20". She put 2-10 back and opened 11-20 to the first entry.

Item: 11

Contents:

- *Viceroy Liam - Jack-in-the-box*

Collection: Public

I picked this up in Brussels, Germany, from an antique shop near Kanaal B-C. It holds a demonic force within the jack-in-the-box. The dealer told me to make sure to never open it because the song played in the cranking summons the creature. Perhaps music or an intonation like chanting can summon other entities like this one…

Lucy's eyes jumped to a word written in the page's margin: *Dodslav?*

There was more written in the entry, but she flipped forward to see the next entry. Item 12, Murman's Train. Item 13, Worry Person.

"This is an inventory?" She put the book back and grabbed 21-30, flipped forward and stopped at

Item: 29

Components:

- *Captain Light & the World of Darkness VHS*
- *King Dark action figure*
- *Beta Ship*

Collection: Private

Acquired through trade with @vice0_pysch0. He got it from a police contact. I'm guessing it was like some of my contacts who could make evidence disappear for the right price.

Lucy skimmed down further.

According to Vice0, the Scorpion Cruiser in mint condition was held by Arnold South as he was bludgeoned to death by Greg Leederman. Greg suspected Arnold of being possessed by an evil spirit imprisoned in the action figure. Argument ensued between the two when Arnold would not put the action figure back in the Scorpion Cruiser.

I tracked down Mr. Leederman, and when I interviewed him, he said the ship was Dark's doorway back to his world. Greg kept saying, "Don't watch the tape. The tape's his eyes. When you see him, he'll see you." I was able to trade the tape, the ship, and the figure with Vice0 for a minor item in my collection. In a few years, this will easily fetch a great return. Putting it in the vault. Everyone online says it must be intact and mint for them to be interested. Broken toys are no good to these collectors. No good to me either.

"Nadia…" Lucy gasped. The room darkened as a cloud blotted out the sun. It was still early afternoon, but twilight came with a dizzying immediacy. Lucy swayed from the sudden change and looked outside through the oval window. The cloud moved on, and the midday sun returned.

There was no doubt she had a toy that got someone killed. If the entry was correct, it was a haunted toy imprisoning some monster, and it was on her kitchen island counter. Was her mom okay? Did it come to life? No, it infected… That's why Arnold was killed. He was infected? "Nadia, I found something."

"Yeah," Nadia panted, her voice cracked into a high-pitch whine, "so did I."

Lucy held the book and ran down the hallway beside the staircase. Nadia was standing outside a workshop. Small tools hung from a pegboard fixed on the wall. Under the pegboard, a work bench had the latest project lying on top of it. There were boxes of small parts lining the room on wheeled carts. No windows lit the room; instead a fast-flickering neon tube cast a grimy sheen on everything. Nadia stood against the wall beside the doorway, pressing herself as far into that wall as she could. Her eyes locked onto the workbench. Sweat flowed freely from her face, dripping in splotches on the floor.

Lucy finally noticed the doll on the workbench. It was a Baby-B-Real like she had when she was little. It had short straight black hair, over-sized adoring eyes, and an enormous smile. The jaw was hinged so it could be fed. This doll wore a farmer's outfit with blue jean overalls covering a pink shirt. Beside the doll was a tented white paper with the number 42 written on it in the same handwriting as Lucy's own toy: 29.

"What's wrong?" Lucy asked.

Nadia shook her head. "You see that, right?"

"The doll?"

"Yeah. I think it's looking at me."

Lucy didn't notice that. The doll's plastic eyes looked like they were looking at everything. That's what made them realistic. Lucy swayed to the side, watching the eyes. They didn't move. Sure, they *seemed* to look at her, but that's what these dolls did. They're supposed to make eye contact to make them believable. Its body laid lifeless on the workbench, while the eyes, full of life, glared at Lucy and Nadia.

A small fanny pack hung over the doll from the pegboard. Written in black marker—in the same handwriting as all the numbers on the two toys seen so far—was the word *Repairs*. Lucy fixed on the fanny pack and thought about "intact" and "mint." She remembered the cracking sound as the ship hit the floor in her room and how Sam— she thinks it was Sam—was feeling the crack last night.

"I think we need to fix the ship," Lucy said, and stepped toward the fanny pack repair kit.

Nadia grabbed her arm, pulled her back. "Are you high?" She pointed to the doll. "That thing's straight out of a nightmare. It's going to come to life and snag you as soon as you get close. Probably as soon as you touch that repair kit."

Lucy handed Nadia the book, but Nadia didn't take her eyes off the doll.

"I'll keep my distance. Besides, it's just a toy." But keeping away would be impossible. The repair kit hung right over the doll's hinged jaw. A quick snap from that mouth would… Would what? Chomp off her arm? Perhaps. But Lucy's heart knew she needed that fanny pack, just like she knew things were wrong here. Like she knew that doll wasn't just a doll, it was wrong. This place was wrong. Good old Neil, a friendly neighbor who didn't talk much, was into some pretty messed up stuff. But isn't that always the case? The neighbor no one knows is the one with the literal bodies in their basement. *Does this house have a basement?* Lucy didn't want to find out.

She took a deep breath, moved quickly to the workbench, snatched the repair kit off, and turned to walk away, but something was holding onto the fanny pack's strap. It was stuck. Her stomach dropped. Her feet turned to concrete on the wooden floor. She gulped as she turned slowly to see the doll holding the strap, but it wasn't. The strap was stuck on the peg it was hanging from. The doll was still lying on the workbench, motionless, its mouth hanging open in a hungry smile. Lucy softly shook the bag to release the strap. It fell from the peg, smacked the doll in the face, and both girls got out of the room immediately.

Nadia didn't hesitate. She headed straight for the door they came in. Lucy stopped at the bookshelf and grabbed the other leather journals. She didn't know why, but she thought the neighbor was right. This house was going to get bulldozed, everything destroyed, and Lucy guessed that was for the best. But what if everything didn't get destroyed? What if…

"Let's go," Nadia hissed in a whisper.

Lucy paused, read the covers of the inventory items: 2-10, 11-20, 21-30, 31-40, 40- That was the last entry. She looked in the journal, saw the last entry was 42.

"Get moving or I'm leaving you here," Nadia said in her detached voice, the one she used when on the edge of an anxiety attack.

Lucy closed the journals and followed Nadia to the door. In the back of her mind, Lucy heard another noise through Nadia's nervous panting, but ignored it. She had to dismiss it right now. *One crazy thing at a time,* she thought, and dismissed the giggling behind her. She shut Neil's door and followed Nadia away from the house.

ELEVEN

Another chatty Uber driver picked the girls up and drove them home. This driver, Lana, tried really hard to talk to the girls but couldn't get a word out of either. Both sat in the backseat, silent and staring out the window. Lucy clutched the journals, replaying the events of 1211 Gordon Avenue in her mind. She missed something at the end, something she thought she heard but couldn't recall.

Nadia stared out the window, her breath finally coming back to calm. The breathing techniques her therapist taught her were working overtime. She didn't close her eyes, tried to avoid blinking for fear of falling asleep. Because her last wind blew out in Neil's house. It was used to escape. And now, she felt the exhaustion expected from someone after enduring 24 hours of extreme emotional distress.

They arrived home in the late afternoon, having spent much more time in the workshop than either of them thought. Building the courage to get the repair kit took time, but their exit was almost immediate.

Both girls went to Nadia's house to check in with her parents. They weren't there.

"Shit. That's right," Nadia grumbled. "They're at my brother's show tonight. Second night of the performance."

"School play?"

"Yeah, he's got a part and they're all excited. He's playing a tree in the background." Nadia sighed, feeling weighty disappointment. She'd rather be watching the play than whatever this is she's doing with Lucy. The streaming stuff was fine, but dealing with evil toys? Monsters in the dark? Insanity-inducing VHS tapes? All this was too much.

"So what now?" Lucy asked, but she knew what. She already started putting the journals and repair kit on Nadia's kitchen counter. The sun was getting lower in the sky. The bay window showed the beginnings of sunset, but they still had a few hours of light.

Winds kicked up harder as a storm moved in. The trees outside danced with chaotic contortions as the freshly budded branches were stripped of their new greens. Clouds came fast and raced over the sun in sheets of passing darkness. Each bout of darkness made Lucy and Nadia jump as they read through Neil's journals, seeing tales of evil, hauntings, mistakes, and the worst of humanity on each page.

Nadia called out, "Hey, Siri, turn on the lights everywhere to 100%."

Siri didn't answer, only beeped, and all the lights came on. A moment later, they shut off as a hard wind shook Nadia's house. Popping and snapping noises came from outside the bay window. Lucy looked and saw a tree in Nadia's front yard straining against the wind.

"Maybe we should go to my house?" Lucy suggested.

Nadia shook her head. "Hey, Siri, turn on the lights."

No answer.

Power was out.

Nadia picked up her phone and tapped to activate her lights, but there was no connection. No internet. No network. No power.

"Shit." Nadia took a deep breath. "Shit, shit, shit." Another deep breath. She closed her eyes, touched her index fingers to her thumbs, making little rings with her fingers, and inhaled deeply. Held it. Exhaled slowly, thoroughly emptying her lungs.

"My mom's home. We'll go over for a bit. We have a generator," Lucy said, remembering her dad's insistence on getting a generator. They'd never needed one before, but there's always a first time.

"Yeah, okay. Front door. No back yard," Nadia said, while still focused on her breathing. She looked to the kitchen cabinet—the medicine cabinet—and remembered her anxiety pills were at Lucy's house. She took them over last night and never brought them back. "Yeah. Let's go."

Outside, the storm roared, but both girls knew it was just getting started. Rain spit down in fat drops as they ran across the front yard. Lucy hunched over as she ran, holding the journals and repair kit tight to her chest so they didn't get wet.

The power was out in Lucy's house too, and Lucy noticed her mom's car was gone. Nadia didn't notice as she sprinted to the front porch. As soon as her foot hit the porch, her butt sat on the swinging rocker. Staying there for a moment, she took a few deep breaths, rocking slowly. Lucy knew what this meant. She was on the edge of an anxiety attack. Her medication was inside. That would help things. Then they could fix the ship and be done. That was the answer. Fix the ship. Return it to "intact" and "mint" condition.

"Need a moment?" Lucy asked calmly. Any anxiety from her would surely push Nadia over the edge.

Nadia shook her head. "Just need to get my meds." She rocked again. "Hard day." Nadia pushed out a laugh to lighten the situation, but it crackled and broke from the day's strain.

Lucy put in the security code to unlock the door. The battery backup worked as expected and they went in. Nadia followed.

"The generator has an ignition switch over here." Lucy turned into the kitchen and stopped. Nadia ran into her, making Lucy stumble forward.

Sam stood in the kitchen. Melted face. Yellow eye rolling toward Lucy and Nadia to track their movement. He smiled and held up his claw-hand. The sun threw a golden ghostly outline around him. His yellowed teeth jutted from bleeding white gums in a smile so tight, Lucy waited to hear ripping flesh. He made a noise, deep and guttural, like he was trying to start a laugh but the engine wouldn't turn over. It just revved and revved in an *eehhhhhh* groan.

The sight of Sam cracked Nadia's anxiety attack. Like a damn, the crack spidered into a fissure, then burst open as a scream vomited from Nadia in deafening fury. She picked up a coffee mug—the one Lucy drank tea from that morning—and hurled it at Sam's smear of a face. It shattered across his mouth, but his smile didn't stop. The chips of ceramic fell out of his teeth with streams of black oozing blood. Nadia was still screaming as she threw another mug, this one hitting the yellow eye, and Lucy braced for something to spray out, for the eye to pop, but it didn't. It just rolled away for a moment, then back like a boulder fixed on rolling over them.

"Your world is so," Sam looked to Nadia, "fresh." He pointed his claw to her as she threw the last mug on the counter at him. The mug she had that morning. Cold tea was still in it.

Lucy froze.

Nadia screamed and turned to run, but didn't. She pivoted back toward Sam. She screamed again and kept turning like she was going to run, but couldn't move. Her feet were anchored to the kitchen floor.

"I'll change that," Sam said. He moved closer to Nadia. She wasn't screaming anymore. She'd stopped breathing. Her anxiety attack chipped away at her. It took her thoughts, her movement, and now her breath.

Sam reached up with his claw hand and wiped away the tea on his face. Chunks of his cheeks came with it, falling in clumps like the spoiled milk Lucy smelled last night.

"Why?" Lucy asked, not sure how that was the only question she had. The only thing she could do. In fight, flight, or freeze, she was frozen, but she had to know the fundamental question: Why?

Sam chuckled, a nasally wheezing sound. "Enough eludes me. A fresh world is a fresh start. A fresh feast."

Nadia's mouth was a frozen scream, but only a hyperventilating pant came out as she gasped for air. Sam's claw clamped around her throat and pulled her face close to his. The yellow eye pressed into Nadia's eyes. She stopped panting, started breathing again, but it was ragged and strained. Her eyes rolled back, spit foamed around her lips and streamed from her mouth, pooling on Sam's claw. Nadia screamed, her body seizing just like Sam's did.

Lucy's mind clicked. *That's what he was trying to do to me last night.* That click restarted her motor controls. Her feet came free from the kitchen floor. She grabbed the shopping bag on the island counter with the tape, figure, and ship in it. The journals fell from her hands, but she held onto the repair kit and ran out the backdoor. Lucy didn't look back, didn't need to. Nadia was screaming in pain, gurgling through her spit or puke or whatever was coming from her mouth. Lucy ran down the center of her street, plastic bag in her hand, rattling and shivering in the hard night wind as the storm, the torrential downpour, finally arrived.

TWELVE

Officer Littleton hadn't had a tongue lashing like Trudy gave him since his mom caught him smoking in the seventh grade. He wasn't the best cop, but he tried to help. Schools invited him to talk to the kids about staying away from drugs and gangs, and he did it every time they asked because that's what good cops do. He volunteered at the firehouse chili cook off and donated his 4th place winnings, a $10 gift card to Applebees, to the fire brigade.

So why did Trudy give him so much crap today? But he knew. She gave him crap because her daughter was scared and she wanted answers. And she wasn't the only pissed off mom right now. There was that missing kid's parents who wanted answers too. But that's a hospital security thing, not a police thing. I guess it's all a police thing when you boil down who has to deal with all the shit.

Littleton thought about these things as he rocked back and forth in his metal desk chair, flicking playing cards across the room into a trash can. He practiced throwing playing cards like that comic book guy Gambit for an upcoming cosplay event where he was going to be, you guessed it, Gambit. The flick was tricky if you wanted your card to fly straight and spin fast. His flick was looking good when the police station door burst open and Lucy Nelson ran in.

"Help!" she screamed through the howling wind and the downpour's angry static drone. "I need help!"

"What's going on?!" Littleton jumped up. The cards fell as his hand dropped to his gun. He'd never had to draw down, but tonight that was going to change.

"He's after me. He got Nadia. He's coming."

"Who?"

"Sam! But it's not Sam. It's Dark. King Dark. He took over Sam's body!"

Littleton didn't know what any of that meant other than she'd seen Sam, and that was good news. Sam's parents said he'd disappeared from the hospital last night and no one had seen him since. Now, at least, he had a lead.

"Okay, sit down." He tried to calm her, brought his chair to her. "Where did you see him?"

The door was still open. Wind battered the inside of the office, blowing Littleton's latest paperwork off his desk. *Man, I should have stapled that.* The pages scattered over the floor. He pushed the door shut, bringing silence back to the inside. Rain tapped hard on the roof but was almost unnoticeable compared to the roaring storm outside.

The station was small, with simple concrete block walls painted creamy beige. There was dark wood trim on the floor and ceiling, but none of it matched. The work had been piecemealed over the years, leaving a disjointed appearance to the place. The only thing that was new was the jail cells, or as Littleton called them, the Drunk Tank. A nice place where drunk people could sober up, because that's all that ever happened in this town.

"Okay, you able to tell me what's going on?"

Lucy clutched the plastic bag to her chest. She rocked back and forth quickly on the chair, sobbing and making a high-pitched wheeze after each panting breath.

"Let's start with the bag." Littleton reached for it.

Lucy jumped out of the chair.

"Don't touch it!"

He took a step back, put his hands up in the universal *calm down* gesture. "Okay. Okay. I'm sorry. I want to help you, but I don't know what's going on. Do you need to call your mom?"

Lucy remembered her phone. She pulled it out of her pocket and tried to activate it, but only got a white battery icon with a red slash through it. *Shit! It's dead! I didn't charge it last night.* She shook her head, unable to remember her mom's phone number.

"Can you tell me where you saw Sam?"

"It wasn't Sam. I told you, he's Dark now. He's King Dark," Lucy said. Littleton didn't understand. "Wait. Wait." She fished in her bag, pushed the books aside, and pulled out a white tape. "This, uh… Do you have a VCR?"

"Ms. Lucy, we are a local government organization. Of course we have a VCR. If it's modern, we don't have it, but the latest tech from the 1980s, we got it." Littleton waved for her to follow. "It's in the coffee room. I'll get you a coffee or tea or whatever while you tell me your story."

"I can show you."

They went to the coffee room, which wasn't much more than a closet built to seat four. A TV was mounted high on the far wall.

"Just put your tape in there and hit play."

Lucy did, and the static of the TV immediately cleared to show a camera looking at the police station outside. The camera panned to the side where a girl—Lucy knew it was Nadia—stood with a melted face and a bulging yellow eye. She smiled at the camera. A tooth fell out as her smile strained against her bleeding gums.

"What the hell is this?" Littleton cocked his head at the screen. "Some kind of prank?" He glanced at Lucy. She was digging in her bag again.

The camera moved around the police station. Rain poured around the view as the camera stopped in front of the station's backup generator. A claw flashed across the camera view, slicing a cable from the generator to the station. The TV and lights went black. Dim emergency lights clicked on with their red glow.

"What the shit?!" Littleton pulled his gun out. "Is this a joke!? Pranking a police officer's a crime!" He scanned the room.

"This isn't a prank, but I need to fix this." Lucy held up the scorpion cruiser. "I think this is all about this ship. It broke, and if I fix it, I can stop all this." Lucy didn't add the words that wanted to follow: *I think*. "Can you put me somewhere safe? Those people are trying to stop me. I need somewhere safe." Lucy spotted the cells outside the coffee room. "Like there. Can you lock me in there?"

"I'm definitely locking you in there until I figure out what's going on," Littleton said, and grabbed Lucy's arm. She held onto her bag as he shoved her into the cell. Littleton locked it. He turned to the station door, panting for whatever happened next.

Lucy sat on the floor and got out the repair kit. Carefully, she took the figure and the ship out of the bag to ensure nothing else got broken. She placed everything on the floor in front of her. *Don't panic.* She thought of the frantic final girl's friend, the one who doesn't make it, and shook her head, committing to avoid their fate.

Opening the repair kit, she took out the components and placed them on the ground.

Plastic cement.

Application brush.

Scraper.

She took a deep breath to focus, but it caught in Lucy's throat when someone knocked on the station door. Sharp, even taps, like something hard scraping against the glass door. She didn't look up. Didn't let herself be distracted. When she heard Littleton gasp in horror, she knew who it was.

The wind rushed in again as the police station door slowly drifted open. Littleton screamed for the two people coming in to stop or he'd shoot, but Lucy didn't have time to see what was going on.

Lucy jumped when the gun fired the first time. It filled her ears with cotton and a high-pitched siren that made it hard to focus. She popped the lid off the plastic cement, filled the crack in the ship from where Nadia dropped it last night. A little accident that no one thought anything of, and now she's in a nightmare. It was just an accident. It was just a toy.

Another gun shot, then another. The popping sounds of bullets became more and more muffled as Lucy focused on the ship. She laid a straight bead of plastic cement, rubbed it in with the application brush, then pressed the sides together. She wanted to see what was happening while she squeezed, but knew if she did, her focus would waver. Panic could set in, and that's what separates a surviving final girl from those who don't. Panic is the ultimate weapon of the monsters.

Littleton choked and gurgled. Lucy kept her eyes on the ship.

"Come on." She blew on the crack to make the glue dry faster.

Littleton's being infected. He choked and screamed in agony, but she didn't look. Sam almost got her last night. She should have been first. *Why wasn't I? Why Nadia and not me?* But these thoughts were distracting her, slowing her exhausted mind with the weight of survivor's guilt. Dark was building his army and starting here, in Lucy's town. She survived his attempt; the others didn't. A hope flickered in her heart that fixing the ship would fix everyone: Sam, Nadia, Littleton. All back to how they were before Dark came, before Lucy brought Dark into their lives.

She ran the scraper over the crack to pull off the excess glue that bubbled up. She tapped the plastic cement, still tacky. Still drying.

"What might you be doing in there?" Sam rasped through a raw throat. "Playing with toys?"

Nadia's mouth jittered, releasing a high-pitched hyena laugh.

"You choose to meet me, to be converted to my glory, while playing with children's things?"

Lucy felt the crack again. It was dry. It sealed. She looked up to see her plan working, but nothing changed. Sam was still melting. Nadia too. Now Littleton was getting up from the floor. His face sagged down as became just like his new master. Fixing the ship didn't stop King Dark, didn't stop Sam. Maybe the glue didn't count as "intact." Lucy ran her finger over the crack. It was invisible with the glue, like the fall never happened.

"Keys." Sam held out his hand to Littleton. Lucy heard the metal-on-metal clanging of Littleton fishing in his pocket.

She looked again at the repair kit for another tool. Another solution. She couldn't look at the three monsters unlocking the cell. She couldn't. They'd start infecting her the moment she saw their yellow eyes. The cell door clicked as Lucy saw Neil's handwriting on the bottom of the scorpion ship: *29.* Neil's note said the murder happened when the one guy wouldn't put the figure back in the ship. Lucy looked at the action figure, forced herself to see it. The hideous features pushed her eyes away, but not before she noticed a fresh scar on the toy. A slash across the mouth, just like what Nadia did to Sam with the coffee mug. Lucy grabbed the figure. It felt slick in her hand, like holding Sam's melting cheesy flesh. The cell door opened, and Sam rushed in. Lucy popped open the cockpit of the ship and shoved King Dark into his seat, then slammed the windshield down with a thunderous click.

Sam instantly fell to the ground. Nadia and Littleton too. Their strings were cut. Their bodies collapsed like broken marionettes. Lucy knew they were dead. Her best friends were dead. She killed them. She could reach Nadia, shake her, check her, but that's when the final girl would find out the monster isn't dead yet. That's the mistake that ends everything.

Lucy gathered her things into the bag and ran from the police station. She ran out into the pounding rain and screaming wind. All the way home, she whispered prayers into the freezing wind that her mom would be home, that she'd have some magic to make this all right.

THIRTEEN

When she got home, she couldn't breathe, but her mom was there. Trudy called the state police. They came quickly.

An incident at the police station, with shots fired, had already been reported. One police car stopped at Lucy's house while many others kept going to the local station. Lucy was in shock. The state troopers called an ambulance and took her to the hospital. She clutched her plastic bag the entire time.

Inside the bag, the Scorpion Cruiser shifted and moved, but Lucy held the cockpit. An iron grip kept it closed, and when she had a moment away from everyone's eyes, she taped it shut with black electrical tape from the repair kit. King Dark was locked in his prison, and if Lucy had her way, he'd be there forever.

After Lucy had been sedated, Trudy told her that Sam and Nadia were found at the police station. Sam was dead. Shot by Officer Littleton. Nadia and Littleton were in the emergency room now. Trudy said Nadia's parents were at the hospital and would keep them up to date. She hugged Lucy and thanked god she was safe.

Lucy didn't feel safe. She clutched the bag and held the scorpion ship tight. *Why did Neil have these things?* Her mind was finally clear enough to process the evening's events. *Why didn't he destroy this?* And then she thought, as if answering her own question, *Why haven't I?* Lucy laid down on her hospital bed, rolled to her side, and rubbed her thumb across the 29 on the ship's belly. "Because they're just toys," she whispered.

Her mom heard, but didn't ask. Trudy finger-combed her daughter's hair to calm the nightmare that gripped them. Sam's mom howled at the news of her son. Nadia's parents were silently crying. And Trudy counted her blessings that Lucy was okay; she wasn't dead or in surgery to save her life. Her daughter survived. With each stroke of Lucy's hair, Trudy swore to be a better person, to repay God for saving her daughter.

Lucy's mind was empty. She didn't make deals, didn't plead for her friends or ask why all this happened. She simply fell asleep stroking the scorpion ship.

FOURTEEN

The next morning, after a series of tests, Lucy was released from the hospital. Nadia was still in intensive care, but was expected to survive, according to her parents. They said she was pretty banged up and that she'd have some scars on her face from where she was burned. Lucy shivered, knowing that Nadia wasn't burned. She was *melted.*

"Is it permanent?" Lucy asked.

"The doctor said they could make it better with some surgery, but yes, it's not going to heal by itself," Nadia's mom said. "Did you see what happened to her? Who did this to them? Officer Littleton has the same burns, and I heard the paramedics said Sam did too."

Lucy shook her head, looking away from Nadia's parents. Their questions, their pleading eyes begging for answers, were too much to bear. Her mother had questions, and Lucy would answer them one day. But not today.

Lucy rode home in silence, holding her bag. Trudy drove and bit the skin around her thumbnail. Lucy noticed this before, when they first moved to this house and their furniture was lost by the moving company. Lately, Trudy hadn't been a nail biter, but the past 48 hours had changed that.

They pulled into the driveway with a slow roll. Trudy said quietly, "When you're ready to talk, I'm ready to listen." She rubbed Lucy's arm.

"I know."

Lucy got out of the car and looked at Nadia's house. *I hope you're okay.*

"Lucy, were you expecting a delivery?" Trudy said from the porch.

Lucy saw nothing but her mom standing by the porch railing. The railing Sam used to sit on and wait for Lucy to get home. He'd never sit there again because of the Life Changing Yard Sale. Because of her.

Lucy slowly walked up the porch steps to join her mom. The plastic bag crinkled in her grip when she saw the Baby-B-Real doll sitting on the swinging rocker. It smiled its hinged-jawed smile as the wind made the rocker gently sway.

"Yes." Lucy nodded. "I'm not going to be streaming anymore." Tears built in her eyes. "Not without Sam and Nadia. I thought I'd get a new hobby."

Trudy reached down for the doll, but Lucy stopped her.

"Don't touch it. It's a collector's item."

"But it's just a toy. You used to have one of these when you were a little girl." Trudy backed away from the doll, finally catching its glare. The eyes moved with her, staring their plastic blue stare past her eyes and into her mind.

"No, Mom. It's not." Lucy picked up the blanket Nadia always used to cover herself on the chilly nights. The memory of how King Dark's action figure felt crawled over her skin. *Do they all feel like that? Oily? Toxic?*

Lucy swaddled the babydoll. *Nadia should be sitting here, rocking. Not you.* But Lucy knew why Nadia wasn't sitting there. Because Lucy was curious, she needed to know, and now the hooks of that need sank deeper.

She repeated, "It's a collector's item," and took the doll inside.

INVENTORY NOTE: 29

Item: 29

Components:

- *Captain Light & the World of Darkness* VHS
- King Dark action figure
- Beta Ship

Collection: Private

Acquired through trade with @vice0_pysch0. He got it from a police contact. I'm guessing it was like some of my contacts who could make evidence disappear for the right price. The officer told Vice0 the whole story too, which I found a compelling reason why I needed it in my private collection.

According to Vice0, the Scorpion Cruiser in mint condition was held by Arnold South as he was bludgeoned to death by Greg Leederman with the Captain Light ship. Greg suspected Arnold of being possessed by an evil spirit imprisoned in the action figure. Argument ensued between the two when Arnold would not put the action figure back in the Scorpion Cruiser.

I tracked down Mr. Leederman, and when I interviewed him, he said the ship was Dark's doorway back to his world. Greg kept saying,

"Don't watch the tape. The tape's his eyes. When you see him, he'll see you." I was able to trade the tape, the ship, and figure with Vice0 for a minor item in my collection. In a few years, this will easily fetch a great return. Putting it in the vault. Everyone online says it must be intact and mint for them to be interested. Broken toys are no good to these collectors. No good to me either.

I wonder at the origin of the tape and from where King Dark originates. Perhaps he is from another planet, but more likely, Dark is like the creature Dodslav. A being just outside of our reality, yet close enough to cross over when the conditions are right. And through this line of reasoning, I must conclude that the ship's effects on Dark could be the same on Dodslav. A prison for one could be a prison for the other.

What would Dodslav give for his freedom? His treasured masterpiece? I dare not hope.

And what of this tape? While recently I obtained an alleged means of travelling between the worlds, I have not tried it yet, and could not imagine how a video camera could record such a thing. A machine lacks a necessary component to observe beyond our material world: a spirit.

My understanding from researching the Captain Light stories is that all three components must be present and in good working order to release King Dark. And with a specific condition for the release of Dark, it seems unlikely to be accidental. Dark was intentionally bound to the ship and the tape. But why?

Vice0 claimed the previous owner saw the tape's contents, and that they were of a strange, blasted world. He used the term "nuclear holocaust" to describe the destruction. Of course I have not, nor will

I, watch such a thing. I know better than to cast my mind into these other places.

Knowing of these things makes you known to these things, as Mr. Leederman indicated. And I am far too well known already. Who knows where Dark originated, but the last thing I need is for yet another dimension to seek my death.

29 will be stored in my private collection. Not to be traded. If it can work as a prison—and I will pursue this logic further—I must have it ready should things with Dodslav proceed in an undesirable manner.

18

ONE

Please return your card to your manager. You are terminated due to HR policy violation. Policy 34: Late Three Times.

Tanya stared at the screen. *Fired? How am I going to afford formula?*

"Nancy?" Tanya shouted toward the manager's office. It wasn't a loud shout; everything behind the kitchen of Burger Boi's was pretty quiet.

Nancy came over, but she already knew what happened. At 6:01am, Nancy received an email from the automated time management system stating employee 963 had violated policy 34 and was terminated. The system provided Nancy directions to "humanely off-board" employee 963 and a voucher for a free Burger Boi combo meal. If the meal was for Nancy or employee 963 was unclear.

"Is there something you can do?" Tanya pointed to the time clock. "Can you override it or something? I'm only three minutes late." Counting the one minute it took to register her termination and call Nancy over, that put her at 6:02 when she clocked in.

Burger Boi prided themselves on their extensive use of automation. Everything was automated, from the burger making to the order taking. Tanya was one of three employees at the restaurant.

"

She was a runner. She delivered the food from the robots in the kitchen to the customers in the front. Her role was to care about the customer experience, and she honestly did. Every order burning her hands, every complaint about the food; it was all good, because at the end of the week she got a paycheck. That check kept her daughter fed, clothed, and on the path to a better life. It was also the only job she could find, with an opposite shift from her dad. He watched Laney, her daughter, during the day while she worked. He worked second shift at the tire factory.

"I'm sorry, Tanya." Nancy sighed, then walked back to her office, motioning for Tanya to follow.

Tanya pleaded for the time clock to give her another chance, that she wouldn't be late again, she promised, but time clocks don't care about promises. In response, it clicked to the next minute. She smacked it hard, stinging her hand, then followed Nancy.

"I need this job, Nancy. My dad had a double. He was running late…" Tanya's reasons poured out of her with the pleading the machine ignored. She sat down in Nancy's metal folding chair, the one for employees. Nancy settled into a creaking swivel chair that once had a leather covering but now only showed yellow foam poking out. "Please. Can't you call someone?"

"There isn't anyone to call, Tanya. Burger Boi is all about the machines optimizing business. I don't get any say in things." Nancy hunted on her keyboard for each letter as she typed the confirmation of humane offboarding into the computer system. "I'm sorry, Tanya, I need your card key. But," Nancy reached around the computer, held Tanya's hand, "I know things are tight, so I'm going to put in an order for you to take home. It's…it's on Burger Boi." Nancy nodded as she continued to poke each key on her keyboard to enter the order. Sending home food wasn't part of the offboarding checklist, but Nancy didn't care. Tanya was an excellent employee, and being a few moments late didn't matter when no one ever came into the restaurant anyway.

"But nowhere else is hiring," Tanya said.

Outside Nancy's office window, Tanya watched the leaves breaking loose from a tree. It was fall. Cold was coming, with heating bills to be paid. Her dad's car needed to be fixed. Laney was just put on the expensive formula because of her digestive issues. More bills came to mind, each mounting heavier until her shoulders sunk from the weight, her back curled under the stress.

Nancy stabbed the enter key with her finger, impotence against the automations turning to anger. "I'm sorry, Tanya. You always did good work. The customers always liked you. I like you and I'm sure you'll find something." When Tanya didn't smile, didn't react at all, Nancy added, "Soon. I'm sure you'll find something soon."

This town didn't have anything. Tanya's best bet was to hope someone got fired at Walmart so she could jump in behind them. Even places that always hired weren't hiring anymore. Burger Boi talked about "the economy" as if it were a dying thing. So did all the other employers she talked to before applying to Burger Boi. "Too bad about the economy." "Real shame people like you get lost in this economy." These statements implied there was nothing anyone could do. This otherworldly force called The Economy was dying, and people like Tanya, people trying to rebuild a life after a rough start, were the human sacrifices necessary to save it.

"Come on, Tanya. I have to walk you out. That's the policy." Nancy looked everywhere but at Tanya.

The two women gathered up bags of burgers, fries, and pies that would last Tanya a week if she ate light. At the door, Nancy heaped the food into Tanya's overflowing arms.

"Sorry I can't do more. Burger Boi's computers, you know."

"Yeah," Tanya said, "nothing we can do against the computers. I know." Tanya nodded and walked home.

TWO

When she got too drunk to drive home, back in her partying days, Tanya knew this feeling. These walks were always at first light, just like now, but always weighed you down with each step. It's the Walk of Shame.

Now the shame was that she'd lost the second job she ever had. The first job, she got fired when she was pregnant. Morning sickness hit Tanya hard, and she'd get sick at work too much. They fired her after two weeks.

A burger slipped out of her arms and fell. She stopped and wondered if she could get it without dropping everything. Bending over would lead to all the bags tumbling out of their precarious position. Tanya froze as a familiar engine roared up the street. It was Rico's Mustang. No one else had a car like that around here; red, black stripes, fiery-orange LED-wrapped headlights, and a bloody neon glow under the car. Vince and Vivian barked and howled from the backseat as the engine revved. Tanya hadn't seen those three since Teddy got locked up. The Walk of Shame was never a good time to see people from your past. Especially these people, who Tanya never wanted to see again.

She looked for an exit, anywhere to get off the road. An alleyway between a construction fence and an old row home was dark enough for her to hide. Three words dripped down the fence in white spray paint: *Doras Dia Leanbh.*

Tanya hurried into the alley with her bags rustling, and another burger spilled into the darkness. Her falling food and crinkling burger wrappers were drowned out by the screaming tires and growling Mustang engine.

Tanya went deeper into the alley's shadows. The Mustang rumbled by; Tanya's insides trembled as it passed. Rancid melted tires covered up the greasy fried food smell. She kept moving into the darkness, waiting for the tires to squeal, come back around because they saw her. They'd come for her. They'd want Laney. Her hip bumped into something. She spun toward it. The Mustang's horn blared loudly as Vivian screamed into the night. Tanya startled, fumbling the bags.

The Mustang kept roaring away, getting farther and farther outside the alley's entrance. Tanya sighed and checked her bags again. They were resting in a basket, but it wasn't a shopping cart. She felt the wax of plastic weaved like a wicker basket. It was long and had a cover over part of the top. Metal chimes quietly sang as she hit something hanging from the cover. Tanya let her eyes adjust to the darkness. A dingy white bassinet emerged from the shadows. The legs ended in wheels. Rings hung from the cover, but Tanya couldn't see them in such deep darkness.

The Mustang's growl faded away as Tanya left the alley. She shrugged, surprise and delight mixed on her face. *Now I don't have to carry the food, and Laney will love this.* After her dad cleaned it up, the bassinet would be perfect for Laney. She never had one this nice before. Laney wasn't rolling or crawling yet, and Tanya loved giving her daughter something so fancy.

Tanya poked the mobile that dangled from the wicker cover. It swayed in the wind with a crisp chime of metal on metal. She wondered if it was safe, but figured her dad would know. The bassinet wheels squeaked and rattled like an old shopping cart as she pushed it down the street, but Tanya thought her luck might be changing. *When life gives you lemons, make lemonade.* She repeated this mantra, but the dread grew in her. How would she face Laney? Another job lost. Laney's mom was turning out to be just like Tanya's mom, and that made Tanya stiffen.

"That's not me. I'm going to get another job," Tanya said to no one around. Sunrise broke the early morning mists at her ankles. "I'm Laney's mom and I'm not going to let her down."

She kept talking to herself as she walked up the street, each affirmation building her confidence to face her daughter. Positivity tried to drown out the fear and worry, but it wasn't working. It did, however, keep Tanya from noticing the curious eyes watching her. They stared from the alleyway she left, unblinking as she pushed the bassinet home. Keeping to the dusky morning shadows, they followed.

THREE

Tanya's home was in the Waterforge Trailer Park on the edge of town. It was what you would expect in a trailer park, with some trailers being beautiful little homes, and others that were more shack than house. The perfect houses were retirees who downsized. The shacks were people who grew up there and never left. Tanya was the latter.

Outside her door sat lawn chairs pocked with rust. Dull gray siding on the trailer looked like dead skin. The lock on her storm door had broken. It constantly swayed in the wind, slamming shut on a heavy breeze. Stairs led to the trailer door, bowing and straining to hold Tanya's slight frame. She held open the storm door, fished for her keys, kept an eye on the food in the bassinet, and opened the front door.

"Marco, can you help me out a minute?" she called in.

"Coming." Marco hurried to her, pulling up his three-sizes-too-big pants as he came to her. It's not that he bought over-sized pants on purpose, but you get what you can find at the thrift store. Tanya's dad always said Marco "had no meat on him," and that made it hard to find fitting clothes. All his weight was in the curly puff of hair on his head, which was almost twice the size of his face. Acne was working into his complexion, but Tanya thought he was doing well for a teenage boy. She imagined avoiding sports and constant reading staved off breakouts.

"Can you help me bring in some of this food?" Tanya pointed to the piles of bags in the bassinet.

"Sure thing, Ms. Lewis." Marco held his pants up as he skipped down the stairs. They didn't creak under his steps, and probably noticed the wind more than his weight.

"Tanya, please. I'm not an old lady…" She trailed off, wondering if he thought she was. Maybe 23 is ancient when you're 16. She couldn't remember those days.

"Yes, ma'am, Tanya." Marco grabbed a few of the bags and took them up into the trailer.

"How's Laneybug this morning?" Tanya asked as he made another trip. She kept to the door, knowing it would slam if she let go. If Laney was asleep, a slamming door would wake her just like it'd been waking Tanya at night lately. Every breeze made her think about Teddy. She knew he couldn't be lurking around Waterforge, but what her mind knew and her heart feared were two different things.

"Perfect as always." Marco took in the last load. "Great listener, as always. I was reading to her and playing Mozart. There was a study about how Mozart makes babies smarter, so does reading."

"What were you reading?" Tanya followed Marco in and closed the storm door softly. She latched the little hook her dad made to keep the door shut, but it always slipped out. He tried to be handy, but his "fixes" didn't always make things better.

"*The Martian*. It's about a guy who gets stranded on Mars." Marco pulled the paperback from his back pocket. "There are some really funny lines in the book and it's super smart. Laney's really liking it."

"Thanks, Marco." Tanya took out a few cheeseburgers and put the rest in her refrigerator. They were cold from the long walk home, but they still smelled like Burger Boi. She didn't eat last night, so everything smelled good. "I lost my job." Tanya opened her purse, but it was empty. "Sorry. I'll get you when my last check comes in. Maybe take a burger as a down payment?" Her cheeks burned as she pushed the burgers to him. She'd never been unable to pay Marco before, and now she didn't know if she'd be able to again.

Marco shrugged it away. "No worries, Ms. Lewis— I mean, Tanya. I like hanging with Laney. She's cool for a baby." He reached for a burger, his lips wet, and then shook his head. "Nah, you keep them. We're going vegetarian in our house. Well, trying. It's not working for Ma too much."

Tanya nodded and smiled. She'd insist, but Marco was proud and took his role as the man of the house seriously. One time, he told her, being the man of the house meant being a helper in all things, including charity and work. He volunteered at the soup kitchen even though he didn't have any food either. He would read to the kids at the library to avoid going home while the gangs were out before the police cracked down at dusk. Marco had a plan for his future and it was far from Waterforge. Tanya knew if anyone could do it, it was him, and that's why she wanted him around Laney. He'd show Laneybug how to do the things her mom never could. Stay out of gangs. Get out of Waterforge. Make a life that isn't paycheck to paycheck with the constant fear of the mailbox and what bills are inside.

"You're a good man." Tanya rubbed his arm and gave him a hug.

He pulled away, uncomfortable with any affection, much less that of an older woman.

"Call me when you get an interview." Marco hopped down the stairs off to home. He paused at the bassinet, the sight of it putting him into slow motion, but shook his head and went off to school.

Tanya chuckled at his last words. "'Call me when you get an interview.' Yeah, that's going to happen." She rolled her eyes and went to check on Laney.

Unlike many of the trailers in Waterforge, Tanya's trailer was a two bedroom with a den model. Her dad was able to get it when times were good and they moved across the trailer park to their new home. That was before Marco was even born. Back when Mom was here and life wasn't so hard.

Laney was on her playmat with Mr. Potmus the stuffed hippopotamus. She chewed on him, leaving slobbery patches of matted plush over his face and snout.

"Hi, baby!" Tanya cooed to her daughter. Whenever Tanya saw Laney, she remembered all the good things in the world and how much one life matters. Not her life, but the life of her daughter.

Laney lit up at her mom and threw Mr. Potmus to the side for better cuddles and love. Tanya scooped her up as she cooed and cheered in garbled baby talk, part drool and part inexpressible love.

"I got you something!" Tanya said with big eyes, as she swayed with Laney. "Do you want to see it?"

Laney made a noise close enough to an affirmative for Tanya. They walked outside. As Tanya loosened the hook for the storm door, the wind ripped the door from Tanya's hands. She startled. That startled

Laney and sent her into wailing tears, the kind only an infant who's afraid of everything can muster.

"Oh, it's okay," Tanya whispered, and swayed slower. "It's okay. Just the wind and this old door. But look." Tanya nuzzled Laney's teary cheeks, smelling her fresh baby. "Look. A new bed."

Laney saw the bassinet and kept howling her fearful cry.

Tanya hurried down the rickety stairs to show Laney the strange wind chime mobile hanging over the bassinet hood.

Laney stopped crying. She stopped breathing as she stared at the strange contraption. Tanya looked at her, worry catching in her throat, and before she could ask, Laney let out a babbling siren of laughter. She reached for the bassinet, eager and joyful. When Tanya didn't move, Laney lunged toward it, making Tanya stagger forward.

"Hold on. It's not clean."

But Laney didn't care. She reached and strained for the bassinet, for the mobile that hung in it. There wasn't anything obviously dangerous, and Tanya was thrilled at Laney's joy. It lit up the morning, warmed the chilly wind, and helped Tanya forget about the hard road ahead, so she lowered Laney into the bassinet.

Laney laid under the mobile and instantly started reaching for it. She batted at it, sending the wind chimes into motion with strange frequencies like glass bells tinkling brightly, but the sound echoed like deep iron church bells. Tanya leaned down to see the mobile, noting the metal rings flowing together in an infinite knot, like the Celtic tattoos her former "friends" had. It was unclear where one ring stopped and another began, weaved together, overlapping and encircling. Some rings were silver, some gold, some copper, one black, but the colors seemed to smear together. *Is this just one ring?* She wasn't sure.

A familiar coughing, wheezing engine pulled up near the bassinet as Laney played. Tanya smiled and saw her dad getting home from his night shift. Their car was a rusty blue station wagon with wood paneling along the sides. Her dad got out and shook his head when he saw Tanya.

"What are you doing home? Where's Marco?"

"Sorry, Dad. I was late, and the computer fired me."

"Computer? Don't you have a manager or something?" Her dad, Zack, was puzzled. His entire career had been working in the factory, and he had never encountered a computer at work. His job was to separate scrap, and it was cheaper for him to do it than some robot. "I mean, how late were you?" Suspicion crept into his voice as it always did when hints of Tanya's old life came up.

"Three minutes." She sighed. The suspicion was clear to her too, and she knew it wasn't misplaced. For too long, she made the wrong decisions. From fourteen to twenty-two, she'd rather be high or drunk than anything else, but Laney changed all that. Being pregnant with Laney and Teddy going to jail. "Honest. The computer don't play." She smirked to avoid crying. "Sorry, Dad. I really tried. I…Laney, wasn't feeling well this morning, and I…"

"These things happen, sweetie. The world's stacked against people like us. Moreso people like you. Trying to do right. Trying to raise your baby." He leaned down and tickled Laney's tummy. "But there's good here too. Just got to work for it, and when you get it, hold it tight." He gave Tanya a hug. "You're on the right path. Keep going."

"Got some burgers in there. But before you go to bed, can I ask you to clean this up for Laney? She loves it and I… I just want to give her something nice."

Zack looked at the bassinet. He hunkered down and examined the legs, the base, the basket, the hood, and stopped at the mobile. He reached for the rings, but Laney smacked at his hands. Tanya and Zack laughed at that, thinking it was cute, and read nothing more into it.

"This looks structurally sound." He pushed on the basket. It whined in response but didn't break. "Yeah, a good scrubbing's all this needs."

Laney stopped cooing, stopped laughing, and reached up to the mobile with a jerky smack. The rings chimed a brain-rattling *DONG* that pushed Tanya back. She grabbed her temples to keep her head from splitting open at the sound. Zack did the same. Laney screamed in joy and looked like she was clapping. A freezing gust of wind blasted through their front yard, pushing over one of the lawn chairs, kicking up dirt and dead leaves as it passed. Tanya snatched Laney from the bassinet, squeezing her tight before it could fall over. It didn't. The storm door slammed shut with a thunderous bang. Tanya jumped, clutched Laney tighter so no one could rip her baby away, and scanned the trailer park for Teddy's car. Slamming doors was always his entrance and exit. All doors. Slammed to announce his presence or departure. Her heart raced with Laney's, but her daughter was still cheering and laughing from the bassinet.

Teddy wasn't around.

"Damn, this weather's gettin' weird," Zack said. "Y'all head on inside and I'll get this scrubbed up."

Tanya did. Laney watched what her grandfather was doing with the bassinet with deep curiosity. She giggled and jerked her hands around in the uncontrollable flailing way babies play. Tanya smiled at her, and the two watched Zack scrub the bassinet from the front window. Laney would whine as Tanya moved away. The little girl focused on the rings, joy brightening her cheeks, obsession darkening her eyes.

FOUR

Zack cleaned the bassinet quickly. He brought it inside and put it in Tanya's bedroom.

Tanya found a blanket that wasn't too big and tucked it under the thin mattress. Laney was in her new bassinet a moment later, playing with her new favorite toy. Even after Tanya put Mr. Potmus in the bassinet, Laney only had eyes for the mobile. She swatted at it, kept swirling it, tapping the metal rings gently, and sometimes getting too excited, then whacking the rings into a swinging pendulum.

Tanya went into the kitchen to prepare some burgers for lunch. Her dad had already gone to bed for the day. He had decorated the den to look like a living room with an old couch, a recliner he found online, and a 42" TV. That TV was his joy and the first thing he showed anyone who came over. It was the biggest TV he'd ever owned, and he thought he was a king when he watched it.

Beyond the den was a galley kitchen. Nothing special, but it had the essentials. The microwave was the most used appliance here, as neither Zack nor Tanya was much for cooking. Heating things up was more their speed. The microwave beeped as Tanya pressed the quick start timer to heat the burgers. She almost didn't notice the soft knocking at her door.

Out the front window, Tanya saw an old lady standing on the stairs. She looked at those stairs with suspicion and a grimace that asked, *Are you going to hold me?* And it was a valid question. She wasn't obese, but she was heavier than anyone who'd stood on those stairs before. The old lady was stout, built solid, old but not frail.

"Can I help you?" Tanya called from the window.

The old lady spotted her, smiled a perfect white toothed smile, an unusual sight in this trailer park. "I'm Carla Geeze from the Burger Boi corporation. I'm here to apologize for your," the old lady shook her head with genuine disgust, "your treatment this morning."

Tanya cracked open her door. "What do you mean?"

"Your termination. Three minutes late. Just awful. And for a working mother. Our records show you are a working mother. Well, a few minutes is just unfair. A bug in our system." Carla waved a white glove as if shooing away the idea of lateness. "If I may speak with you, I am here to discuss a severance package."

"Severance?"

"That's a term used by our fancy lawyers to say 'apology money.'" Carla grinned. "I'm not a fan of lawyer types."

Tanya smiled and opened the door more. "Me neither." She remembered her many run-ins with the public defenders and prosecutors. Neither wanted to help her. Just wanted to get through whatever trouble she brought to them. Tanya stepped back to make room for Carla to come in, but she just stood on the stairs. The old lady shivered in the wind. Tanya took another step back and held the door so it didn't swing closed. A moment later, a silent moment of confusion for Tanya, and she asked, "Would you like to come in?"

Carla smiled and stepped lightly into the trailer. "Why thank you."

"Please, have a seat. I don't have any coffee left." Tanya blushed.

"I'm more of a tea person anyhow. Regardless, I'm here to express the deepest condolences for the way our system treated you. To express our regrets, I have been given instructions to provide you with a severance package. This package is to help you while you search for other opportunities." Laney cooed loud and cheery from her room. "Or perhaps with babysitting services." Carla smiled broad and joyous like a grandmother should. Tanya smiled in return, tearing up at the sight of someone so happy her baby was happy. No judgement, no questions about the daddy, no wondering about how she was going to make it, just joy to hear Laney.

"What does this mean? Like, I've never heard of this kind of thing. Maybe I should get my dad?" Tanya stood, but Carla rested her hand on Tanya's arm so gently it felt like a fallen leaf settling for a winter's sleep.

"Oh dear, you needn't bother him. We ladies are more than capable of handling ourselves." Carla pulled a large stack of paper from her purse and a black pen with a golden fountain tip. Reaching into her purse again, Carla produced a small pot of ink and uncorked the lid. Tanya had never seen a pen and ink set like this outside of the movies. "I just need your signature to give you this check."

The stack of papers was intimidating. It put Tanya in mind of a Bible, and not the short Jesus stories but the long, long version starting with let there be light and ending with fire and brimstone. Never being the church type, she wasn't sure about the stories in between, but knew the Bible was a long book. She started reading the first page and, while it was English, it was totally foreign to her. Tanya didn't know the term "legalese" but that's what this document, this contract, was written in.

"If you sign the last page, I can give you this check." Carla pushed a much smaller and easier to read piece of paper toward Tanya. There were not as many words on this one, and only one number that made reading the rest unnecessary. Tanya gaped at Carla.

"This is a mistake." Tanya pushed the check back to her. "This is…" She did some quick math in her head, but was never very good at math. "I don't know, more than I would make in a year at Burger Boi."

Laney cooed again as the chimes of the mobile clinked and jangled.

Carla smiled at the noise. "Here's the bottom line. We give you money. You don't talk to the press or sue us." She pushed the check back to Tanya. "And I'm sticking around town to check in and help you with any," Carla's head bounced from side to side, making Tanya smile, "transition that might be necessary."

"Transition?"

"You know, new job stuff." Carla crinkled her nose and shrugged away the word. She flipped to the last page of the book that was the legalese contract and tapped a line that said *Signature*. Holding the pen out, Carla smiled an inviting grin as she sat calm and patient.

Tanya's hands jittered toward the pen. That much money would be just what she needed to get Laney's college fund started. They could get good groceries. Pay Marco more. Maybe even get Laney a nice crib for when she got a little older. Her dad said things would get better, and maybe this was it. She wasn't going to sue Burger Boi anyway, didn't even think about it. The pen was light in her fingers and pressed to the signature line before Tanya even realized she was doing it. But nothing came out of the pen.

"You must dip it first. I like the old ways." Carla pushed the ink pot toward Tanya. The smell of whatever was inside burned Tanya's nose hairs. It put her in mind of the time a skunk got caught in their car's axle. The poor thing was wrapped around the metal under Dad's car, reeking of death and burning from the spinning tires. As she pressed the pen into the ink, there was an audible pop as the skin over the ink broke. Tanya pulled the pen from the pot and watched a slow strain of dark red ink drool from the tip back into the pot. She wiped it on the lip of the pot, looked to the check, and signed her name on the signature line.

As she wrote, she noticed Carla had already signed her name to a line beside her's. Over Carla's line, the word *Granter* was written. Over Tanya's line, *Inheritor*. Carla sprinkled something on the wet signature and shuffled the papers away.

"Excellent. Here's your check. Remember, no legal stuff, and no telling others what's happened here. If anyone asks, say you quit Burger Boi and received an inheritance from a long-lost relative." Carla nodded and smiled her perfect smile. "I must be going now, but I'll be around to check in. Remember, if you need anything, just call me." She pushed a business card across the table, but it only had a handwritten phone number on it.

"Thank you," Tanya said as the quick shuffling of papers confused her. *Should I have read all that?* But then the check was in her hands. The numbers were so large that she couldn't help but smile. It was the lottery. "I...I can't thank you enough. This is such an amazing thing. Thank you."

"Oh, dear, we just want you to be happy." Carla glanced back to the laughs and coos coming from Laney's room. "And to be the mother you want to be. That money is yours now. Use it how you'd like."

Carla saw herself out as Tanya looked again at the check, unbelieving that her luck had finally turned.

Outside, Carla went to her black Audi sedan and climbed into the backseat. Tanya hadn't noticed her car when she arrived, but now saw she had a driver waiting for her the whole time. The windows were tinted, but the front window showed a young man's face, a gorgeous man dressed in formal wear. He drove away carefully and quietly into the afternoon clouds. As he turned out of Waterforge, the first drops of rain fell, signaling the storm which had been blowing all morning had finally arrived.

FIVE

The check cleared. It wasn't from Burger Boi, it was from Carla. Tanya didn't notice during the discussion, but her dad did when he looked at the check.

"Probably to keep them out of all this," Tanya said, but her dad was worried.

"Did you get a copy of what you signed?" he kept asking, and she kept telling him no, but it was hard to hear over Laney screaming in the back. Her car seat kept her locked in, but Tanya could hear little Laney thrashing and screaming her lungs out.

The screaming started when Tanya took her out of the bassinet. Laney wanted to keep playing with the mobile and that was clear because she hadn't stopped screaming since.

In the cramped car, Tanya's couldn't tell what would give first, her ear drums from Laney or her patience for all her dad's questions.

"Look, we need the money. There are no other jobs, Dad."

"How do you know?"

"Because there wasn't when I got this one and not much has changed around here," Tanya growled.

"Just saying it ain't right. They're pulling a fast one on you." Zack rolled down his window a little to let some fresh air in and let the breeze drown out Laney's screaming.

Sheets of rain crashed on the window, adding another noise trampling through Tanya's head. They got to the shopping center in town as the storm picked up steam and dropped a downpour on them. Rain roared over the windshield and dripped through the broken seals on the edges. Windshield wipers stuttered across the front window but couldn't keep the rain clear.

"Need help with Laney?" Zack asked. "I can wait here with her while you run in." He pointed to the grocery store.

"No, she's my daughter, and I'll get her to calm down. I'm her mom." Tanya didn't say the rest: *Moms don't leave their kids behind.* "You get what you need in TractorSmart and I'll get dinner for tonight." Tanya opened her door and hustled to open Laney's. Icy rain drenched her as she struggled to unhook the car seat cradle. Laney screamed in her face as she leaned in to unhook the car seat. "Please, Laneybug, please, it's okay." She found the latch for the car seat, pulled it, released it, and lifted Laney out of the car. Tanya hurried to get out of the rain, turned, and bumped Laney's head on the car door. The screaming intensified, drowning out the howling wind and driving rain.

"Oh my god!" Tanya gasped. "I'm so sorry! I'm sorry! I didn't mean to do that!" *I didn't do that on purpose.* But she wondered if it was true the way many mothers at the end of their rope from stress and screaming wonder. It was an accident from being distracted and rushed, but that didn't stop Tanya from blaming herself, questioning her ability to be a mom. The rain soaked them both as Tanya checked Laney's head. A little bump was forming. Laney kept screaming.

"I'm sorry." Tanya hurried into the grocery store, escaping the rain, but Laney didn't calm down. Her wailing continued in the store. The looks came as soon as the doors slid open and the rain was silenced when they closed. Familiar stares of old ladies and teens wondering why Tanya couldn't control her baby filled the store's entrance.

"Shhh, shhhhh, shhh." Tanya rocked Laney, begged for her to quiet down, but she didn't. People shifted away from her quickly, glancing, disgusted at the bad mom who couldn't handle a crying baby. "I'm sorry," Tanya said to anyone who looked, and she thought they were all looking, all judging, all deserving an apology that she wasn't better.

"Oh, someone sounds sad."

Tanya recognized the voice and turned to her. Carla came toward her, ready to take Laney. "Can I help?" Her face was joyous and excited, not judgmental and dismissive.

"She bumped her head." Tanya's voice cracked. Tears rolled down her face as the rain streamed from her hair. "I was getting her out," her voice caught in her throat, "I hit her head. It was an accident."

Carla nodded and smiled. "Let me help you."

Tanya held Laney tight, swaying faster to calm her. The screaming didn't stop.

Now people were stopping, pointing with their eyes and grumbling about how that poor baby had such a terrible mommy. Tanya thought she could hear them, but by now Laney's screams were a constant siren in her ears. She didn't notice when Laney stopped.

Carla gently scooped Laney out of Tanya's arms and cuddled her with cooing noises. Laney was playing with Carla's necklace. It was a black glass pendant hanging from a silver chain. She cooed and looked at the teardrop shape with curious wonder.

"There we go," Carla whispered and swayed.

People were still staring at Tanya, but now they gave thankful glances to Carla. All the appreciation they sent her was reflected in disgust and malice.

"Don't look at those beasts, Tanya. They don't understand. No, they don't. No, they don't." Carla snuggled Laney, who cooed and giggled back to her happy self. "Are you giving Mommy a hard time? You shouldn't do that. She's a good mommy."

Tanya looked away, tugging one of the blue shopping baskets from the pile. It was stuck. Another thing she couldn't do. Her head shook slightly, sending flicks of water around her. A drop hit an old man walking by. He glared at her in disgust.

"What? You don't like water. Get out of here!" Carla barked. The man skittered away. "Don't take their shit, deary. They'll always have it to dump on you, but that doesn't mean you have to take it. No." Carla's voice shifted to baby talk. "No, it doesn't." Laney laughed. "Now, tell Mommy you're sorry for overreacting."

The store entrance was filling up as people waited for the rain to break before going to their car. They eyed Carla about her baby talk, but she paid them no mind. Laney reached for Tanya with a pleading whine. Tanya took her back with a smile and a gasping cry.

"I'm sorry," Tanya said.

"She's fine." Carla waved away the idea and took the shopping basket. "Now, what are we here for?"

We? But Tanya took the help and sputtered, "I need some dinner for tonight. Something that's not Burger Boi."

"Yes, then let's get to it." Carla strode into the store. Two people stood beyond the automatic doors in the produce section and she shooed them away as Tanya followed.

I guess people listen to old ladies? Tanya wondered, but the expressions on people who saw Carla weren't those of respect or reverence, but fear. They were creeped out by her, but why? *She's just a nice old lady, and not even that old. Older than Tanya's mom, but not wicked stepmother old.*

As Tanya, Laney, and Carla went down the produce aisle, Tanya noticed how everyone moved to the other side of the aisle. *They're avoiding me. The single mom. The failure at mothering and relationships.*

Laney kept reaching for Carla's necklace. The black glass raindrop shimmered in the fluorescent lights over the apples.

"Laney, leave that alone." Tanya pulled Laney back.

"No, it's fine." Carla put the basket down and handed Laney the necklace. "It was my mom's." Laney shook it and laughed at the high-pitched rattling of the silver chain.

"Is it something? I mean, it looks like a drop of water."

"Yes, that's what it is. Well, a tear. My mom said it was a frozen tear from a pooka, a shapeshifter." Carla lifted an apple for Tanya's examination. Tanya shrugged. Carla looked at her, puzzled. "Firm, no bad spots, top of pile. Good apple." She winked and placed the apple gently in the basket. "Pookas were thought to be troublemakers and monsters, but my mom thought they were just misunderstood."

Laney sputtered a spitty raspberry and put the black tear stone to her mouth. Tanya stopped her from trying to teethe on glass with a patient smile and worried glance to see who saw that. Did anyone see her baby try to eat jewelry? But no one looked at them now. Carla's glare, a warning for any who dared look their way, made sure of that.

"Well, let's get some veggies."

"So, were the pooka monsters?" Tanya held the black glass which was much heavier than it looked. The silver chain jangled and sung in her hands as Carla smiled. She showed Tanya colorful peppers and bright orange carrots. With each item she picked up, she made an *Oh, did you see this?* expression that made Tanya smile. She'd never been shopping with anyone who helped her pick healthy foods.

"No." Carla sniffed a box of strawberries. "Like most of us, they're misunderstood. These are good. You can tell because they smell like strawberries."

Carla shoved the box under Tanya's nose, and she took an involuntary sniff. The smell stole her mind away from questions about the existence of pookas and threw her into the ecstasy of being with someone who genuinely cared for her. Carla put the box to Laney's nose and Laney busted into laughter.

"Come, come. Let's get done." Carla hustled them through the store, letting Laney play with the pooka's teardrop. Tanya followed in awe as Carla navigated the store, the people, the world with confidence, certainty, and a deep sense of not giving a shit what other people thought. She felt something with Carla that she hadn't felt in a long time. She felt safe. Tanya forgot that, not long ago, she felt safe with Teddy too.

SIX

The rain calmed as Tanya and her family drove home. Everyone was relaxed after the shopping trip. When the rain stopped, Tanya opened her window to let in the fresh fall air. She rested her head on the car door and let the cool breeze wash over her. From beneath the car, the tires droned a sleepy white noise of wet static.

Her eyes were getting heavy as they pulled into Waterforge and stopped in front of their trailer. After a quick stretch and deep yawn, Tanya took Laney inside to the bassinet.

"There you go." Tanya smiled and tickled Laney's little toes. "Enjoy, Laneybug." She pushed the bassinet into the den while they unpacked groceries.

"Hey, Ms. Tanya." Marco came in with a handful of groceries. "Big shop?"

"Yeah. Thanks. Here, let me—"

"Nah, I got this. You can chill." Marco motioned to the recliner then hustled back outside to get more bags. Tanya shook away the thought and grabbed some bags with him.

Zach went into the trailer, got his work gear, and returned to the car. He waited for Marco to finish taking groceries in and drove off.

Tanya watched him leave and shook her head. *Not even one bag.* Years ago he would have helped. He'd insist Tanya and he be out there when her mom got home to carry in groceries. Now, he couldn't be bothered with anything but his TV, sleep, and work. Even when he was supposed to be watching Laney, he was just watching TV or sleeping.

What happened? But Tanya knew. She only had to look around at the trailers here to see. Time breaks down everything in this place. That's why Laney can't stay. If you're here too long, this place's rot sinks into you. *Is it already in me? Too deep in me to leave here?*

"Wow, look at all this." Marco's cheer brought her back to the good things in Waterforge. A laughing baby, and a helpful boy unpacking her bags. "Like, you hit the lottery or something?"

"Or something." Tanya joined Marco in the kitchen.

Laney played with the mobile. Her hands flailed in jerky slaps, spinning the rings with deep, iron bell sounds. The dong from each collision hung in the air longer and longer. Tanya turned from the groceries, watching the rings for a moment.

Weren't they brighter before? She thought the rings sounded more like chimes than old church bells, but now she couldn't remember.

"Where do you want all these?" Marco held up a spiky yellow fruit, unsure if it would cut him. "Whatever this is?"

"That's a jelly melon. And they can go on the counter."

Laney smacked the rings hard, but the resulting ring was quiet. She laughed and Tanya returned to unpacking her massive shop.

DONGGGG!

Marco jumped. Tanya's attention snapped back to Laney's bassinet. The sound hung in the air, rattling Tanya's back teeth with a gut-twisting resonance. She grabbed her stomach, then grabbed the counter to keep from crumbling to the ground. Marco collapsed and squeezed his watering eyes shut.

That's the same noise. The loud noise. Tanya remembered the first time the rings made such a deafening sound. Laney's ecstatic giggles mixed with the reverberating pulse wobbling through everything.

Tanya stumbled to Laney. Marco followed.

"You feel that?" Marco asked as his hand rose to his mouth. He pressed on his jaw, feeling the bone.

"Yeah." Tanya rubbed her jaw. "In my teeth. Is that from the bell?" Her mouth buzzed like she'd eaten ten packs of PopRocks.

Marco shook his head, shrugged. "Where'd it come from?" He glanced quickly at the mobile but dismissed it. Nothing that small could make such a big noise in his mind. And while he spent a lot of time with Laney, he'd never heard one of her screaming fits, thus not understanding that little things can make very, very big noises.

They searched for the sound, keeping their eyes far from the mobile. Laney kept laughing.

"Mmmm!" Marco moaned. "I can still feel it."

Laney screamed in delight as Tanya picked her up from the bassinet. With a sigh of contentment, Laney curled into her mom with a smile.

The three went to the kitchen as the vibration in their teeth settled and the groceries started to thaw. Marco moved quickly to put things away as Tanya swayed with her baby.

"Reading anything new?" Tanya asked.

"Yeah." Marco paused from putting away a jar of strawberry jam and plucked his newest read from his back pocket. "A collection."

"*Call of Cthulhu and Other Tales.*" Tanya shook her head. "Cover looks creepy." A giant octopus man attacked a little ship, but the ship wasn't all that little, nor was the octopus man giant—it was incomprehensible. Once, Marco told her the right word for something so massive you couldn't imagine it was "prodigious," and that's exactly what this octopus man was. "Don't be reading that to Laneybug." She chuckled.

"Do you need me to watch her for a bit?"

"Would you mind? I'd like to maybe have some 'me' time." Tanya choked back the idea. *That's selfish. I don't need "me" time.* After this morning, she thought it might be good, but she didn't want to be a bad mom. Didn't want to leave her daughter behind. "You know, never mind. I'll—"

"No, you go," Marco said. He closed the last cabinet. "I'll hang here with Laneybug and you have some Ms. Tanya time. It's good for you and good for Laney. I was reading online that if the momma doesn't take care of herself, then she can't take care of her baby." He smiled.

"You're reading parenting stuff?"

"YouTube." He shrugged. "Now go and have fun. We'll be here." Marco took Laney. She cheered and reached for his book as she always did.

"You have something else to read her?"

He pulled another book from another pocket in a flourish of pride. "Always."

"*A Brief History of Time?*" Tanya laughed as she gathered up her purse. "No wonder Laney's so smart." She didn't notice it, but Tanya stood a little taller when she talked about Laney. Never about how beautiful Laney was—and she was a beautiful baby—but always proudest when remarking about her intelligence. Tanya knew, learned the hard way in her own life, that beauty fades faster than you'd like, and with it, how others see you. Smarts are forever and only get sharper with age.

Marco sat on the floor with Laney. He cleared his throat and opened the book. "Chapter 2, Space and Time."

SEVEN

Without a car, there were not many places Tanya could go during the day that weren't the grocery store. There was a Walmart, and that's where she went. Not to buy anything, just to look around, but remembering her newfound fortune, she grabbed a cart and headed to the baby aisle.

There were a few other young moms in the store, but all with their babies and pretending to be cheery no matter how miserable their kid was. No mommies want to look like they're failing. Tanya knew this well, but she made it a point to smile at each and give some compliment.

"You look nice," Tanya said to one mom. "Your baby's clothes are so clean. I wish my daughter could stay that clean," to another. "What a fun outfit for your little guy."

All the comments she never received being a single, stressed-out mom. Maybe if she gave more compliments, more would come her way.

Tanya put a new stuffy—an elephant—into the cart, as well as some new pacifiers and some fresh bedding for the bassinet. She wasn't sure what size to get but assumed it's all probably standard.

A box of diapers, a rattle, and a few chewy rings finished out her shopping, but she took a lap around the store to just relax.

In the electronics section, she saw a 52" TV and knew her dad would love it. It was black and sleek and something out of a rich person's house. If she got it for her dad, he'd know she'd turned over a new leaf. Now she could get him things like a new TV. Tanya could take care of him, like he took care of her. She stopped at that thought and questioned if it was true, but abandoned it quickly, remembering this money wasn't for her dad. Tanya moved out of the electronics section.

As she passed the clothes section, a dress she liked jumped out at her along with a fun top. *When I get my new job, I'm going to get those.* She smiled; *when*, no longer *if.* Carla was right. This money was a chance to reinvent herself. To be someone she never could have been without it. She could reinvent her family's world.

A man was in front of her in the checkout line. His flushed face and scraggly beard stank of beer, even from a shopping cart away. The checkout worker was a young man with Down syndrome. He scanned each item, checking the price that rang up as he placed the items in the bag.

"Can you go any faster?" The customer's voice was a slurry growl. "Don't want to be here all day."

Tanya watched the checkout guy scanning and bagging. He wasn't moving slow. He was being accurate.

"I want to make sure all the prices are right. Our system's been having issues—" the clerk started, but was cut off by the beer-stinking man's hand slamming down on the credit card machine.

"I don't care about your retard problems."

"Hey!" Tanya roared. "Don't be a dick. He's looking out for you."

"Shut up, bitch, or I'll show you a dick."

The clerk stopped scanning and raised his hand with three fingers up. Another man came over quickly, older than the clerk and wearing a tie—a manager if Tanya had ever seen one.

"What seems to be the problem here?" the manager asked.

"This retard—"

"This man is being offensive to our guests," the clerk answered and gestured toward me. "He threatened assault. Ma'am, would you like us to call the police?"

"Oh, wait now! I didn't say nothing—"

"Sir, perhaps you'd best step out of line and let her go while we sort this out." The manager invited him toward the office.

"No, your boy here is—"

"Sir." The manager stepped back and waved. "Perhaps we can discuss this over here."

Two other men were now watching near the manager's office. The rude customer noticed them and stepped over to the manager.

The clerk tossed the man's bags to the side. They were taken by one of the security guards now moving toward the situation.

"And he thinks I'm the retard." The clerk shook his head as the man, the manager, and security had moved out of earshot.

"I'm sorry that happened," Tanya said, but the clerk waved it away.

"Assholes come in here all the time." He scanned slowly, checking the prices as he went. Tanya looked around to see what happened, but everyone had disappeared into the manager's office. Two other security people were watching her but pretending to be shopping. One was a man with scruffy black hair, another was an older woman with long blonde hair turning white. Both seemed more interested in Tanya than the clothes they were pretending to look at.

"Do they think something else is going to happen?" Tanya nodded to the security people.

"Who?" the clerk asked as he double-checked the price tag on the diapers.

"Those guys." She pointed to the people at the clothes, but stopped when she saw they'd moved on. "Oh, never mind. I thought…" She trailed off, realizing the words "*someone was watching me*" sounded a little paranoid.

A few minutes later, she wrapped up in the line and left. In the parking lot, she pushed everything in her cart until the last cart return. She pulled out her bag, hefted the diaper box, and prepared for the long walk home.

Walmart shopping carts are so loud that she didn't hear the wheezing growl of the Mustang engine creeping up behind her. As she loaded her arms, the engine roared, filling her world with dark images of drunk nights and bad decisions. It was Rico's red Mustang, with Vivian hanging out the side.

"Where you going, mama?" Rico whistled. "Need a ride?"

"No," Tanya said, and started walking back toward the store.

"C'mon, we can't let Teddy's girl walk home with all that stuff.

He'd be pissed. Get in the car," Rico said.

"Yeah, you don't want Teddy pissed, do ya?" Vivian said. A smile wanted to burst through, but she held it back behind a pouty face.

"No, thank you. I'm fine. I forgot something in the store."

"We can wait," Rico said. He revved the engine again, making Tanya jump again.

"I'm not Teddy's girl no more," Tanya said as she walked. The Mustang crept along beside her, Rico's head and arm hanging out the window lolling toward her.

"That ain't what he says." Rico chuckled.

"He's in jail. Don't matter what he says," Tanya whispered.

"Oh, is that what you think?" Rico straightened up in the driver's seat. "Well, you might want to rethink that."

Tanya stopped walking. She stared at the Walmart sign. Clouds had moved in quickly, blotting out the sun in an inky patch of darkness.

"Now you thinking." Rico tittered. "But our offer has expired. My kindness only goes so far, and you being rude on Teddy just ain't good." Rico sighed as if to say, *So sad, so sad is this world.* "Teddy's gonna hear about this." Rico revved the engine into a deafening roar. He barked at Tanya. She shrank from him. Vivian cackled laughter as the two raced away, tires squealing and smoking.

Tanya stood frozen. She looked for Teddy. He was always around when you didn't want him to be. He was vicious. He played with his victims, tormenting them. Whether it was someone he robbed or a junkie he shook down. Teddy delighted in cruelty and often turned that mind to Tanya when the drugs or drinks hit him right.

She didn't go back to the store. She ran home.

EIGHT

On the hurried walk home, Tanya looked for someone behind her more than she watched where she was going. Teddy knew where she lived. His *friends* didn't need to follow her. They knew no one ever left Waterforge, certainly not a single mom who couldn't keep a job.

When she saw her trailer, the buzzing orange light over the door, she sighed in relief. But the sigh caught in her throat. Marco was sitting in one of the lawn chairs, tapping his foot like a jackhammer.

"What's wrong?" Tanya asked.

"I had to—" Marco bit his lip, his hands jerking around in confused swirls. "I had to get out. I can't listen to it anymore."

"Listen to what?" She glanced into the trailer, but the door was closed. The storm door hung open, creaking quietly in the gentle breeze. "Was Laney crying?"

"No." Marco stood up and quickly blocked her from going to the door. "No. There's something in there. I think Laney's fine. She was—"

"*Think* she's fine?" Tanya bristled. "You think she's fine? Marco, you left her alone in the house?"

"She's not alone." Marco shouted the last word. "I don't think she's alone. There was another of those bells, another." He rubbed his jaw, pressing hard into the skin over his back teeth. "Then she was talking, like babbling on the baby monitor, but something answered. It was a…" He reached for the words, his hands thrusting toward the ground to pull them up as if the deep earth were the only place to find a word to describe the sounds.

"You left her alone." Tanya pushed past him and went inside. Marco didn't follow. He stood outside, still digging for the words.

The baby monitor hissed with its normal static in the den. All the lights in the house were on. The monitor's green light flickered as it received Laney's cooing. Tanya paused for a response, to hear what Marco heard. But there was nothing. Laney kept cooing. No voices replied.

Tanya scooped her out of the bassinet. Laney didn't protest but gave a parting whack to the mobile, which chimed and jingled its discordant tune.

"Is she okay?" Marco asked from outside as he peeked around the door.

"You can't leave her alone," Tanya barked at Marco. He shrank from her. "What if she got hurt? What if she ate that mobile?" Tanya knew this was unlikely and ridiculous, but her mom instincts screamed about all the things that were possible. In her mind, without supervision, Laney might fly off the face of the earth, vanish into the night, or worse: grow up to be like her.

"I'm sorry. I'm sorry. It was talking. I thought it was just static or feedback, but it was talking to her." Marco pointed to Laney. The baby smiled, but his face didn't echo her joy. It twisted in fear and pain. "She was talking to it."

"She can't talk, Marco," Tanya shouted. "Your book just freaked you out. I can't believe you left her! She was your responsibility! You said you'd watch her!"

Marco shrank with each word, their weight breaking him down, eroding his fear with acidic shame, dissolving every reason that drove him outside.

"What if she needed you?! You weren't there!"

"I'm sorry." Marco hung his head, avoiding Tanya's burning eyes. "I—"

"Just go." She bent down to pick up the bag and diapers she dropped by the lawn chair. Laney clung to her and reached for Marco with a cheery grin. She raspberried at him, but Tanya pulled her away.

He didn't leave at first. He stood there, staring at the ground. There wasn't much to look at on Tanya's lawn. The grass was mostly dead, and where they were standing was all mud from the storms last night. He wasn't looking at that though. Marco was looking at how he screwed up. How his book spooked him and how Laney could have gotten hurt. He didn't apologize again. He walked away.

Tanya took Laney and her packages from Walmart inside. The baby monitor's low static still buzzed in the living room as Tanya put Laney down on the floor.

"I can't believe that." Tanya suddenly noticed how hot the room was. She opened a window. The cool breeze leaked in, but didn't help. The room wasn't hot, she was. Anger literally boiled inside her. Trust was broken, and by Marco, the one person she could count on.

Laney cooed again and clapped. The baby monitor buzzed louder, but Tanya didn't notice. She was too busy trying to take a deep breath, trying to let her disappointment go, but that's hard to do when the walls are closing in around you.

The check from Burger Boi, from Carla, was great news, but then Teddy's crew showed up. And now Marco lets her down. Just when things start going well, there's something that throws you off. One step forward, two steps back.

The baby monitor buzzed again, but Tanya's deep breaths drown it out. Laney babbles something and claps as she lies on the carpet. Tanya took her to the bassinet so she could play more.

"Okay, here we go, Laneybug." Tanya bent to put Laney in the bassinet. In the corner of the room, two long ears, like a black fox's head, twitched. She straightened and looked. The ears were gone. Maybe never there. *Marco freaked me out. That's all.* She bent again to put Laney down when Laney babbled something and a sharp chirping sound came from behind Tanya.

She didn't jump, she just ran. Her grip on Laney tightened and she left the bedroom, running straight out to the lawn chairs outside her trailer.

Nothing followed her out. Nothing peeked out of the bedroom. The baby monitor was quiet except for its steady hum and solid green light.

"Marco," Tanya said. She gritted her teeth, cursing him for freaking her out.

"Problem, dear?"

Tanya screamed and spun to see a familiar face standing behind her. Carla had stopped by.

NINE

"What are you doing here?" Tanya panted. She pulled Laney away from Carla without realizing it.

"Sorry to scare you. I saw you walking from the store and thought I'd check in. You looked very," Carla scrunched up one side of her face, "paranoid." The word came out high-pitched and nasal.

"Yeah… Well, now I think there's something in my house. A fox or racoon or something in Laney's room."

"Ah, critter trouble." Carla went to her car, a black sedan that gleamed in the late afternoon sun. Her driver, a twenty-something guy with large sunglasses and a black suit, white shirt, and black tie, sat staring out the front window. When Carla knocked on the trunk, the driver quickly pressed a button above his head and returned his hands to the wheel, ready to drive.

The trunk clicked open, and Carla pulled out a baseball bat.

"Let's go see what's what." Carla pointed into the house with the bat.

"Are you going to smash it?" Tanya asked, staring at the bat, and wondering why Carla had a bat in the trunk. Did this sort of thing happen often to her?

"Heavens no. Ewww. We don't need all that mess. Going to make noise and get it to run away."

Tanya headed into her trailer, and Carla trailed close behind her. The storm door slammed shut as soon as Carla let go of it. Of the three, only Tanya startled at the sound. She jerked around, seeing Carla calmly following with the baseball bat hanging loosely at her side. The old lady had her normal, carefree smile and easy feel about her. It calmed Tanya a little.

"It was in the bedroom." Tanya pointed down the little hallway to where she and Laney sleep. "I mean, maybe it was."

Carla grinned and calmly walked back to the bedroom. Tanya stayed in the living room, staring at the baby monitor.

The green light blinked. "Come out, ya rascal," Carla said through the static of the baby monitor. "No hurting you, but want you out."

In the living room, Tanya swayed with Laney and watched the monitor for anything. Carla groaned the familiar sounds of an older lady bending down, getting back up, crawling to look under the bed and behind furniture. She came out a moment later.

"Nothing. I guess whatever it was got spooked and got out of there."

"No, I was watching the door. Nothing came out."

Carla pointed to the open window in the kitchen. "Probably slipped out before you even left the room."

Tanya nodded. *Yeah, that's probably it.* Her heart wanted that to be true, no matter what her head believed.

"Can you help me move the bassinet out here?" Tanya asked. "I just don't want Laney sleeping in there if there's some animal hiding."

"I checked thoroughly, but I understand what you mean." Carla went to the room and wheeled the bassinet out into the living room.

"Thank you," Tanya said.

"No problem. Like I said, I was driving by. Is there anything else?"

Tanya thought about Teddy. Thought about Rico's comment when she said Teddy was in jail. *Is that what you think?* Is that what he said? Did Teddy get out? But all this was more than the nice old Carla Geeze signed up for. She had already helped, already done more than most.

"No. I'm okay. Spooked a bit. Thank you."

"Well, that's fine. It happens to us all. You still have my number?" Carla plucked a blank business card and pen from her pocket but put it all away when Tanya nodded. "Call if you need anything else. Now get some rest."

Tanya thanked her again as she left. Laney laid in her bassinet playing with the mobile as it made wind chime sounds and Tanya ate a burger for dinner. While she ate, Tanya watched *Unsolved Mysteries* on her dad's TV—the old episodes—and sat on the couch. She kept the volume low to not disturb Laney. So low, the chimes and Laney's cooing took Tanya gently into the darkness of sleep.

TEN

SLAM!

Tanya leapt from the couch, her head whipping from side to side while she searched for who was making that noise. She half-ran, half-stumbled around the room until she was sure only her and Laney, still sleeping, were in the trailer. Through her panting, she couldn't hear the chirping she expected. But she stood by Laney, calmed her breathing, and listened.

SLAM!

It was the storm door. Hard winds outside whipped the door open. She hurried to it before another slam woke Laney.

Didn't I latch that when Carla left? She couldn't remember.

When she opened the front door, the wind blew hard and ripped the handle out of her hand. The storm door slammed into the trailer wall. Tanya shielded her face from the wind blast, cold and biting as early autumn winds can be at night.

She latched the door just as two headlights came up the street. They lit up the street a few trailers down from Tanya. Fast food wrappers blew through the lights as the car sat, its engine running quietly. A high-pitched whine came from the car as something strained to keep the engine running. Tanya couldn't see anyone through the headlights' white beams.

The car drifted forward, made a sharp turn, and drove by her trailer on the road out of Waterforge. A shadowy driver looked at her as the beat-up gray car rolled by, but she couldn't see him in the moonless night. It sped up past her trailer.

Tanya held the door a moment longer to see the car turn out of Waterforge. A sudden scent of mint and cloves came on the wind. The smell sparked memories, as many smells do, but these memories weren't pleasant. They were memories of Teddy and his aftershave and cigarettes. The potent stench that always followed him stung Tanya's nose as she slammed the door quickly.

Laney didn't move. She kept still, sleeping her peaceful dreams. Tanya grabbed the biggest knife she could find from the kitchen. She took it to the window, held it up so anyone looking in could see it, and looked out for any sign of movement.

Nothing.

She took a deep sniff of air but didn't smell anything. *It's just in your head.* But she didn't wait to find out. Tanya put the trailer in lockdown. Every door and window was locked and double-checked. She even shut the bedroom doors and turned off the baby monitor. As she hurried around the trailer, checking that everything was locked, the phone rang.

She jumped and swung the knife toward it. The phone was in the kitchen and not in her slicing range. It rang again. She answered it.

"Hello?" Her voice jittered. Men were shouting on the phone.

"Hey, Tanya!" her dad screamed into the phone. She ripped the receiver from her ear.

"Oh, hi, Dad." She sighed in relief recognizing the tire factory's normal noise level.

"Hey, gotta work a double tonight. Won't be home until tomorrow afternoon. You good with that?"

"Yeah." She took a deep breath. "Yeah, do what you need to do. We're okay." She looked at Laney's bassinet. Her knife was pointing toward the kitchen window. In Tanya's head, she screamed, *Come home! I'm scared!* But she knew they needed the money. Carla's check wouldn't last forever, and every penny they earned now could be saved for the future. "We're good."

"Love you!"

"Love you too, Dad."

She hung up and returned to the couch. Turning on the TV, she flipped through channels for the rest of the night, watching nothing as her eyes jumped between the windows, door, and knife.

Mint and cloves hung around her nose like a wreath of regrets. It didn't leave her until the sun came up and she awoke from the light chimes of Laney's mobile.

ELEVEN

Morning came slowly as Tanya stared at the door. Hours ago, her arm grew too tired to hold up the knife. It rested beside her leg, fingers still wrapped tight around it, as her eyes stayed on the front door.

She had never seen a sunrise while sober and was thrown by the grayness of it. Before the golden light, before the purple sky, a gray twilight flowed through her windows. Streetlights were still on, casting their orange haze through a misty morning, but outside the mesh of light, the world was drowsy. Waking, but not yet ready to open its eyes. Not refreshed from a night of sleep, but contemplating a return to the pillow and letting go of starting the day.

An hour later, sunrise had turned from gold to the dull light that accompanies coffee and morning commutes. Tanya got up from the couch and started on her coffee. The knife hung limp at her side as she dragged herself into the kitchen and stared at the cabinet with coffee filters. Her knife clinked against the glass coffeepot as she tried to pick it up with the same hand that still held the knife. Silently, she put the knife down on the counter. The handle hung over the edge.

Laney laughed. The chimes from the mobile started. Tanya glanced over and saw her little hands turning the mobile like a steering wheel.

Coffee sizzled on the pot's hot pad as she poured the dark caffeinated goodness into her mug. Marco got her the mug; it said, *World's Okay-est Chef.* She laughed at it. Another drip sizzled before she put the pot back to catch the rest.

Flopping on the couch, she turned the volume on the TV up and flicked over to the news. Nothing good. Bad storms expected today. Bad people doing bad things. She heard Laney's cooing and thought, *Not everything's bad.* Tanya smiled.

A light knock on the door didn't startle Tanya, but her hand groped for the knife that wasn't by her leg anymore. She snorted a laugh at her ridiculousness. *It's Marco. He always comes over before school.*

Her stomach ached as she remembered how hard she was on him last night. He was spooked. Laney was fine. No harm done. And he's a responsible boy. No need to be on him. Tanya answered the door.

"Hey, Marco," she said, but it wasn't Marco.

It was Carla.

"Hi, deary. I hope you don't mind me checking in. You seemed very strained last night." Carla looked her over appraisingly with a concerned tilt to her mouth. "And you look worse this morning. How can I help?" Carla walked into the trailer. Tanya stepped aside and smiled, thankful for her visitor.

"I'm sorry. I thought you were Marco," Tanya said, and checked for Marco up the street. His trailer was dark, as if he'd already left for school. *I was too hard on him.*

"Well, let me help you, please." Carla went to Laney and tickled her. Marco was never late. Never missed a morning. Laney's laughter made Tanya forget about her worries. "What's going on?" Carla cooed to Laney. "To be clear, I'm asking you, not Laney."

Tanya chuckled. "I…" She didn't know where to start. The worries about Teddy being out of jail mounted up through the night and she didn't really know Carla all that well. Something about the old woman—her motherly smile, her calming presence, how Laney took right to her—all these things made Tanya trust Carla and not question anything someone else might have noticed as odd.

She started again. "I made a lot of bad decisions before Laneybug came along." And that's how she started her story. Carla sat with Tanya on the couch, bouncing Laney on her knee as Tanya recounted her life since high school. A life of bucking authority and seeking the approval of everyone around her. A life focused on pushing boundaries and parties and self-medication to numb the pain of absent parents. Her dad worked constantly, her mom was an alcoholic. Tanya suspected her mom of doing more than drinking.

Carla sat perched on the couch and listened with the attentive ear of a patient friend. She was, Tanya realized, her only friend. Certainly, she was more present than anyone else, including her dad, and definitely moreso than her mom.

Toward the end of the story—as everyone can feel the end of a story coming—Carla reached for Tanya's hand and held it. Laney had transitioned to the floor, pulling her toes to her mouth.

"Teddy got arrested for possession and they got him on charges of being a dealer. I wasn't around for that. I left when Laney was born." Tanya took a deep breath to push through the rest of the story. "But before Laney came, I wasn't making good decisions, and my mom, she said she wasn't raising another kid. She was done raising kids, and she left."

Carla winced at that. Tanya recoiled, almost pulled her hand away, but Carla held firm. The pain in the old woman's face was beyond empathy. It was genuine disgust.

"I'm sorry," Carla said, but Tanya wasn't sure if she was apologizing for squeezing her hand so hard or empathizing. "Life hasn't cut you a break."

Tanya smiled. "It did." She scooped up Laney and bounced the chubby little girl on her knee. "Life gave me a break and so much more."

"Well," Carla wiped a tear that hadn't yet streaked her mascara, "Laney's lucky to have you. But she won't have you for long if you don't take care of yourself. I'm free for a few hours. Why don't you go get some sleep? I'll stay with Laney and you can rest."

A cocktail of exhaustion mixed from a sleepless night and retelling her story broke down any inhibition. Tanya agreed. *Laney loves her, and she's so nice.* Before Tanya realized it, her hand was on the baby monitor. *I don't need this.* But she took it anyway.

"If you need anything, just call." Tanya shook the monitor and forced a smile.

Carla nodded. "We'll be great, won't we, Laney?"

Laney cooed, laughed, and clapped as Carla took her from Tanya and put her in the bassinet.

The bedroom door opened quietly. Tanya had forgotten why she closed the door, forgotten the sounds from last night, and collapsed on the bed. *Before you lay down, put away…?* What? There was something she meant to do, but the idea died as sleep came quickly.

TWELVE

My mom never sang to me. Tanya listened to the soft tune coming through the baby monitor. Static didn't interrupt the gentle lullaby.

Gealacha ag clamhsán ó, a iníon,
Cén ceol a thabharfaidh an ghaoth leat?
Tá mé ag dul i bhfad ó anseo,
cén ghaoth a thabharfainn duit?

Ní bheidh mé ar ais go luath,
Aislingeoidh mé thú go deo.

Tusa, a iníon, tabharfaidh mé mo ghaoth
Tá sé ag déanamh cinnte go mbeidh muid le chéile.

Agus baileoidh na clingíní sinn,
ag iompar thú as ar tháinig muid.

"I think Mommy's awake." Carla stopped singing. Laney made a happy baby noise.

"Sorry I slept so long." Tanya joined them in the kitchen. Laney was on Carla's hip. The smell of spicy ground beef, lime, and seared peppers drifted through the air, drawing Tanya deeper into the kitchen.

"Wow, that smells amazing."

Laney was reaching for something on the counter, making her *I want* noise. Carla wasn't far from what Laney was trying to reach. Tanya couldn't see it, just that it was shiny, and Laney always loved shiny things. *That's probably why she loves that mobile so much.*

"I hope you don't mind us making you dinner," Carla said.

Something tingled in Tanya's mind. The thing she was trying to remember before her nap, but what was it?

Laney picked up what was on the counter and shoved it in her mouth.

"NO!" Tanya screamed, and grabbed Laney's hand, remembering the knife, the thing she left on the counter. Laney screamed, scared and startled, dropping the wet metal to the floor.

"What's wrong!?" Carla stepped back from the clattering.

Tanya stared at the spoon on the floor. Checked Laney's screaming, wide-open mouth for cuts.

"I thought that was a knife. I left a knife there. I, she, what if—" Tanya's face flushed, eyes instantly filled with tears as she imagined Laney's mouth slashed open all because she was too lazy to put away a knife.

"Don't worry. I found that before we got started, washed it and put it away." Carla bounced Laney to calm her. "No big deal." She shook her head.

Laney reached for Tanya. Tanya took her. The crying stopped as they squeezed each other.

"See, all better with Mommy." Carla flipped the meat in the skillet with a quick flick of her wrist.

"I'm sorry."

"You say that too much." Carla chuckled as she flipped again. Some of the meat didn't make it after the flip and fell on the floor. "I'll get that later. Never be sorry for protecting your daughter."

Tanya nodded and tried to push away the images that flooded her mind. Laney with the knife in her mouth, blood drooling out from deep gashes; they flashed in her mind, battering with cruel, unrelenting force. Each image was a reminder of what could have happened because she was tired, because she wasn't a good mom. Carla saved the day.

"What was that song? Was that another language?" Tanya went to the fridge and pulled out a bottle for Laney.

"My mom used to sing that to me." Carla sighed as she flipped again, this time catching all the meat. "She was from the old country."

"What's the song mean?"

"It's a song about a mom going on a trip and leaving her daughter." Carla stopped stirring, sighed deeply. "My mom traveled a lot."

Tanya heard the pride in Carla's voice as well as the thick sadness. The air grew heavy and dense between them.

"I'm sorry—"

Carla turned and pointed the stirring spoon at Tanya.

"I mean, I bet that was hard," Tanya said. "You loved your mom?"

Carla nodded. "She was amazing. Smart. Kind." She shrugged and took the meat to a colander in the sink. Steam burst up around her face as she dumped the meat in.

"Is she still around?"

"No. She passed many years ago. I still miss her, still hear her songs, but a mother must prepare her daughter for the world, and she did just that." Carla put the meat back in the pan, the pan on the stove, and patted Tanya's upper arm softly. "Just like all good moms," Carla winked.

Tanya blushed.

"Okay, tacos are ready. Just need to put the meat in the shell. Oh! Will you look at the time! I must be on my way." Carla scrunched up her face and smiled at Laney. "Are you okay from here?"

"Oh, yes! Thank you. I really needed that sleep."

"No problem." Carla gathered her purse from the couch and hurried to the door. She opened it and Tanya saw the black Audi.

"Thank you again," Tanya said.

Carla waved away the words and walked to the car. "Remember, call if you need anything. I mean it. Your well being is important to me." Carla got in the car and the driver drove away.

Laney reached for the bassinet.

"Not yet, Laneybug." Tanya pulled the curtains over to see Marco's trailer. His mom was outside in her garden. The kitchen clock said it was 2:32pm. Marco should be home by now. So should Dad. *Where are they?*

THIRTEEN

"I haven't seen him," Marco's mom, Debbi, said. "He's not helping you?"

Tanya shook her head, but stopped quickly. "I'm sure he's…" She smiled to diffuse the panic building on Debbi's face. "I was a jerk. I want him to know I didn't mean it. He's a great guy, and I was such a jerk." Laney straddled Tanya's hip and bounced. Normally that made Laney smile, but today all she wanted was to get back to her mobile.

"He loves you and that little girl." Debbi reached for Laney, who cooed her cheerful laugh. "I'm sure he's at the gym."

Of course! Tanya sighed in relief. "I didn't even think about that. Yes. That makes total sense." *He went to the gym to blow off steam. Probably lifting weights or punching a bag or something. Or the library to get a new book.* All the reasonable possibilities came to her now that she could think, now that she wasn't so tired. "Well, if you see him, send him over. I owe him an apology and some tacos." Tanya replaced her fake smile with a real one.

As the girls walked back, Tanya's dad arrived home. He looked beat and surprised when he saw Tanya and Laney coming up the street.

"Everything okay?" he asked.

"Yeah, hadn't seen Marco and got freaked out."

"Well, sorry I'm so late," he said, "Gotta get that overtime when I can."

"I have tacos inside."

They both went in.

Tanya made two tacos for her dad, set aside two for Marco, and then made herself two. Carla had also made boiled black beans and fried rice.

"Wow! You outdid yourself," Zack said.

Tanya smiled and nodded, not wanting to tell her dad that Carla did the cooking while she slept. Something about that didn't seem right, seemed like a bad idea, and she couldn't deal with judgement from her dad right now.

"Hey, Dad, do you still work with Mr. Donaldson?"

"Yeah, his shift and my shift overlap some. Why?"

"Is his son, what was his name? Is he still at the jail? I mean, still work at the jail?"

"Last I heard. Uh, Nathan," Zack snapped. "Yeah, Nathan. Why you thinking about him?"

"Can you do me a favor? Can you ask him if Teddy's still in there?"

Zack straightened at the name. "Why?" His chewing slowed as he remembered all the bad that Teddy kid brought into Tanya's life. Bad for her meant bad for him. Always did, and now he turned to stone, waiting for the latest bad news.

"I thought I saw him last night, and it really freaked me out," Tanya said. That wasn't quite true. She thought she smelled him, but maybe it was all in her mind. The run-in with Rico, that car last night, the smell of Teddy in the air, all of it was too much. She had to know if he was still in jail. "I want to make sure he's still locked away from us." Tanya glanced at Laney in her bassinet. The chimes of her mobile sang a bright tune through the living room.

"Yeah, okay. I'll call him later. I mean, I'll see him tonight, but sounds like this can't wait." He relaxed some that Tanya wasn't inviting that troublemaker back into their lives, but this is how it always started. She heard he was around, she'd swear he changed, she'd run off with him. Zack shook his head and chewed his taco, knowing there's nothing he could do if that's what Tanya wanted.

Tanya looked at her taco. The shell was cracking. "If you can."

"Yeah, yeah. No problem. I don't want that trash around you. I'll call in a bit. Petey probably isn't home yet. Long drive."

"Thanks."

While her dad wondered about Tanya going back to Teddy, she had no doubt about what would come next. Laney was her choice. She hoped he was locked away, but hope had never gone far in her life. Like her dad said, hope in one hand, shit in the other, and see which one fills up first. When it came to Teddy, the hope hand was always empty, and the other was always overflowing.

They finished their meal—not quite lunch, too early for dinner—and her dad went to bed. Tanya sat with Laney, played with her, but Laney wanted her mobile. The chimes it made were bright and cheery. No more deep church bells, now more like thin silver bells. The sound made Tanya want to sleep and dream of far-off places where Teddy couldn't find her and Laney could be anything. Her dad and his doubt wouldn't be there. No bills, no worries, just taking care of Laney and enjoying the gifts of life.

But she didn't sleep. She stayed awake and listened to Laney play her mobile's ethereal music. Tanya smiled at the sounds, wondering if Laney would be a musician.

Outside, Marco's mom was still in her garden. She milled about the tiny row of boxes, but didn't really do anything. *She's worried.* Tanya wheeled Laney in with her dad.

"Dad, can you keep an ear on Laney? I need to run to the store."

He grunted a tired agreement and pulled the bassinet to the edge of his bed. "Be safe. What time you coming back?"

That question hit Tanya in the gut. It was the question her dad asked when he planned to check up on her. The question he asked when he wondered what she would be doing.

Tanya took a deep breath, smiled, and kissed Laney. "See you soon. I'm going to check on Marco."

I'm not going back to that life. But it was an easier life. A life without responsibility, without everyone wondering if she'd fail because they knew she would. Without anyone but her and Teddy. Laney looked at her, reminding her that that life was without joy, without purpose, without hope. *I'm not going back.*

Laney didn't say anything. She was too enthralled with her mobile, making it chime the sleepy tones and staring into the intertwined rings with intense ferocity.

Outside, Tanya listened for Laney to cry, but she didn't. Too busy playing.

"Where are you, Marco?" Tanya checked the streets. Her eyes stopped where the headlights were last night. She sniffed the air. The smell of nothing should relax her, but her body tightened in high alert. The smell of nothing meant Teddy was being careful. She knew him. She knew he wouldn't let her be. He was coming for her, coming for her and Laney.

FOURTEEN

Marco wasn't at the library or the gym. No one had seen him all day. While at the library, Tanya ran into Mrs. Cables and asked if Marco was in school today. Cables was an ancient teacher who taught Tanya and Tanya's dad, but her memory was sharp, and her attention to her students was acute.

"He was in school this morning, but very distracted. Came in very early and left for his work-study early too."

Left school early? That didn't seem right at all. As she talked to Mrs. Cables, a man three bookshelves away kept glancing at Tanya. He was a good-looking guy, middle-aged, clean cut, but eerily familiar. Tanya thought she'd seen him before…but where? Her tired mind was still running slow.

"Can you tell Marco I'm looking for him?" Tanya asked, almost pleaded. Worry was building and about to burst through her frail calm.

Did Teddy see Marco leaving last night? Get jealous? That would be something he'd do. He'd want everyone away from Tanya, isolate her, make her need him and only him.

Outside the library, from her car, Tanya noticed the guy a few shelves over had followed her out. He kept his distance but watched as she got in her car. When their eyes met, he quickly walked off toward the 7-Eleven a few doors down.

Tanya waited for the man to do something in 7-Eleven. He bought a fountain drink. She sat in her car and waited for him to come out. He didn't. He read magazines. He shopped for candy. When he glanced toward her, he'd go somewhere else in the store quickly.

Is he with Teddy? Teddy always could get people to follow him. Maybe that's some junkie that owes him. Just a nice-looking one.

The idea made her laugh. She knew few addicts who could look that put together, but it was easy to slip into the jittering junkie mess that flocked around Teddy. She dismissed the idea as paranoia and exhaustion. Her car started with a grinding whine, as it has been doing more and more lately, another expense waiting to happen.

She drove to the last place Marco would go: the bowling alley. He wasn't much for doing things around town and preferred to keep to himself. Sometimes he'd throw a few balls, mostly in the gutter. That's where Tanya first met him.

Please be here, she kept repeating as she walked in, and there he was. Sitting in a racecar game in the little arcade, Marco had headphones on, staring blankly at the game screen.

There wasn't much happening at the bowling alley this afternoon, but a few elderly couples were on the lanes. The lights were on and bright, unlike the first time she came here when the lights were neon and the other-worldly blacklights cast everything in a deep purple. With the lights on, this place looked dingy and mostly broken. The dark and neon of Glow Bowl hid the reality of this neglected place.

She climbed into the seat beside Marco. "Watching the races?" Tanya said.

Marco looked at her. His eyes were heavy, dreamy, his lips wet, face dry.

"She was talking to them," he said. "And last night, they came to talk to me." He shook his head. "But I didn't answer."

Tanya's heart sped up. Her mind was thrown back into Laney's room last night. The shadowy ears in the corner. They moved when she wasn't looking. The chirping sound.

"I checked. Nothing was there." Tanya shook her head and hoped her words would crack his face into a smile. *Just joking*, he'd yell, and they'd laugh. But he didn't. He looked at Tanya with the game's flashing lights strobing off the slick spit on his lips.

"I just want to sleep, but they're going to be there. They want to talk, but if I talk to them, they'll stay." Marco yawned and looked back at the screen. The cars flashed and pulsed in bright lights, each pulling his eyes open as they slowly closed.

"Why don't I just call you mom and she'll come get you?" Tanya rubbed his shoulder, and he bristled, jolting away from her touch. "Sorry! Didn't mean to scare you."

He slowly calmed and returned to staring at the cars on the screen. They raced around the track, crashing, spinning out in a visual barrage of flashing lights and blaring music.

Tanya climbed out of the car and went to the pay phone near the entrance. She called his mom. The irony of the situation wasn't lost on her. When she met him, she was drunk out of her mind and Marco thought it wasn't safe for her to leave with the people she was with. He called her dad, and Zack came to pick them both up. Good thing too. That was the night Rico smashed up his old Mazda. If Tanya had gone with them, she would have been in the accident. Sometimes she wondered how that would have turned out. She was pregnant already and didn't know it. Laney wasn't even a thought yet, but if she was in the accident, would she have lost her baby?

"Hello?" Marco's mom answered.

Tanya told her she's found Marco, but he's exhausted and needs a ride home. "I'll bring him."

"No, I'll come get him. I've gotta come by there and don't want to bother you no more today."

Tanya tells her it's no bother, but quickly hears the truth. A mother needs her son. It isn't about bothering Tanya; it's the need to make sure her little boy is safe. Good mothers care about their kids.

"I'll wait here with him."

"Thank you. I'll be there soon."

Tanya hung up. Outside the bowling alley, the man from the library walked by. He glanced toward her and that was enough for Tanya to throw another quarter into the phone and call her dad. *If he sees me calling someone, he'll go away.*

"Hello?" Zack answered the phone.

"Hey, Dad. Just calling to let you know I'm at the bowling alley with Marco. His mom's coming by to pick him up and then I'll bring home some dinner." Tanya watched for the man to come into the bowling alley, but he was gone.

"Sounds good. Oh, and pick up some super glue. I think Laney broke that mobile."

"What do you mean?"

"There was a loud crack, like a really loud crack, and it woke me up." Zack sighed. "She's fine. Didn't break into the bassinet or anything, and it didn't look broken, but it sure sounded like something broke. Ripped too. Like, I thought she ripped her onesie."

"Cracking, ripping sound?" Tanya thought about the sounds of the mobile: chimes, the deep bell, but cracking was new.

"Oh, and I called the exterminator. Y'all got a mouse or something in Laney's room."

"Did you see it?" The image of two long ears in the shadows flashed in Tanya's mind. Those ears were too big to be a mouse, maybe a large fox. "Did you see the mouse?"

"Nah, heard it. Never heard a mouse chirp like a cricket, but crickets don't have toenails clicking on the floor. No doubt. Mouse. Maybe a rat. Either way, you two should sleep in the living room tonight."

Chirping? Mice don't chirp. Tanya didn't have any plans to sleep in her room tonight. She knew whatever was in her room, it wasn't a mouse.

FIFTEEN

When Tanya arrived home, Laney was in the den, laying quietly in her bassinet. The mobile rings swayed above her, colliding like hollow wooden wind chimes.

Weren't the rings metal? Tanya held the takeout bags as she watched the rings slowly drift like a pendulum. It moved hypnotically, turning as it swung, clacking as it danced above her daughter.

Laney's little hands reached for it, almost touched it, then pulled away as she looked over to her mom and smiled. Tanya wanted to smile back, but Laney's movements were too slow and Laney wasn't looking at her.

"Hey, Dad," Tanya said and turned, but he wasn't there. She looked back to Laney, followed her eyes to the kitchen window. "You see something out there?" But Tanya didn't go to the window, she didn't want to see. Just wanted to eat dinner and put on a movie to relax for the evening.

"What'd you bring?" Zack walked into the kitchen. She kept her eyes off the window, away from what could be outside. Laney stared out, a curious smile on her face.

"Breakfast for dinner." Tanya kept her eyes from the window and put the boxes from IHOP on the counter. *Don't look.* She glanced back at Laney. Her big baby eyes were wide and staring out the window. One of Laney's hands raised up to the mobile and then slowly retracted back down as if told not to touch it.

"I'll take mine to go. Gotta get to work." Zack grabbed his pancakes and bacon, took the keys from Tanya. "Oh yeah. I talked to Nate."

"Nathan?" Tanya stared at the counter. Her fists curled, bracing for the answer. "What did he have to say?"

"Well…" Zack took a deep breath. "Can't say I don't like this news, and that don't make me a good person. Teddy's dead. Hung himself in his cell earlier today. Right before I called, apparently."

"What?" The shock broke Tanya's will. She looked out the window. None of the streetlights on that side of the road worked. It was dark with only a sliver of moon to light the night. *Teddy's dead? Teddy…killed himself?*

"Yeah, sounds like he used the sheets or something. He wasn't on watch or anything, so it took everyone by surprise. Sorry, it's not real Christian of me, but that boy's been the worst thing that happened to you. Not Laney. I mean, she's amazing. You two'll be better off without him."

Tanya stared deeper into the night, trying to see what Laney saw. But there was nothing out there. Nothing in the dark. Laney saw something though. Something curious. Tanya squinted, trying to figure out who's out there or what they're saying to her little Laneybug.

"Are you going to be okay?"

"Yeah." Tanya kept looking into the dark, hoping her eyes adjusted. But they didn't, and she saw nothing. *Maybe if I open the window?* She reached for the latch, but pulled her hand away. *I don't want to know.* "Have a good night, Dad."

"Hey, that stuff about Teddy's heavy news, so if you need anything, call Marco's mom. She can chat with you."

Or you could stay home. Not go to work. Stay with me tonight and see how I'm doing. But that was like asking her dad to stop doing what he thought mattered. His work was everything to him, and without it, who was he? Her father. That wasn't enough for him. Never was.

"We'll be fine."

"You can be happy he's gone. It's okay for people like us to be happy. First you get the payout, then Teddy. These aren't bad things. Maybe life's turning around." He gave her a kiss on the forehead and headed off to work.

Without wasting a moment, Tanya pulled an old rusty cookie pan from under the sink. She put it over the kitchen window to block out the night. No internal discussion, no dismissal of the act, just certainty that she needed to cover the window.

Laney returned to the mobile and studied it. She didn't squirm in the white plastic bassinet. No rolling yet. No crawling. Sitting probably wasn't too far away, but for now, Laney was mostly on her back or tummy. Currently, she had her feet outstretched to the mobile, her hands up but motionless.

"What are you thinking about?" Tanya asked as she got out a bottle and warmed it up. "Is it like a puzzle to you?" She quietly chuckled. "Isn't everything?" Again, the thought never far from her mind, she was reminded of Laney's brilliance. Brilliant in both mind and spirit. Her laugh could light the world, but tonight she was quiet and contemplative. Fortunately, Tanya knew the cure for that. She pulled out the *Elmo in Grouchland* movie from her drawer of DVD boxes and slipped the disk into their player.

"This will get you laughing," Tanya said, as the blue federal warning appeared. "Let's get some yummy dinner and watch our movie." The opening music to the movie and the bottle made Laney go gladly to the couch with Tanya for movie night.

The milk was gone before Elmo was in Grouchland. Tanya propped her up for a burp and felt Laney pawing in her hair. It was a strange sensation. Her stubby little fingers seemed longer, her nails sharper than Tanya expected. Laney flailed and whacked Tanya in the face, but not hard enough to distract her from the feeling of the fingers still in her hair. Tanya leaned forward and looked behind her, seeing the gap in between the couch and the wall. It was small. Too small for anything to be down there, but too dark to see if anything was.

All in your head. She shook away the idea and moved to the recliner. There, she and Laney watched Elmo escape Grouchland with Elmo's blankee and a wonderful lesson on sharing. Laney laughed most of the way through the movie. *Maybe one day you'll be on* Sesame Street. Tanya smiled at that.

"Okay, kiddo. I've got to get new pajamas for you. You want to play while I get them?" Tanya's voice hit the high notes common when talking to babies. She put Laney in the bassinet, which took all the cheer out of Laney, making her astute, deep-thinking, wrinkly forehead return. "Be right back."

Clothes for the girls were in their room. Tanya approached cautiously, remembering the noises from last night. She flicked on the lights before stepping inside. When the yellowish light filled the room, she watched the floor for anything to scamper away. Nothing did. She moved quickly to the dresser across the room. Opening the third drawer, one of Laney's drawers, Tanya shuffled through her onesies to find one warm enough for how chilly tonight was supposed to be. When she found the pink one with a white elephant, she knew she had the right one.

Laney babbled through the static of the baby monitor. Tanya remembered bringing it in earlier for her nap. That seemed like days ago but was only earlier today. The green light flickered as Laney cooed and giggled and raspberried.

A chirping noise replied through the baby monitor.

Tanya jumped. She scanned the room, heard the chirp again. It came from the baby monitor and melted into the static with a constant buzzing. The green light flickered, pulsing with the chirps that grew from a quick, high-pitched sound to a sharper, deeper sound. A throaty noise that garbled something. Tanya froze. Her mind was too busy processing the familiar sound to tell her body to run. Laney laughed a loud, hearty belly laugh of pure joy. The voice—now that's what it was—kept talking, and the sound wasn't English. It was so familiar, but Tanya couldn't place it.

Laney grew quiet. The voice kept going. Then paused. Was it a song? Another language? Laney burst into laughter like she heard a joke, but Tanya wasn't laughing. She couldn't move. She couldn't breathe. All she could think, all she could do, suddenly came out of her mouth.

"Laney! What's going on?" The words broke the spell, and she ran out into the living room. Tanya looked at the bassinet. Laney was fine. Playing with her mobile.

BANG!

The cookie sheet fell from the kitchen window. Tanya jumped, screamed, and ran to Laney. Out of the corner of her eye, she saw two long ears dart out of the kitchen. She screamed again and grabbed Laney. Now Laney was screaming, torn away from her mobile. The chirping came again, a screeching howl from the bedroom. It echoed with a static warble as the baby monitor in the living room heard the noise and played it back with the momentary delay. Whatever was making the chirp responded to the echo in a snarling scream that made Tanya's teeth vibrate like the first loud sound the mobile made. The vibration buzzed in her bones as it got louder.

The doorknob was in her hand before she realized; she ripped the door open and screamed at the little shadow waiting outside. Bright lights blasted Tanya, blinding her. She screamed again, her throat now raw and coppery as the lights shut off and Carla put one finger to her lips and shushed Tanya with a slow, hissing shhhh.

"Calm, calm. You'll scare Laneybug," Carla scooped Laney out of Tanya's arms while she was blinded, her eyes readjusting to the night.

"There's something in my house!"

Carla stepped aside for Tanya to come out. She did.

"Would you like me to check, or would you like to just get away for a moment?" Carla's voice was quiet and soothing. She balanced Laney on her hip as Tanya looked back into her house.

"Get away. I…" Tanya moved to the car quickly. "Get away.

Laney and I need to get away for a bit." The weight of the news about Teddy, the noises, Laney's staring outside, the cookie sheet, the voice, the song—Tanya's back sprang straight, tension in every muscle firing at once, as she matched the voice in the baby monitor to Carla's song. The creature's language, it was the same as Carla's song. *That can't be right. That's just because Carla's here now. Why is she here now? Why always when I need her?*

"What is it?" Carla asked as she opened the car door for Tanya to climb in. "I don't have a child car seat, but we can get one from Walmart before we do anything else. My treat."

Carla put Laney in the backseat of her shiny black sedan and stepped aside for Tanya to get in. Tanya looked at her daughter, now in the car. *Carla's been good to me. Why am I so scared? She's here just when I need her.* Tanya remembered what her dad said: *Good things can happen to people like us.* Carla was one of those good things. The fairy godmother of her story, but real. Not sent by a magic star, but by a company that didn't want to get sued. Tanya chuckled at that. *This isn't a fairy tale, but a simple case of cause and effect that has ultimately led to me having the supportive mom I needed right now.* And with a smile on her face, Tanya got in the car.

SIXTEEN

Walmart was their first stop for Laney's car seat. It wasn't the cheap one either. It was the nicest one in the store. Carla's man servant/ driver took care of the purchase. He was like all the other drivers: young, gorgeous, well-dressed, and silent. Tanya wanted to make a joke about Carla being surrounded by the perfect men, but she kept those thoughts to herself.

As the man hooked up the car seat like a seasoned pro, Tanya wondered how many drivers Carla had. This was the third one she'd seen. All different, dressed exactly the same, but with different colored skin, different cheek bones, slightly different haircuts, but all short and well styled. Black suit. White shirt. Thin black tie. Black sunglasses. Of all the things that she found strange, the strangest was the efficiency of the man placing the car seat into the car. No instructions needed. He got it in place in seconds and locked it tight, along with a safety check that would have made any paranoid parent relax.

"Alright, how about some greasy comfort food?" Carla said, and touched Tanya's arm to pull her attention toward her. "Where would you like?"

"This might sound weird, but Burger Boi?" Tanya had a sudden craving for the BacoStacker 3000, named for all the bacon and calories in the burger. As a naturally high-metabolismed twenty-something, Tanya hadn't needed to worry about a 3,000-calorie burger yet, but her arteries would remember this far longer than her waistline.

Carla's smile faltered for a moment but quickly recovered before Tanya noticed. "Sounds wonderful. Let's do drive thru."

Tanya agreed, not wanting to see her old coworkers. Being with Carla might be awkward with how everything went down at Burger Boi. Tanya climbed into the backseat with Laney and smiled at her happy little girl. Carla got into the passenger seat, the driver got in last.

"To Burger Boi," Carla said, and the four drove off.

There weren't many restaurants in town. Burger Boi was one of the few. It was fairly central and not too far from Walmart. The ride there was silent until Laney ripped the loudest fart Tanya had ever heard. She laughed at first, but when the smell followed, all the funny was choked out of her. It was eye-watering, and led to the driver opening all the windows a little. Tanya pressed the button to open her's more, but it didn't move. The window was locked.

"Oh, Laneybug, that's horrible." Tanya waved at her baby to clear the air, but it spread the stink more. "I think I need to change her. I'll just run in." As much as she hated the idea, it seemed unavoidable now, and who knows, maybe it wouldn't be that awkward. Carla glanced at her driver, who kept his eyes on the road. She nodded. He nodded in return.

"Diapers are in the back. I was bringing you some supplies when I stopped by," Carla said with shallow cheer.

"Thank you." Tanya smiled and leaned toward her window to get some fresh air. "Sorry Laney bombed us out."

"It happens," Carla said with the same relaxed dismissal of all the stressful things in her life. "Have you been back to Burger Boi since your unfortunate event?"

Tanya watched Carla carefully, the faintest smirk tugging at her lips. She'd seen this before—the way people would word their questions to make it seem like they were asking for information when really they already knew the answer. This tactic was common in the many interrogation rooms Tanya had sat in throughout her life from frequent run-ins with the police.

"Uh, no. No. Had my fill, I guess."

"Oh, well, would you rather go somewhere else?"

The Burger Boi sign was ahead.

Tanya said, "No. I've got it in my head now and it's close, and Laney needs a change." They parked. Tanya extracted Laney from the car seat and went in.

"We'll wait right here," Carla said with a smile.

Tanya hurried straight to the bathroom. Nancy was running food out to some kids and stopped as Tanya ran through the seating area.

"Tanya?" Nancy gasped. "Are you—"

"Hey, Nancy," Tanya said cheerily but rushed. "Sorry, be right back. Emergency." She pointed to Laney and waved her hand in front of her nose. The gesture was funny to Tanya, but apparently not to Nancy. The manager of Burger Boi stared at her, mouth hanging open in disbelief.

In the bathroom, Tanya carefully took Laney out of the car seat to avoid anything horrid leaking out of her diaper. She laid her daughter on the changing table—Nancy always kept it spotless and sanitized—then began the careful operation of removing a full diaper without drenching her hands in the foul output only a baby can manufacture.

As the extraction of diaper from baby was successful, the bathroom door opened. Nancy came in, checking behind her as the door closed.

"Tanya?" Her voice trembled.

"Hey, Nancy."

"Are you…" Nancy came closer, reaching for Tanya's shoulder but not touching. "Are you okay?"

"Yeah, I'm sorry I haven't come in. Thanks for making things right."

"What are you talking about? Make what right?"

Tanya slowed down as she fastened the new diaper. The processing power of her brain was redirected from finishing the diaper to analyzing what Nancy was saying.

"The check? The help from Burger Boi?" Tanya resumed the diapering. "The check, so I don't have any legal recourse or whatever."

"I don't know about that. I thought that lady got to you and that's why you weren't back."

"What lady?" But Tanya knew. *What did I sign?* Her pulse quickened as the questions surrounding Carla started to solidify. *Why would Burger Boi care about me? Why was she always there when I needed someone? Why didn't she come in until invited?*

"Some old lady. She came in and said she was from Burger Boi corporate and needed your information. Said you were being investigated. It was after you left. Like a few hours later." Nancy shivered at the memory. "She freaked me out. Told me I'd be fired if I didn't give her what she wanted, but I—" Her fingers wrapped around Tanya's arm, pleading for Tanya to look at her sweat slicked face. "I don't remember giving her your info, but it was on my computer. Like, I woke up, and it was on my computer, but I don't think I fell asleep. I was serving a customer and then I was at my desk." Nancy groped in her mind for what happened in the gap between the service floor and her desk. She pawed at Tanya's arm like a cat kneading a blanket.

Tanya would have pulled away if she wasn't battling her own thoughts, her own doubts about Carla. *She's not who she says she is.* Not a question in her mind. *Would a regional manager have an army of drivers? Maybe because she's older. Needs help to drive. And she's a nice lady. More of a mom to me than my mom ever was. And Laney loves her.* Tanya stomped out all the questions that were bubbling up in her heart. Like she did with Teddy so many times, Tanya could see the good in Carla, the helpfulness. She was there when no one else was. Just like Teddy. But he always wanted something. What did Carla want?

"Did she find you?" Nancy clenched Tanya's arm. Now Laney was getting upset by Nancy's frantic jitters. "I'm sorry. I didn't mean to give your info to her. I don't know if I did, but I guess I did. I don't know."

"I'm good. No creepy old lady has kidnapped me." Tanya put her hand on Nancy and gently rubbed her fingers. "I'm better than I've ever been. Laney's good too, aren't you?" Tanya held up her little girl, and she babbled something Tanya took for agreement. "But I've gotta go. Gotta get home." She gathered up the diaper bag and hurried out of the bathroom.

Nancy followed. "Wait. What check? You said something about a check?"

Tanya didn't stop, didn't want to explore any more thoughts, and headed straight for the door. Nancy reached for Tanya, but ripped her hand back when she saw Carla. Nancy stopped chasing Tanya. All the manager of Burger Boi could do was gasp a high-pitched whining siren. *Danger! Danger!* that siren said to Tanya, but she didn't stop. She went straight to the car, hooked Laney in, and sat down beside her.

Carla stood outside the car for another second. Nancy ran back inside Burger Boi. Tanya stared at Laney. *We're going to be okay.*

Laney cooed.

"Drive thru?" Carla said, cheery and satisfied.

"No. I've lost my appetite. Can we go home?" Tanya asked.

Carla smiled and nodded to the driver. "Absolutely. Take us home."

They drove off.

Inside Burger Boi, Nancy watched them leave. She cried in the dining area. The customers didn't matter to her. She didn't care that everyone saw her blotchy face and streaming eyes or the fountains of snot coming from her nose. That lady standing at the black car, the car that took Tanya away, that was the crazy lady. She'd found Tanya. She got to her. And whatever that lady did to Nancy to make her forget, she was going to do to Tanya.

Tanya and her baby were in trouble, and it was all Nancy's fault. That thought would never leave Nancy. It would be a weight she carried forever. If she had seen Tanya again, perhaps she could have forgiven herself. Tanya glanced back from the black car, smiled as they drove into the night. That was the last time Nancy, or anyone, ever saw Tanya and little Laneybug again.

SEVENTEEN

They drove home, but not Tanya's home.

"I just need to take care of something real quick," Carla answered when Tanya asked where they were going.

They drove out of town, through a dense forest, and finally arrived at a grand mansion on top of a hill. The dark canopy of trees hid the night sky as they wound their way through the secluded road. Tanya thought they could be anywhere now, she had never seen these woods before, and she'd lived here her entire life. Rico and Teddy always stayed in town. Where were they now?

Tanya explained away this turn of events for the evening as a quick stop so Carla could do whatever she needed. Tanya, thinking she had already put Carla out enough, didn't protest driving so far in such darkness.

Clouds had moved in as a storm built ahead of them. They drove into a sheet of pouring rain as they left the trees and started up the mansion's long driveway. It crashed on the windshield like a wave with a summer storm's rage lingering into autumn. Tanya could not grasp the mansion's size other than it was huge. When they drove through a large metal gate surrounding the house, Tanya pointed at it and told Laney to look. The gate closed automatically behind them.

Tanya watched it shiver shut in the bloody taillight glow.

The road was well maintained and smooth, with lights marking the path at close intervals. Tanya watched the lights pass as the car moved up the winding drive toward the house. Their repetitive flash was hypnotic, making her window feel more and more like a pillow as they drove. The car vibrated like a massage to her brain, inviting her to relax, to lie back and just enjoy.

Laney was talking up a storm. Tanya responded with baby talk: "Yeah!" and "Is that right?" The drive felt right with Laney in the car. She made the world right, no matter how wrong it was. No matter how dark the destination or how dangerous the companions.

Arriving at the house, three men met them with umbrellas at their car doors. All dressed the same. Black suit. White shirt. Thin black tie. Black oversized umbrella. The man at Tanya's door opened it for her, held the umbrella over her, and led Tanya to Laney's door. Carla went to the mansion's door with two men holding umbrellas over her.

Without saying anything, the umbrella man guided Tanya to the massive oak front door. Not wanting to be rude, thinking that inappropriate for all Carla had done for her, she entered the house, ignoring the voice inside screaming, *Run!*

Carla's mansion was what Tanya imagined a mansion to be. The entryway was bigger than any house she'd ever seen. The walls were dark wood that glittered from a crystal chandelier hanging above. Red carpet with intricate gold threadwork squished like a pillow under her feet. Gas lamp fixtures lined the walls, lit to full, making the entrance glow in golden light.

"Come, come." Carla waved for Tanya to follow her as she walked up the left side staircase to another floor. The staircases—one on the left, one on the right—curved around a large marble fountain that was shaped like the glass teardrop on her necklace. Laney reached for it and laughed.

"Don't touch anything here," Tanya whispered to Laney. "We can't afford to replace any of this." She chuckled and baby-talked, "No, we can't. No, we can't." Laney laughed.

They followed Carla upstairs and listened to the quiet bubbling of the fountain. It was calming. As she got to the landing, Tanya wondered what Carla thought of her trailer. *Is she sorry for me?* But Tanya never sensed that from Carla. Never felt pity except for when she mentioned her mom leaving. Over the entrance door, clearly visible from the landing, was a painting, perhaps ten feet tall, of three women. One was an old lady, sitting on a throne. A slightly younger lady, Carla, stood beside her, and a very young woman, about the age of Tanya, sat in front of the two. Carla and the young one smiled, but the old lady did not. She was regal. Demure. All three wore the black glass teardrop necklaces. The older woman had an animal curled near her feet, while the youngest woman reached to stroke the creature. Those long, pointy ears of the black fox animal reminded Tanya of the shadowy creature in her trailer.

"Right this way," Carla called from ahead.

Tanya hurried along, her eyes staying on the painting as all three sets of eyes followed her into the room where Carla was waiting. Before going in, Tanya turned Laney to see the painting. Laney gasped in adoration, the sounds usually reserved for Tanya's dad or the one time she met Tanya's mom. It was only a quick glance. As Tanya turned Laney back around to go into the room, Laney squealed in joy at her bassinet and mobile.

Tanya did not have such a happy reaction. She shrieked, the scream ripped from her by surprise and confusion. But when she saw Carla's hands resting on the bassinet, saw the slight smile crack the old lady's face, the voices in Tanya's mind finally broke free.

Coming here was a mistake.

Suddenly, memories of Teddy giving her her first taste of heroin came back to her. She knew taking it was a mistake, but it was Teddy. He'd never do anything to hurt her. He only wanted to help her relax from dealing with her screwed-up family. She took the taste. And then took the rest.

Carla was the new Teddy. The taste wasn't the money. It was the love. And even now, facing what Tanya knew was something dangerous, something horribly wrong, she didn't want to leave the taste. She wanted to take the rest, and so she walked into the room. Behind her, two of Carla's man servants closed the doors with a bright metal click as the lock fastened.

EIGHTEEN

"Are you going to hurt her?" Tanya's voice quivered.

"Absolutely not," Carla responded in her calming way. "Please, let her play while we talk." She motioned to the mobile.

Tanya took Laney to the bassinet and placed her gently on the mattress. She stayed with her, staring at her to get one last look at the perfect light in her life. Laney grabbed her finger and squeezed as her cooing made Tanya tear up.

The room was large, but not as cavernous as the foyer. It was a library with floor-to-ceiling bookshelves. The walls were easily twenty-feet high, and ladders spotted the shelves to reach the higher-up volumes. No dust could be seen anywhere. A velvet couch sat near a molded fireplace. Another high-back leather chair sat across from the couch, and this is where Carla sat. In the fireplace, a warm fire was blazing, casting strange shadows into the room. Around the fireplace, those long-eared creatures were carved in various positions, from hunting crouch to sitting attentively to running and playing.

"No, I do not work for Burger Boi," Carla said with a dead-pan face. After a moment, she smiled, but Tanya wasn't sure if she should smile back. The woman had lied to her for days, stringing her along all to get to here. And the outcome was becoming clear. She wanted Laney.

"Why are we here?"

"Your daughter is," Carla smiled wide, her eyes sparkling in the firelight, "very special. She's about to do something that few others have done." She pointed to the mobile. Laney batted at it. "And when she does, the world will never be the same."

"Don't take her." Tanya leaned toward Carla. "You've got all the money. Please take someone else. She needs me and I need her. A girl needs her mom."

"And a mom needs her girl." Carla sighed. Her eyes drifted to the fire. "I saw you looking at the painting. That was my mom, me, and my daughter Zelia." Carla rolled her eyes and waved her hand. "My mom named her. Old family name. Well, she was the light of my world, like Laney is yours. Zelia died in a car accident when she was twenty-one. Not a story of irresponsibility or tragedy, purely an accident. A deer ran in front of her, she swerved, hit another car. The other driver was fine after a bit in the hospital, but Zelia died on impact." Carla's face reddened deeper than the fire, her eyes glittering, cheeks flashing in the flames. "I know a mom needs her baby better than you realize, but sometimes, life puts the mom in a place where she cannot be a mom."

Carla stood and went to the fireplace. She plucked two tissues from a box on the mantle and blotted her eyes. Tanya stayed seated and heard a hollow knocking coming from the mobile's rings. They clattered together like wooden sticks.

"And so you have a choice," Carla started again, her voice wavery but strengthening. "You can have your daughter, or you can have everything." Carla waved to the house. "This is my family's property. We own it. There's enough money to be whoever you want, do whatever you want, and give the world to everyone you want. There are secrets here that you will be obliged to maintain, but they will not obstruct your fancies."

Tanya stood from the couch. She pushed back against the offer. *It can't be true.*

"In fact, you have already signed the paperwork to own this property." Carla tapped a wooden box on the table between the couch and the chair. She pulled off the lid and exposed the book of papers Tanya had signed when she first met Carla. "This made you the inheritor of all."

"But I'll leave Laney?"

"Well, technically, she's leaving. You'd be choosing to stay."

"Where's she going?" Tanya stepped toward the bassinet. "Where are you taking her?"

Carla laughed loud, echoing in the room. "Taking her? No, she's making her own way. Now, time is short. If you choose to stay, I will take your place with Laney. You'll never see her again. But she will have everything and anything she could ever want. She will have the future that you never did, but always wanted."

"But I'm her mom." Tanya went to the bassinet.

Laney's intense concentration blinded her to everything else. Heat radiated from Laney as she focused all her will into controlling her jerky baby movements.

One of the man servants approached Carla and whispered something into her ear. Tanya noted, *That's the first time one of them has spoken to her.* Carla nodded, and the man hurried off to get a tray of tea from near the fireplace. The tray had two tea pots on it, a black pot and a purple pot. He poured two cups of tea from the purple pot and brought them to Carla and Tanya.

"Drink. It will help you focus." Carla motioned to the tea and took a deep sip from her cup.

Tanya took a small sip.

"Could you really provide for Laney in the long term?" Carla asked in her calm tone. Tanya would normally bristle at such a question, but here, she didn't. She wondered, could she? Would Laney turn out to be just like her? And Tanya become the next version of her own mom? Is there a way to break the cycle of poverty and addiction?

"Do you believe in fate?" Carla asked.

Tanya shrugged.

"Why did you go into that alley when you left Burger Boi?"

"I was hiding." Tanya remembered Rico's Mustang roaring down the street. She ducked into the alley to avoid being dragged back into her old life.

"And you found this in that alley." Carla ran her hand gently on the bassinet.

"I needed help carrying the food home." Tanya shook her head. "That's not fate, that's just things happening."

"One of the secrets you will need to maintain if you stay is that of my family's religious order. We…" Carla measured how to say the next words. "We provide for others, and part of that was leaving this mobile in a random location. We left it there. You found it. Laney knew what to do with it. That's fate's hands busily working."

Tanya watched Laney working on the puzzle in her mind. The rings vibrated. It wasn't the tooth-numbing vibration from before, but a resonance like a tuning fork. The rings were discovering the frequency as Laney struck them together.

"She's gotten further than anyone in a long time. I think she'll solve this soon, and you need to answer before then," Carla said.

Could I provide for Laney? Tanya watched her daughter manipulate the rings. She aligned them, turned them, tapped them together. *No. Waterforge has infected me. It's taken root.* She thought of her mom, how she never tried to leave. How Tanya's never tried to leave. She'd just settled down, grown roots, but those roots were shallow. With Teddy dead, those roots were just her dad and Marco. With Teddy gone...

"Did you kill Teddy?"

Carla shrugged. "Do you care?"

Tanya didn't. She sighed, relieved that he was gone, one less thing could disrupt her future with Laney. She knew that's why Carla did it. To remove anything that could get in the way of this decision right now. Teddy would have been a threat to her dad, Marco, anyone, but now he's out of the picture.

There was nothing holding her back, except fear. A deep fear that she now gave voice to.

"I don't want to be like my mom." Tanya breathed the words that had lived in her heart so long. With those words out, it opened the way to release the darker words that festered in her soul. "But I am. I am. I've been a terrible person. Laney will be so ashamed of me when she understands who I am." Tanya didn't tear up. Her words were calcified from years of fear, doubt, and self-hatred.

Her dad doubted her. Her mom left her. Only Marco had ever believed in her. He was smart. He had a future, and he thought Tanya could too. What if he was right? When Tanya was at her lowest, Marco didn't judge her. He helped her. He still helped her. Dad only saw Tanya's past. Marco only saw her potential. What if Marco was right?

The hollow clacking got louder. Faster. The vibration turned to a hum.

"I can't change who I am or what I've done." Tanya took Laney's hand. "I'm her mom. A mom needs her daughter, and she needs me. She needs the best me, and I'm going to be that. I'm going to be that." Tanya's tears broke free. "No, Carla. I can't stay."

Carla nodded. "So be it."

The fireplace's dancing shadows solidified into two large foxes with three tails each. Their eyes crackled with blue electricity, their teeth were bared, yellowed and pocked from ages of decay. Both creatures came to Carla and crouched at her feet. They watched Tanya carefully and chirped their high-pitched sound.

Laney's brow creased in focus. She whacked the innermost ring with a controlled smack that made the hollow clacking echo deep throughout the room. A chirping noise came from the rings. Tanya almost moved away, almost pulled Laney from the bassinet, but instead leaned in. She didn't realize the shadow creatures were ready to pounce, to remove her if she interfered in these last moments. Tanya was too busy staring at the bright reflection in Laney's eyes. It looked like stars, like a spiral galaxy whirling in her glossy eyes.

"See what she sees." Carla motioned to the mobile. Her voice was too far for only being a few feet away.

Tanya leaned down and looked up into the rings. Inside, the universe unfurled in majestic splendor beyond Tanya's ability to vocalize. She said what she understood to be true: "You're making the stars."

"They've been searching for Laney for a long time." Carla's voice fell further away. "Those who solve the rings are destined to be their gods. They will worship Laney and sacrifice for her. She is the creator, and she will be benevolent, with joy and hope from her mother."

Belly laughs erupted from Laney, and glee gushed from her, infecting the room with her joy. Singing filled the universe around Tanya, but it was her voice singing. She sang Carla's song to Laney. The words were changed. The words weren't about leaving, but going together, and Laney looked at her with the love only a baby can give its mother.

Tanya tried to see Carla, but she was so far away now. She faded through the blazing rim of a black hole's horizon.

Before Carla vanished, Tanya said, "Take care of my dad."

Laney screamed in joy, and the shadow foxes chirped a howling siren that echoed through the mansion. They sang the song of praise and worship for their newest god. Tanya's clothes were empty on the floor. Laney's onesie was empty in the bassinet. They were gone. The mobile slowly swayed, chiming its triumphant silver bell ring one last time.

The shadow foxes trotted to the fireplace and vanished.

After the creatures departed, one of Carla's servants came to her.

"Are they pleased?" he asked.

She took a deep breath and held it, feeling the energy of the room crackling through her old bones. It tingled like bubbles of champagne catching your nose before a drink. "Yes. We've restored their faith in us. They'll let us continue on, and why wouldn't they? Their new god is good. Brilliant. Devoted. With a mother to match." Carla smiled. "Please take this," she tapped the bassinet, "to the vault. We will not need it for quite a long time."

"And when we do? Will we find another to sustain them?" he asked.

"We always do."

INVENTORY NOTE: 18

Item: 18

Components:

- Baby bassinet (whicker, white)
- Baby mobile (interweaving rings, bronze?)

Collection: Private

I obtained this piece after the Geeze Estate burned down. There was suspicion of arson, which makes for a great sales opportunity. Pieces can vanish without many people noticing. My contact, a police officer, told me this case was very crazy.

Apparently, some kid and the father of a missing woman burned the house down. Police said both insisted that the owner, Carla Geeze, had kidnapped the woman and her baby for some kind of human sacrifice. Whenever I hear about a human sacrifice, I have to get involved.

Emotions run high in such events and, as we all know, emotions are the bridge between the body and the soul. The chemical transfer into the spiritual energy at the moment of distress can create a powerful binding. In this case, I assumed the woman was sacrificed and the binding would have been her soul to the bassinet, but one look at the mobile hanging in the bassinet and I knew I was wrong, as were the police.

Swinging in the bassinet was a baby mobile with a complex ring design. It was clearly modeled after the Portal of V'ahur, which legend states can open gateways into other dimensions. My first exposure to the portal was through Sister Wendy's journal, in the section on dimensional design. Some days that book haunts me, its origin a reminder of my brother, but on this day it was a true gift. I acquired the Portal of V'ahur for only a few thousand dollars.

Unfortunately, Ms. Geeze died in the fire and so I will need to find answers elsewhere. Only one place comes to mind, and I know I will not be welcome there. Sister Wendy cast me out once, and with the ferocity of leaving an impression thirty years later. I didn't scare easy at 18 having seen what I had already seen in life, but Sister Wendy… the Nightshade; such a person, such a place is only for the desperate.

Thirty years…

Perhaps my desperation has peeked? How much longer must I wait? Must I prepare? When will I have enough for Dodslav to come?

There are numerous collectors interested in this piece, but it will stay in my private collection. Too many religious nuts want to get their hands on it. I'd never get a fair market price from the likes of them. Faith always contrasts profit.

Note: I did dust the rings for fingerprints and found a few distinct sets. One set was very small, probably the last baby to play with this death trap. Seriously, who'd let their kid play with a bunch of metal rings? Not safe. Especially when they could whisk you away to another world.

ONE

Mrs. Louise Cathmun was a nasty bitch, and everyone knew it. As her husband would say before he joined the angels, God rest his soul, *They can't push you around if you push first.* So she nudged, gently but firmly, the moody teenager out of her way at the yard sale.

The girl, all brooding and indignant as only a teenage girl can be, scoffed at Louise. That earned another nudge, this one hard enough to motivate the young lady to get out of the way. The teenager moved on and found her own curious treasure: a VHS tape and spaceship.

No one would have called Louise Cathmun intimidating when they saw her, but a quick interaction, verbal or not, taught everyone otherwise. She wasn't short, wasn't tall, wasn't quite skinny. Only her tightly pinned white hair betrayed her age while deep lines under her eyes betrayed the exhaustion of recent years.

Life Changing Yard Sale my ass.

Louise talked to herself more and more since her husband died. She found the voice to be the only person smart enough to carry good conversation. *More like Bottom Feeding Frenzy Yard Sale.*

This yard sale was normal, no matter what the sign advertised. Tables with junk. Blankets on the grass with junk. Tubs of junk everywhere and only a few toys. People milled about the yard sale, each with their own wish, the thing they're secretly hoping to find, but Louise had no such wishes. Wishing was as fruitful as shitting. At this age, both usually produced nothing at all, but when they did, it stank to high hell. She came here to restart an old engine, an old hobby, but the engine wasn't turning over. Nothing was starting but her frustration at being around all these stupid people.

"Oh, did you see this?" some lady squealed.

Louise rolled her eyes. *Is she blind? Anyone could see that tacky piece of shit from across the lawn.* Another lady asked where the seller was. Louise didn't see anyone either. There was a jar with some cash in it. Mostly crumpled and thrown in like balls of trash. *Who the hell treats their money like that?* Her neck hairs tingled as people looked at the jar, searched but not too hard, for someone to give their money to, and then just left. *Thieves.*

A new inventory started in her mind, tracking all the things all the people were holding. She associated the item with an assumed price based on its condition. *Stupid lamp, $5. Old book, $3. Toaster, $2.* Louise kept inventories because that's how her mind worked. She tracked everything, and once it was in her mind, there was no getting it out.

She spat on the ground to ward off the bad karma swirling around these people. Not that she believed in such things, but her mom did, and some habits you simply pick up when you're around them enough. A fleck of spittle landed near the kind of thing she was looking for. If she was any closer, she'd have spit on the big wheel bike shining in the midday sun.

Never having kids, she didn't recognize this big wheel was in fabulous condition. Most kids would have ridden this three-wheeled personification of adventure and freedom into the ground, but this one looked like it came straight out of the box. Two white wheels in the back, fat and rough from driving on stone or pavement, but not too badly damaged. The front wheel was bright white, massive and pitted. A baby blue body connected all three tires with white handlebars. Ribbons, silver and flashing with the slight breeze, dangled from the handlebars. Under the white seat and along the side of the big wheel's body were a series of purple lightning bolt glitter stickers. They looked like racing decals. Louise wondered if this big wheel was originally for that show with the little blue people who wore white pants and hats, but she didn't know. It looked like it would fetch a lot of interest on eBay, and that's all she wanted.

Louise checked for a price but didn't find one. There was a *6* drawn in white on the bottom of the bike, but she doubted that was the price. *Haggle for a price, I guess. Think this bozo's up for haggling with a Cathmun? Probably not.* But no one was around to haggle with. *What kind of business is this?* She shook her head and went to the money jar, dragging the big wheel behind her. Among the bunched blankets, mindless conversations droned on, their words chipping away at her intelligence with their stupidity and pointlessness. *If you've got nothing to say, then shut the hell up.*

"Hello!?" she shouted to the house. It was run down and dark. "You going to take care of your business or let all these shitbags steal from you?" *Yeah, shitbags.*

"Excuse me!?" one lady cawed. Her sensibilities were shattered by an old lady using the S word.

"I said," Louise locked eyes with the lady, "these shitbags are stealing from you! Get a damn hearing aid if you can't hear, you dumbass." *She should consider a hearing aid.* The voice repeated. Louise smiled. "Yeah, that's what I said." She mumbled.

"Well," said the lady and her friend, equally stupid in Louise's observation. "I," she choked on her reply, "I hear just fine." Then she stomped off, junky trinkets in hand.

"Don't forget to pay," Louise grumbled. "Yeah, you too!" She pointed to the other shoppers staring at her. "Just because this business is run like crap doesn't mean you get," she pointed to a weird lamp or bookend, Louise couldn't tell, "crap like that for free." She shoved the money jar at the lady. "Pay up!"

"Crazy old bat!" another lady said as she rushed off.

"Crazy? You're about to find out." Louise ran after the lady, who sprinted away from the Life Changing Yard Sale like an insane person was chasing her. Louise tired out quickly and stopped before getting past the last blanket of junk on the ground. *You could have caught her.* Louise shrugged, unsure.

She slammed the money jar back on the table and stuffed in a twenty for the big wheel. After digging in her purse, she stuffed in another fifty to pay for the people who weren't coughing up their own money. Her mental inventory put the amount stolen at about $48. *You shouldn't do that. Bad business gets bad results.* "Maybe the owner's got a good reason. These thieves are taking advantage of the situation." Louise knew all about being on the receiving end of that and how it sucked. The voice didn't reply.

In the house, the darkness behind the windows was uninterrupted. She took the big wheel to her car and loaded it into the trunk. Before she shut it, she checked the yard sale to see who was crying.

It sounded like a little girl, but there were only old ladies, all of them staring at her, at the yard sale. The crying faded in the wind.

"What the hell you looking at?!" Louise said. *You. They're looking at you.* "Don't remind me," she grumbled quietly.

They all looked affronted. They whispered. They scoffed. Nothing new for Louise. But another thing her husband used to say came to mind. *I'm all out of shits to give.* And so was she.

TWO

She parked on the street in front of her house, went to the trunk, took out the big wheel, and placed it on the little patch of concrete that was supposed to be a driveway. The bleached concrete pad didn't make for good contrast against the white wheels, but Louise thought a picture of the bike on the driveway would be good for eBay. She snapped a carefully staged shot and then moved the bike to the grass, positioned the wheel at an angle, and clicked another pic.

A young couple jogged by, both on their phones. They glanced up at her. She scowled them away. They ran faster past her house.

Louise pulled her car onto the driveway and then dragged the big wheel into her house. The small rancher was spacious inside. Any house can be spacious when you minimize your possessions to the absolute essentials. Too much furniture made getting around tough for Simon. After the third time finding Simon standing at the corner of the couch, trying to remember where he was going, Louise knew it was time to downsize everything. Smaller house. Fewer things.

Some kid could have driven the big wheel around this little rancher with ease. Few corners. The floor plan was open. No rooms. Louise had most of the walls removed when they moved in so she could see Simon at all times. But without him, the house was just a cavern. No longer their house. It didn't even feel like her house anymore.

She took a few more pictures of the big wheel on her kitchen counter and in the house, then loaded up the sales page on her computer.

For Sale: Blazing Blue Big Wheel

Condition: Amazing

Description: Lightning fast and totally safe big wheel in amazing condition for one lucky kid. It can take them anywhere! Fun for them. Safe for you. Pics attached. Message me if interested. Price negotiable.

Price: Contact Seller

When she clicked submit, there was a satisfying *ding* that reminded her of an old phone ringing. While she had a smart phone, Simon had insisted she get it for her eBay business. She never liked it. Nothing in it was real. Just chips and sensors, nothing like the old phones which had stuff that could be fixed in them. These phones, once they broke, were done, and Louise thought that was a bunch of bullshit. She thought most things nowadays were bullshit.

Her phone dinged almost instantly with an interested buyer.

From: funguyToad821

Message: That's a Blue Bolt! I'm very interested. What's the price? How did you find one in such good condition? Does it support a rider? Often these bikes' back axle is rusted to crap. Can you show someone sitting on it to show it is in "amazing" condition? Sorry to ask, not trying to be a creep. Want this for my son. I had one when I was a kid. Want to make sure it works.

Thanks!

Tommy

Of course it's a guy. Louise scoffed. *Boys always need their toys.* Simon was never much for toys. He was more a trips kind of person. He loved to travel. That was something they shared. Their last trip was to Ireland. That was when Simon was still able to hold a conversation. After he lost his focus, they stopped traveling abroad. After he lost his memory, they stopped traveling in the US. Slowly, Simon's world shrank until it was only the empty openness of this house. And now Louise was the only resident of this tiny world.

But she always had a line out. She had her eBay customers. For a while, even those vanished, but now Louise was trying to cast herself, slowly, gently, back into the world one auction item at a time.

Customers were fickle, but this one seemed on the level. Seeing pictures of the product being in the condition stated was reasonable. Louise set up her phone holder, a tripod Simon bought for her last year, and positioned the big wheel on the floor. She wasn't a large lady, but was definitely bigger than most eight-year-olds, and so she thought she'd make a good demonstration.

"Okay, here we go, Tommy," she said as she started recording. The big wheel was laughably small for her. She took a moment to process the best way to sit on it without the bike shooting out from under her.

Don't break a hip like those old bitches back home.

"That's not my home."

It was. You made it exactly what you wanted, and now look at this place. This isn't you. Nothing on the walls. No walls! Maybe a plant would be good?

After a calculation, she pushed the bike's two back wheels against the kitchen counter so it wouldn't roll backward. She moved her camera.

"Hello, Tommy. The bike's in great condition. Here you go." Louise carefully lowered herself onto the white seat. The bike didn't move. It sank with her weight, letting out a little squeaking sigh. Some dust floated up from the seat. The wind blew open her front door, startling her. She jerked to see what was happening, and her back popped in a burst of pain and relief. Outside, the sun was bright. Clouds had left the sky, and where her street should have been was an infinite emerald-green field of wheat.

"What?" She stood up. Her feet sunk into the mud. Her hands brushed through long shafts of spring wheat as she climbed to her feet. "Where?" Louise's house was gone. She was standing in a large field under a cloudless sky. Behind her, three-wheel tracks matted the wheat in a trail. A gnarled tree twisted not too far from her. A bud of pale green drifted from the tree to her nose. Louise pushed it away and searched for where her house went, but it wasn't anywhere. She wasn't on her street. Seeing the big sky and long fields, she wondered, *Where am I?*

THREE

Three thoughts sprinted into Louise's mind, with only the first one lingering.

Oh god, it's come for me.

God didn't listen to Simon. He ain't listenin' to you.

But I haven't had other symptoms.

The first thought hooked into her brain and tore deep into her thoughts as the other two ideas floated along their way.

She took inventory of her surroundings, like she'd learned to do when walking into any new situation. See what's there.

A field. Big sky. Creepy tree. Trail from the bike. Other things appeared as she turned. A road close to the field. A motel up the road. She was off the road, probably about half a mile. A warm breeze blew toward her. It carried with it the smell of rain. On the horizon, clouds were building. There was matted wheat around her feet.

Was I laying there?

She replayed the first moments she had noticed being here, but couldn't remember getting up from the bike or the ground.

Memory. A new inventory list began in her mind. *How did I get here?* But nothing filled the inventory. She had no idea how she got here and didn't remember anything from when she sat on the bike until now. *Missing time.* The inventory was trashed in her mind as she dismissed the need for it now that she was wherever she was.

How long have I been standing here?

With that thought, she knew the time for standing and thinking was over. Time for action had begun. Louise dragged the big wheel behind her as she backtracked the trail to the road. Suddenly, her legs felt the exhaustion they knew from running to find Simon when he had an episode like this. Back then, she'd run up the street, down to the lake, over to each neighbor, and those were not close distances. Before her current house, Simon and Louise lived in the wealthy part of upstate New York. Not mega-millionaires, but not far off. Their house was a horse farm with a private dock on the lake. Too many places for Simon to get lost, so they moved to a small town, small house, small life. The neighbors at the old farm probably threw a party when they left. Simon's episodes terrified them, and Louise didn't blame them. They terrified her too. Who wants the constant reminder of death, or worse, the death of who you were, lurking around? No, she didn't blame them for being afraid, but she did blame them for abandoning Simon. Turning their backs on him when he needed them most. Turning their backs on her after all the years and all the favors; nothing makes you *persona non grata* like having your mind stolen from you.

These thoughts played in Louise's head as she trudged along to the motel. There was nothing else around. The motel would be a good place to call for a ride. Her phone was missing. All the questions she had couldn't push out the one thought still cinched deep in her mind: *It's coming for me now.* But dwelling on that didn't help anything, so she pushed on. Every step was a strain on her heart. The ticker was getting tired from all the stress and strain over the past two years.

The motel parking lot was empty. No traffic passed by. The motel sign flickered neon pink with a smiley face flashing side to side like it was bouncing to a merry tune no one else heard. It was high enough to be seen by whatever highway was on the horizon. On the ground, the building was a single-story antique from the seventies with a color scheme to match. Brown and beige stucco walls stretched between orange doors with gold numbers on them. Some doors lost their numbers, with only the yellowed mud of dried glue remaining.

Louise sighed. *If the outside is this bad, what's the inside look like?*

She walked to the door marked *Office* and knocked. The big wheel sat in the empty parking lot.

"Open," an exhausted woman said from behind the office door.

Louise opened the door. A new inventory sprung into action: the desk was a mess of papers, receipts scattered over the table, the lighting was piss-poor for reading a computer screen, the office chair was obviously lifted from a dumpster, and the lady sitting in it was the apotheosis of burnout. Her gaunt, spectral face had a frantic, twitchy feeling about it. The lady's brown hair was pulled up in the sloppiest bun Louise had ever seen, and considering her own history with indifference toward physical appearances, that was saying something. Every fingernail was gnawed down to the cuticle, with some lined dark, crusty red.

"Can I help you?" the lady asked with a joyless smile.

"Probably not with this office. But I need a room for the evening and access to a phone."

Heaps of bills and final notices suggested an attempt to organize, but a lack of discipline eroded those piles into paper landslides. Even after retiring five years ago, she couldn't stop being the consultant. To Louise, this desk screamed for help. Pleaded for her to put it in order. She had fixed billion-dollar businesses. This little hotel would be a weekend project. Organization. Focus. Communication. Commitment. Those were the seeds to grow success. Chaos is poison.

The lady wrinkled her nose, but still tried to smile. A customer is a customer, and she desperately needed customers.

"Yes, I have a room available. All the rooms have phones." The lady reached for a key over her computer. Louise noticed the computer's browser tabs; another habit she'd never left behind. *Observe the leadership to see what's important and how to motivate them.* This lady's browser had so many tabs open that her digital desktop was as chaotic as her real desktop. The active tab was Google. She was searching for missing people reports.

"How's a queen-sized bed for tonight?" The lady picked up a key, checked its number, then dropped it on her desk. She picked up another one, checked, dropped, continued.

Louise knew this was how all mail, bills, work orders were treated. They were examined. Dropped on the desk. Then buried by the next thing. Her jaw clenched, squeaking a quiet grinding as she curled her toes and reached for the desk.

"That's fine!" Louise's tone was sharp. "I'd like to get on with my evening. Can I just get whatever you pick up next?"

The lady winced. She bit back what she wanted to say and tossed the last key she pulled toward Louise.

"Are you paying cash or card?"

"Direct wire. I don't have my wallet. My accountant will take care of the bill if I can ever get a room or a phone."

"No money, no room. This isn't a charity."

"A charity would be run better. And by someone who cares. Give me your phone and I'll get your money."

The lady slammed down an old push-button phone. It dinged when it hit the paper-covered desk. She huffed, smiled an inviting sardonic smile for Louise to make her call and get out.

Louise snapped up the receiver. She tapped out Theodore's number and wondered when the last time she used a phone like this was. Her smart phone was her only phone since work.

"Hello?" Theodore was drowsy and coming out of sleep.

"I need you to do a transfer."

"Oh, Mrs. Cathmun." Her voice snapped him awake. "How can I help?"

"I just told you. Transfer. Pay this lady for a night in this hotel." Louise shoved the receiver to the lady behind the desk.

She took it with surprise. "Hello?"

The lady sat quietly and listened. Theodore was speaking, barely audible.

"Yes. Motel Magnificent. Yes. We're right off Route 43."

Louise perked at that. *Route 43? Where's that?*

"It is $100 a night. That's special pricing for," the lady smirked at Louise, who returned the smirk, "special guests."

"Just give her the money, Theodore. I'm tired and getting pissy," Louise barked. *You're always pissy. More and more every day.*

Theodore said something. The lady giggled, smiled, and entered the payment information into her billing system. *APPROVED* flashed quickly on the screen.

"We done now?" Louise said. She thrust out her hand for a key.

"Yes, room 4." The lady dropped a gold key with an oversized diamond key ring in her hand. "Wi-fi password is on the TV stand."

"Do I look like I have a computer?" Louise growled as she stomped away.

"I'm Rachael, by the way. If you need anything, let me know. Everything's additional, including talking to me." Rachael smiled, happy Louise was leaving.

"I won't." Louise went to room four and opened it with her key. To her shock, the room was clean. But as expected, it was ugly as sin, with brown and gold bedding, ancient furniture, and a water stain on the wall leading to the bathroom. She shook her head and closed the door. Her first stop in the room was the window, where she closed the blackout curtains, but she froze as her eyes landed on the big wheel still sitting in the parking lot. The front tire was tilted like a puppy looking naughty, but puppies and babies never moved Louise. Still, she went out and dragged the big wheel into her room. One thing that always moved Louise to action was business. She had a customer for this bike, and she'd be damned if she lost a sale because she was lazy.

Her body was ready to quit for the day. Exhaustion hit her in waves, each tide pushing her to the bed, inviting her to lie down for a minute, but before she did that, she got out the phone book to figure out where the hell she was. On the cover was the word *Billston.*

"Billston? Where the shit is that?" She scanned the cover, finding the state. Two states over from where she lived. Inside the phone book was a map showing the United States. There was a star on the map marking Billston. A quick eyeball measurement put Billston about 500 miles from her house. Louise looked at the big wheel. The back tires were scuffed, darker than she remembered them. *Can you trust your memory?* That thought made her growl in denial.

"Bullshit."

She wasn't disagreeing with anything, just declaring that this was all, in fact, bullshit. Louise flopped down on the bed; her body thanked her for stopping. Her heart clenched, a pain getting more common since Simon died, but it relaxed, as did the rest of her. Sleep came quickly, but it didn't come alone. Before her eyes shut, she saw a little girl peeking through her window. *Someone else came to this crappy place?* Louise heard the little girl at her window crying as sleep took her.

FOUR

Stars weren't what Louise expected to see when she opened her eyes. A cool breeze and the rustling wheat woke her up. She was in the field again. The afternoon sun was gone, replaced by a crescent moon, pre-dawn dark, and wisps of clouds on the horizon.

"Shit," Louise said. She sat up. The big wheel was beside her, its giant white wheel askew, again putting her in mind of a shameful dog. Mud was clumped in the treads.

It's here for me. It took Simon, and now it's here to take me.

"Bullshit."

Is it? Didn't you start forgetting things while Simon was still alive? This isn't new.

She grumbled disagreement with the voice in her head and climbed up to her feet. The same trail of mashed wheat was behind her. Over the wheat, the hotel sign flashed, making the field look orange in the pink light. The sign flashed "notel." Louise shook her head and grabbed the big wheel, now known in her mind as the *god damn big wheel.* She stopped as another wind blew, rattling the knotted tree. More buds flew off and floated toward the motel. Louise tossed the big wheel to the side.

"You're the problem."

The little bike sat, wheel turned, purple glitter lightning bolts catching the first crack of dawn. Another breeze blew, this one harder. Buds fell on the seat in a silent invitation to sit and go for a ride. That was the last thing on Louise's mind. She busily pushed out the idea that Alzheimer's was chipping away at her, and instead believed that a child's bike was to blame for her problems.

"This crap never happened before you came along."

Untrue. Remember the time you forgot Simon's medications? Probably not, since you're forgetting everything nowadays.

"Shut up."

This is like Simon's episodes. He'd wake up in strange places, didn't know how he got there. Sound familiar?

The big wheel didn't infect her with Alzheimer's, she just never noticed it until things got this bad.

"Good thing someone wants to buy you." Louise grabbed one of the handlebars and dragged the bike back to the motel.

The light in the motel's office was on. Early start for Rachael. Dawn was growing on the horizon. The pink dusty colors of morning were now turning to the golden light of sunrise. Behind Louise, the big wheel scraped along the pavement. She couldn't carry it with her aching muscles, still sore from yesterday.

She knocked on the door.

"Yes. Open," Rachael said.

Louise didn't go in. None of the chairs were open to sit in, they were all covered in papers or cleaning supplies.

Once Rachael saw who it was, she continued sorting through her receipts and papers, trying to find something more pressing than helping this rude customer.

"I need a ride home. Can you call and book it to my room?" Louise dropped the big wheel with a plastic crack on the sidewalk. Rachael stretched her neck to see what hit the pavement, but couldn't see anything.

"That's extra," Rachael said without missing a beat in her paperwork.

"Yes. Fine. Do it." Louise waved away the cost. "How do you work in this?" Louise stepped in and reached for some papers hanging on the edge of the desk. They were about to fall from Rachael's shuffling. "You need to—"

"I'll call for your ride. You can go back to your room and wait." Rachael put her hand up to block Louise from touching anything. The quick motion, the breeze from her hand, sent the papers drifting to the floor. "See, look at this," Rachael grunted. "I'll let you know when your ride is here."

"Fine." Louise shrugged, letting go of her attempt to help. Some people value experience and knowledge, but, according to Louise, Rachael was not one of them. And if Louise's episodes worked like Simon's, time was too short to deal with assholes like Rachael.

Louise waited in her room, but not for long. Rachael knocked on her door and shouted, "Your ride is here!"

"Fine," Louise shouted back. She grabbed her big wheel, dragged it along behind her, and opened the door. Rachael stood on the other side with her hand out.

"Tip?" Louise scoffed and shook her head.

"Key," Rachael sneered. "Your money boy already tipped me."

Louise pushed the key into her hand and walked by with the big wheel. Rachael dropped the key. It hit the concrete with a crisp clang.

"Where did you get that?!" Rachael screamed. Her pale face bloomed bright pink as she thrusted her finger at the big wheel. "Where did you get that?"

Louise, never having shrank from anyone in her life, pressed into Rachael and screamed back, "Yard sale! Now bug off."

Rachael staggered back from the big wheel, her face contorting between horror and preparing to scream, but nothing came from her. A high-pitched whine was in Rachael's throat. Questions wanted to jump out of her mouth but couldn't. The unreality of that bike being here, being with this old lady, was paralyzing.

Louise didn't look back. She got in the car, glad to be done with this place. Her mind was clear for now, and she wanted to get home and get normal as quickly as possible.

"Let's go," Louise said. The driver didn't wait. He hit the accelerator and left the motel behind. Rachael watched the car merge onto Route 43, frozen from the sight of that big wheel.

FIVE

One stop for gas and eight hours later, Louise arrived home. The driver, who Louise thought of as Larry even though neither exchanged names, wore headphones and bobbed his head along to the music all the way home. Louise wondered if this was farther than Larry's normal route, and assumed Theodore compensated him for both the silence and the trip.

Her house was just as she left it. The door was closed, which was a surprise. She expected it to have been left open or unlocked. A spare key was kept by the shed in the back yard in case she or Simon was ever locked out. Getting older, it was possible that Simon could wander off without her knowing or that she'd be unable to keep up. Louise's heart wasn't what it used to be, and Simon was quick for his eighties.

The back yard had fallen to long grass and dead weeds since Simon passed. Gardening was his thing, not Louise's, and she didn't have the heart to restart after his passing. The outside was never for her. She was more of an inside-the-office kind of gal. He loved growing plants. She loved growing businesses. Both were alive, and both were apt to die without proper care and feeding. Much like Rachael's motel. Without the proper skills and knowledge, growing anything was impossible, and keeping it alive was difficult.

The key was there. The back door opened. The house was how she left it. Open, empty, and alone. Louise's phone was still set up on the tripod, and that sparked an idea. She pulled her phone from the stand, took it to her charger in the kitchen, and plugged it in.

"Dead from being left on."

Nothing lasts forever.

"Tell me about it."

Louise recognized that she talked to herself more out loud since Simon's diagnosis. He never was one for conversation, and so his silence wasn't such a change. But Louise talked to herself so she didn't live in complete silence after Simon lost his ability to speak. She missed hearing his voice, hearing any voice other than her own.

A red battery sliver showed on her phone. That was enough to power it up, and so she did. Once on, she tapped her camera to see the last video recording.

The bike sat in the kitchen, close to where her phone was set up moments ago. It just looked like a bike here in the afternoon sun and the well-lit, soft yellow house lights.

On her phone, she opened the video and hit play. It was a few hours long, but the first few minutes were all she needed to see.

The camera focused on the big wheel, then on her as she lowered herself, carefully, onto the seat. When her butt hit the white plastic seat, a puff of smokey dust blew out. She didn't remember seeing that, but remembered what Simon's doctor said about *triggering events.*

"Episodes of memory loss like you're having, Mr. Cathmun, can be caused by many things. There's a lot we are still learning about the brain, the mind, and how it all works. There are triggers to make

symptoms flair up, such as dehydration, exhaustion, depression…"
The list went on. Louise thought it would be easier to list the things
that didn't cause an episode, but the doctors didn't know that and
thus couldn't say it. Alzheimer's was a greedy thief with many doors to
enter your mind.

"Yes, exhaustion and dehydration from the yard sale." Louise
nodded. She held the phone as she went to the refrigerator and pulled
out a bottle of water. Still watching the video, she popped the lid and
took a deep drink. "And yesterday, I was so thirsty. Dehydrated." She
shook her head, admonishing herself for the foolish behavior.

*You know what invites that bastard, so don't be so stupid. Don't invite
it in.*

After the dust cloud from the big wheel seat cleared on the video,
Louise smiled and started peddling. Off camera, Louise heard the
front door open, close, and the big wheel's three wheels grind on the
sidewalk away from the house.

"That must have been quite the sight." She imagined someone
seeing an old lady like her riding a big wheel down the sidewalk for
miles. Hundreds of miles.

Did I stop for a drink?

"No. I was so thirsty. Still am." She took another deep swig of
the water bottle. "Well, mystery solved." On the refrigerator, she
still had the contact information for Simon's doctor. "I'll make an
appointment on Monday."

Yeah, why do it now?

Monday always seemed like the best day to start something new. It
also had the great power of not being today, right now. This allowed

Monday to have the magical power to never come. Sure, Mondays come and go, but the Monday that will start something new, that Monday can easily be some other Monday, always coming and never here.

Louise opened eBay on her phone. A message from Tommy, the buyer interested in the big wheel, was in her inbox.

She opened it and read it out loud. "Sorry if my message freaked you out. I didn't mean anything other than just wanting to make sure the supports hadn't rotted out. Sorry if I came across creepy. Just send me a picture of a few books on the seat. That's perfect. Again, I'm very interested in the bike. My son will love it."

The message went on about how he's not a creeper, and Louise chuckled at this. Tommy was clearly not a creeper. Just a concerned prospective customer. She respected him for that.

A quick trim of the video on her phone cut out the hours of dead space after she peddled away. Flipping back over to the eBay app, she sent her response to Tommy.

"I don't think you're creepy. Here's the video. See me riding it away to show it's not staged or anything."

She sent the video and gulped more water, draining the bottle.

No more episodes. Another voice chuckled inside her. *Yeah, we'll see.*

The declaration was as effective as telling a storm to just stop storming. What was in motion could not be paused—only endured. She drank another bottle of water. Ate a bowl of chicken noodle soup. Drank some of Simon's Pedialyte she hadn't thrown away yet. He needed it constantly late in his condition to avoid episodes.

An eight-hour car ride will take the energy from a forty-something, much less a seventy-something. She felt exhausted, and sleep was knocking on her door. Louise ran through the playbook she used to use for Simon when she had to leave him for a trip to the store, or just to have a moment away to cry in the shed.

From the bottom drawer of her dresser, she pulled out the fanny pack Simon used to wear to sleep. Toward the end, he slept fully clothed and wearing this fanny pack. Inside it was his phone, his ID, some cash, and a note telling anyone who found him who he was and who to call. Louise strapped on the fanny pack and went to the kitchen for a piece of paper to make her own instructions.

"Bullshit." She sighed as she wrote her name, her address, Theodore's phone number. "Might as well say, *If found, put down.*" She shook her head. "No, being put down is the humane thing to do to an animal. People aren't humane to other humans." She crumpled the note and shoved it in the fanny pack, now hanging from her hips. "Bullshit."

Before she laid down, she put her phone and keys in the fanny pack. Every bone in her wanted to sleep, every muscle needed to go slack. Exhaustion had played her out. Her butt hit the bed, her head rolled to the big wheel. Its wheel turned toward her. Louise sat up. The big wheel was pointing at her.

It's always been like that. Don't be stupid. It hasn't taken your mind yet. Don't let it screw with you.

And she laid down. Sleep came fast, deep, and with a quiet sob from a little girl in Louise's kitchen.

SIX

Louise knew she was dreaming because she was flying. Clouds washed over her feet as she peddled. Her shoes had soaked through, making her socks heavy and dense. Rain fell below her, but she only felt it when her foot went down into the cloud. Her butt dragged through the mists, drenching her jeans.

It's going to look like I peed myself, she thought gloomily, but was able to remind herself that she only looked like she was peeing herself. Many of the old bags back in New York were needing diapers when she left. Louise assumed a strong bladder was her reward for dealing with those snotty bitches.

The big wheel, her flying machine, descended through the clouds, soaking the rest of her. A little girl was cheering her from the ground as she flew down through the dark night. The girl was a shadow on the ground, waving lights that looked like fireflies pulsing softly in a late spring evening. Her pigtails whipped around as she shouted and danced in joy at Louise's arrival. Louise waved, easily taking her hand off the handlebars as the big wheel gently touched down at the edge of the field.

"Welcome back," the little girl said. Her voice was high-pitched, but muffled like she was talking through a rubber Halloween mask.

Louise kept pedaling into the field. Mud sprayed up behind her but didn't get on her clothes. She let out her own joyful scream. The little girl ran to her, but the girl's pigtails didn't flip around anymore. The night was moonless, with only a faraway flickering neon light to illuminate the field.

"You found me!" the little girl said as she shoved her face into Louise's. Plastic cling wrap strained over the girl's face, smashing down her nose, forehead, and cheeks as they tried to burst through. Tense white creases stretched through the plastic, but it was too thick to rip. It sucked into the girl's mouth, flapping as the girl tried to breathe through it. Her eyes were open, screaming for help. The girl lunged for Louise, grabbing for her as she fell off the bike.

The muddy ground splashed around Louise as she woke up. The sun was blinding white, but her eyes adjusted quickly. She was in the field, laying in mud this time. The matted wheat had been ground down, broken apart to bare earth.

"Bullshit."

Like before, a trail stretched behind her to the road, but this time there were more tracks. These branched off from the trail. Louise stood. The big wheel was behind her this time, the wheel pointing toward the left track like a puppy ready to go fetch.

"You are shitting me."

She followed the dirt path, leaving the big wheel behind. The path was a circle, a small one at that, and led back to the big wheel quickly.

This is stupid. I'm breaking down. That bastard is chipping away at me. I'm acting out dreams now. You're losing, Louise. You're losing to that bastard. The other voice was back. *Not a bastard, just...* But she couldn't finish the thought. Her mind argued with her. That had never happened. The voices agreed with her. They were her voice. But not just then.

All the rational reasons about what was happening stamped out the supernatural reasons her heart was secretly hoping.

"Fine." Louise grabbed the big wheel and dragged it to the motel. "Bullshit." Mud caked her pants and shoes as if she were gardening on a rainy day. She hated this as much as gardening.

Wait, Simon's garden? Louise stopped and went back to the mud circle. *Simon's garden.*

The pieces came together slowly but firmly as she held the wheat on the right of the circle, the wheat toward the road. It was green. She then took the wheat that was within the circle in her hand. It was greener. Not just a piece, but all of it she could see.

"You couldn't get the new grass to match," Louise said. "Even when you replanted, it always looked off." She chuckled, remembering how frustrated that would get Simon back when he got frustrated. When he got anything other than tired.

"Are you telling me something?" She looked at the big wheel and immediately growled at her stupidity. *No, this isn't a magic bike. You're sick. You're being eaten by that bastard. By me.* The other voice was back, but Louise ignored it. She ripped a stalk of wheat from the soil. Then another. Then handfuls as she screamed at the wheat. "Bullshit! Shitting bullshit!" She stomped the wheat, kicked it, threw the shredded bits into the surrounding mud.

"What the hell are you doing!?" Rachael said. Her eyes dropped to the big wheel. The purple lightning bolts warned her from looking too closely, and Rachael turned her attention back to the old lady raging in the wheat field.

Louise rounded on her. The tinge in her chest made Louise grimace, but she recovered quickly. "Is this your field!?" she demanded.

"No! It's old Farmer Butcher's field, and he's going to be pissed that you're screwing it up."

"Well, he can go screw himself with his shittin' corn!"

"It's wheat!" Rachael stepped around the big wheel, getting closer to Louise. Deep set, sleepless circles were etched in Louise's eyes. Rachael wondered if she was sick, maybe lost. Maybe crazy. A hint of pity slipped into Rachael's eyes, and that was enough to send Louise over the deep end.

"Don't! I know what this looks like and it isn't!" *Lies.* "Get that look off your face before I smack it off!"

"Fine. I don't care about whatever's going on with you. Where'd you get that bike?"

"I told you, a yard sale. What, you can't remember anything?"

Can you?

"Shut up!" Louise spat. A spike of pain sliced through her chest, but burned out quickly. She clenched her teeth while it passed.

"I didn't say anything! What yard sale? Where?"

Louise's breath caught in her chest. "Why do you care?!"

Rachael's glances at the bike sparked Louise's hope for the unlikely, the supernatural, a reason for her episodes other than the onset of Alzheimer's.

"That looks exactly like my sister's bike," Rachael said. Louise's calm was infecting her now. The two women's emotions fed on each other, and now the calm of the one was a cool drink for the other.

"Maybe your family sold it?" Louise said. The lightning bolt stickers glimmered in the sunlight.

"I'm all that's left of my family." Rachael turned away from the bike and Louise.

"But you said—"

"My sister disappeared ten years ago. She was riding that bike the last time I saw her."

"How do you know it's her bike?" Louise wasn't challenging her, but was genuinely curious. The lightning bolt stickers were the only thing on the bike that looked unique. Everything else was boring blue plastic or white plastic.

Rachael bent down to the bike seat, pointed to the front of the white plastic. Clearly etched in the seat were the letters *LB*. Louise assumed those letters were a stamp from the manufacturer because of their precision and cleanliness.

"Lily Brown," Rachael said. She stood back up and bit her lip. Words wanted to come out of her, but Rachael said nothing. Her face contorted and twisted to find the shape of those words, but only a rattling sucking sound came out of her as she swallowed the spit flooding into her mouth.

Louise bent down, her knees popping loudly as she did, and checked the initials. Now that Rachael pointed it out, it was clear. Some kid made this mark. *How did I miss that?*

How do you miss a 500-mile trip? You're not playing with a full deck. That voice again. *I'm surprised you saw it at all.*

Louise ignored the voice. "Disappeared and never found, or—" She stopped there, letting the rest of the sentence be unsaid but understood.

"She's missing." Rachael turned back to the motel. "Come on, you look like hell. I'll call your guy."

Louise stood for a moment longer, watching Rachael. The midday sun was getting hot, and Louise's mouth was dry. Not a good sign when it came to dehydration. Rachael pushed through the wheat. Louise grabbed the big wheel, grumbled to it, "Come on," and dragged it through the field toward the motel.

Every few steps, Louise glanced down at the big wheel and wondered, *Are you in there, Lily? Are you bringing me here?* Never had Louise ever thought that she would hope a ghost was possessing her, but now it was the preferable option. She'd rather be infected by a spirit than devoured by that bastard.

She saw it in Simon, but something he said echoed in her mind as she walked. "It eats at you. Silently chomping away everything about you until you're just hollow. You don't know where you are, who you are, why you are there. Just empty until it's done and throws you away like the invisible trash you've become."

Louise stepped out of the wheat. The motel was just a few feet away. Rachael went into the office and waved absently for Louise to follow.

I know where I am. Who I am. But not why I'm here. She looked at the glittery lightning bolts on the big wheel. *You going to help me figure that out?*

But part of her mind chuckled at the foolish hope that she was in a ghost story and not a monster movie, the monster biting off a piece of her mind one wet chomp at a time until she was hollow, just like Simon.

SEVEN

"That's Lily." Rachael carefully placed a picture frame on her chaotic desk. It was a family. Rachael was a teenager with all the angst and grump Louise would have expected. Two parents suffered through the photo with smiles, but Louise saw plastered happiness after a long car ride with lots of threats to turn the car around. Probably bickering between the teen and her much younger sister, a little blonde girl with tan skin and bright eyes. She's happy in the photo. The background is this motel. Louise sees the "notel" sign behind the family.

"Was this taken here?"

"Yeah." Rachael returned the picture to a shelf behind her. "We stayed here on the way to a little vacation in the mountains. Just stayed a night. Never mind." Rachael cleared her throat, shook her head. "What's your guy's number again?"

Louise, never being one for tact, said, "You want to talk about it, so talk about it."

Rachael, surprised but not put off, shook her head. "I don't want to talk about it. Just waiting here." She motioned to the desk as if to say, "This is what I'm doing until Lily comes back."

Louise picked up a pile of the papers and shuffled them to a neat stack quickly. "Waiting's bullshit. About as useful as punching a concrete wall with a sock on your hand. It doesn't help."

"What else can you do?" Rachael answered. Her voice was the resolution Louise knew so well. Every time Simon got lost, forgot who she was, couldn't remember his name, what else was there to do but sit and wait for the Alzheimer's to finish having its fun and release his mind?

"So, you are working here waiting for her to come back?" Louise tried to keep out the tone that crept into her voice when she thought something was ridiculous.

Rachael laughed a dry, humorless laugh. "Owner. Not employee."

Louise nodded, stamping down the overwhelming urge to yell at Rachael for letting her business go to shit, or yell at her for buying a business she had no idea how to run. Bad decisions compound and get slippery with each new decision, making the next easier and looking like it can't get any worse than the previous.

"Your guy's info?" Rachael pivoted the conversation.

Louise let it pivot. "I'll just write it down. Keep it this time. And look, I'm not good at all this," Louise waved toward Lily's picture, "stuff. I'll say this, my husband Simon died not too long ago. I did a lot of waiting myself. Probably still am. I don't think he'd want me doing that, but it isn't up to him. You do what you need to do, but for shit's sake, clean off your desk." Louise stood. "I'll take four again."

Rachael sat, taking in what Louise said. The last sentence took longer to sink in than Louise's patience could last.

"Room four. The room I had last time. I like the bed." Louise flapped her hand for the key.

Rachael sifted through the papers on her desk. The key made a metallic scraping noise and then fell to the floor out of a pile of unopened mail.

Louise sighed her loudest, most disappointed sigh, and bent down to pick up the key. Her chest cramped with the too-familiar pain, the sudden shortness of breath that she was getting used to after one of her episodes.

"Let me get that." Rachael hurried around the desk and swiped up the key before Louise protested. The key plopped into Louise's hand as she unconsciously rolled her shoulder like she was trying to work out a sore muscle. She nodded a wordless thank you and walked to room four.

Rachael watched her go, expecting Louise to collapse. But the old lady didn't collapse until she got to her bed. The door to room four was still open when Rachael heard Louise shout, "Black coffee!" A moment later. "Please."

Rachael made the coffee and took the pot with two cups to room four.

EIGHT

Before Rachael brought the coffee, Louise had a message from Tommy, the buyer. She opened it while lying down. A sudden thought of the phone falling out of her hand and smashing her face came to her, so she sat up. The lift was a struggle. Her chest ached. *A heart attack would probably hurt more than this.* She ignored the pain.

The message read, "This is perfect, but what's with the special effects? I'm not paying more for a haunted bike. LOL! The face was a nice touch."

Face? She looked again at the video she sent. There's no face, only smoke. *Maybe he meant my face?* Louise rewound the video, played it slowly, and watched the smoke come up from the seat—the dust cloud that rose when she first sat on the bike did indeed have wisps that could be a face if you stared at it long enough. It could be a face like that piece of toast someone sold on eBay had the face of Jesus on it. She watched it again, this time at half speed, and saw what could have been a face smiling in the smoke, but probably not. Probably dust and her mind constructing a face now that Tommy suggested it. Louise was a logical person and didn't believe in the supernatural until this big wheel came along.

"Are you in there?" Louise said to the bike. She wondered if she showed the smoke face to Rachael if she'd see her sister.

"Um, I'm out here," Rachael said from outside the door.

"Yeah, yeah. Come in. Coffee?"

"Black. But," Rachael took in Louise's posture, her face, "are you sure you should have coffee right now?"

"Why shouldn't I?" Louise straightened up, suddenly aware of her slouch.

Rachael shrugged away the question and sat in the low-back chair that faced the TV. Nothing was far from anything in this room. The chair, a yellow-orange leather armchair, was close to the bed, with a scratched-up wooden coffee table in between. Rachael set the coffee cups between them and put the pot on the table. Louise scowled at that, knowing the pot would burn the wood and be yet another thing to fix in this place.

"So, why do you keep coming here?" Rachael asked. "It's weird."

It was now Louise's turn to study Rachael. The younger woman sat with her coffee at her lips. Steam floated around her sharp, worn-out face.

"I don't know." Louise shook her head and picked up her own cup. The pain in her chest had left. She sipped the bitter mud Rachael passed off as coffee. It was as horrible as Simon's attempts at making coffee. He was a tea drinker and never understood the appeal of coffee, much less how to make it. He could grow anything in any garden, but never brewed a passable pot of coffee. "Simon would say my feet took me here."

"Your...?"

"Husband."

"Oh," Rachael said, and looked away.

Theodore must have said something. Louise read Rachael's response as trying to hear this news for the first time. She let it go.

"How did he—"

"Theodore told you so cut the coy shit." Louise took a drink of coffee and watched Rachael for a reaction. She didn't flinch.

"Yeah, he did. He asked if I noticed anything concerning about you," Rachael said. Her coffee cup rested on her stomach, a thin thing that didn't have enough meat on it to allow the cup to sit flat or even still. It shifted, trying not to spill over. "I'd say showing up in the middle of nowhere with no way to get here is pretty weird. Pretty concerning."

Louise shrugged it away like these things happened all the time. That's what Rachael understood from her apathy and dismissal.

"Are you seeing anyone about your symptoms?" Rachael asked. There was a hint of care in her voice that distracted Louise from her question.

"No." Louise again stretched her arm and chest. "Nothing that bad. I've always had a good—"

"Wait, are you still having chest pains?"

"Wasn't that what you were asking me?" Louise stopped moving. Her cup steamed around her face, hiding the reddening cheeks. *Of course that's not what she meant. How could I have missed that?*

"I'm sorry, I meant your… Theodore called them *episodes*."

Louise put her coffee down to avoid throwing the steaming drink in Rachael's face. "I'm not having episodes. I'm not having anything other than the pains a normal seventy-year-old person would have from dealing with frustrating people." Louise bristled. "And I'd appreciate you stay out of my business when yours so desperately needs your attention."

"There's no shame in needing help," Rachael said. Her tone hit Louise the hardest. Rachael wasn't angry or defensive. She was pitiful. Pitying Louise.

"I don't need help." Louise glared at the big wheel sitting in the corner. It still looked bright and happy, with the giant white wheel pointing right at Louise. The silver tassels sparkled in the air conditioning breeze.

"My grandmother had dementia," Rachael offered. "It was horrible, but at least she got to forget Lily. Sometimes I think that's not all bad."

"Shut your shit-spewing mouth," Louise roared. Rage exploded in her, sending pain crackling through her chest like heat lightning splitting her insides. "You weren't there all the time, were you? Were you?! You didn't see days where she lost years in her mind, gone forever. Gone! And you think she…" Louise stood, leaning toward Rachael, fingers itching to slap the younger woman who had so many years until she had to face that bastard. The bastard who came for too many and now came for Louise. "You think she was thankful to rot away like that?"

"No—"

"Get out." Louise's boiling rage simmered into a seething heat. "Take your shitty coffee with you and this goddamn bike!"

Rachael got up, said nothing, went to the door. "If you're not having a problem, then why are you so mad?" She paused, twisted her face at the bike. "You keep it. It was never mine." Rachael slammed the door as she left.

Because you know there are no such things as ghosts. You know what's happening. You know why you're coming here.

"Shut up." Louise clenched her eyes shut. "Shut up!" The voice wasn't hers. Another voice was talking. She'd never heard it so clearly before. Who else could it be but that bastard? That bastard who's come to take her piece by piece.

You knew it was me all along. You just didn't want to say it. Now you have and now we can move on.

"No." Louise went to the bike, sat on it. Nothing happened. No smoke. No ghost. No field. "No."

I don't want to go anywhere right now. Just want to talk to you. Just want to remind you I'm here. But you won't be much longer. Soon I'll be here and you'll sit and drool and no one will care. I'll eat you like I ate Simon. You had to watch. Now you have to rot.

"No! You shitting shit ass!" Louise pushed the petals to get the bike moving, but it didn't move. The white wheel spun, unable to get a grip on the carpet. "Go! Go to the field!"

No, we're not going anywhere.

Louise got off the bike, kicked it, went to the bathroom and looked at the mirror to see who was looking back.

I'm still me. Her voice returned. It was her voice again in her mind. *I'm me. I'm me.* She washed her face. It was still her. *I'll go lay down. I'll go to sleep and I'll wake up in the field. The bike will take me there.*

Hopeful with a wish on her lips, Louise laid down on the bed. She reached over and clicked off the light. Sleep didn't come quickly. It waited. Wandered through her mind, trying to decide if she was tired or not. Her muscles were exhausted, but her thoughts wouldn't slow down.

Louise didn't look at the clock. Didn't look at her phone. Didn't see the time, just waited for sleep. After hours, maybe minutes, sleep settled on her, uneasy and restless. In what felt like a blink, she awoke.

NINE

"No." Louise sighed as she rolled over in her bed. "No. I should be in the field." She sat up and looked for the big wheel. It sat where she kicked it last night, in the corner, the giant white wheel turned to the side, looking away. The morning sun poured through the large window.

Think you'd be somewhere else? The other voice was back. It sneered in her mind as much as a faceless voice could. Louise tried to visualize someone to own the voice but, in her mind, the face was always blurry. Its body was clear, a well-dressed man in a black suit with purple pin stripes. He moved around with ease and grace, every motion dripping in smug confidence, but his face was always blurred like someone dragged their thumb over a photograph before it dried.

"No," Louise said. "This is where I should be."

Is it now? The faceless man laughed.

Louise stood over the bike, hands on hips, all her weight on one leg as she considered the thing.

Looking for someone?

"No," Louise whispered. "Just thinking."

Thinking I'm not here. I'm not eating you yet. The last word was so delighted, it transformed into a giggle. *I'm not here yet. You're hoping I'm not here yet.*

Louise didn't answer. She grabbed the bike and dragged it out of her room with the back two wheels grinding along the sidewalk.

Rachael was working in the office, trying to make sense of some paperwork, but Louise didn't stop. The field was waiting for her, and the mid-morning sun was still cool enough for a walk. A chilly breeze helped Louise ignore the chatter in her head as the voice kept asking what she was doing. She didn't know yet, but thought she'd figure it out when she got there.

"If I were losing it, I'd go somewhere I knew." Louise remembered Simon and how he never went too far. She didn't know if that was common for people suffering from that bastard, but took her experience as the only one she had. "Simon never went somewhere he'd never been unless he wandered, and when he did that, it was never the same place twice."

Louise pressed through the wall of green wheat at the edge of the motel's parking lot. The field absorbed her into the tall stalks, and she dragged the big wheel behind her. "So why here?"

You've forgotten this place.

"I've never been here." But the doubt had set like a seed. The voice fertilized the seed while she kept walking toward the gnarled tree that twisted and stretched into the blue sky. "I'd remember that tree." The voice just laughed at that. Louise kept rationalizing why she's not randomly coming here, and the conversation with herself hid the sounds of rustling wheat following behind her.

The wheat was broken by the mud tracks she remembered from yesterday. Louise put the big wheel bike on the tracks toward the road.

"That's where I keep finding you." Louise pointed to the bike, her finger tracing the mud track. "And that's—"

"What are you doing out here?" Rachael asked from the wheat, then stepped out onto the mud track.

"Figuring it out." Louise didn't look at her. Two deep tracks were carved into the mud, but they were smooth. "The back wheels." And another track in the center of the smooth tracks, which was rough like the front wheel. Her finger dipped into the mud and felt the cool, goopy trail.

"I called Theodore. He's sending someone here to take you home," Rachael said. She kept her distance. "He made an appointment with your doctor too."

Louise ignored that. Her mind was too busy sorting through the screaming voice, the faceless man's voice, telling her there are no such things as ghosts, that she's making excuses because Alzheimer's had her. The disease that she had known as that bastard had her. "Bullshit," she declared, and faced Rachael. "You have a shovel?"

TEN

"A shovel?" Rachael leaned back, her arms folded and tight around her. "Planning on—"

"Digging. What else would I use a shitting shovel for?" Louise said.

"Digging up the field?"

"Not the whole field." Louise scoffed at the absurd idea. The darker green wheat on the inside of the muddy circular track parted around her as she stepped into it. "Just a little in here." She walked toward the center of this circle of wheat. Each stalk swooshed around her as she went.

Rachael didn't follow. "You look like you haven't slept in days. I don't think digging's a good idea."

"Shovel or not!?" Louise snapped back. "I know what's a good idea: you getting me a shovel. That's a good idea."

"Why don't you come back with me to the office?" Rachael said in the best *trying to be calm* voice she could muster. "I'm sure your ride will be here soon."

"I'll be going to hell sooner than your office or any car unless you get me that shovel," Louise shouted from inside the wheat.

"Fine. I'll get the damn shovel." Rachael stomped off. "You're going to kill yourself out here, you stubborn old bat."

She's right.

"Old bat? I haven't been called an old bat since…" Louise tried to remember, but she couldn't. "Since…"

Missing something? Forgetting something that just happened a few days ago? The lady at the yard sale called you an old bat. But you don't remember that because I don't want you to. That memory was a treat I slurped up just when you wanted it. It was delicious. The voice laughed. *What else can I take…?* A long pause hung off the words as that bastard sorted through the files of Louise's memory. A picture of Simon came to mind and the voice laughed a throaty, vile chuckle.

"Shut up."

Louise kept walking until she came out the other side of the wheat, back to the round mud track she found yesterday. She quickly turned around and walked back, stopping at what she thought was the center.

You sure this is the center? You didn't wander off?

"You still out here?" Rachael called.

"Here. Shovel?" Louise waved over the wheat's feather-like tops glistening in the sun.

Rachael huffed and brought her the long-handled shovel.

"Here. You'll need these too." Rachael handed Louise heavy work gloves, like Simon wore. Once, he forgot his gloves during one of his episodes, and the blisters got infected. Louise had to put on the antibacterial cream, and when he'd forget why his hands were covered in the cream, she would have to put it on again. Without her constant supervision, he would have lost his fingers from infection going gangrene.

And who would watch for you?

Louise pulled on the gloves and grabbed the shovel. "You sticking around?" She thrust the shovel into the soft dirt. Shafts of wheat tumbled down as they were sliced at the root.

"You're crazy! You're going to kill yourself out here," Rachael said.

"I'm not crazy!" Louise shouted, and pointed the shovel at Rachael. A quick stab and the rusty metal head would be in Rachael's stomach, but Louise hadn't lost it that much yet. She threw the shovel's tip into the ground to pull out another clump of dirt.

"Well, I'm not going to watch you die. I'll get you water," Rachael grumbled as she stomped off. "But I'm not sitting out here all day. I've got work to do."

"Yeah, I've seen your desk. It'd take days to get out from all that shit."

"You want the water or not?"

"No, I want to dehydrate! Of course I want the water. If you had less attitude, I might even say thank you," Louise said as she dug.

Rachael grumbled something as she walked away. The swooshing wheat became distant as she went.

The dirt moved effortlessly as Louise dug. "Rain makes mud. Mud makes digging easy."

But there's dry rock down there. That won't be so easy.

"I'll deal with it when I get to it." Louise glanced up to where she thought she'd left the big wheel. "I think you're down here."

Or you'll dig your own grave. The voice laughed. *This is going to be fun to watch. I don't even have to do anything. You're not even going to wait for me to finish you. Oh, did you feel that?*

A slice of pain lanced over Louise's chest just as the voice said it. She shook her head, denying that bastard the satisfaction of being right.

"Just dig," she told herself, and kept moving. Her pace was slow. Intentional. Focused. "If you're not down here, then I might as well die in this ditch."

The voice laughed in her mind as her chest burned, her hands strained, and Louise kept saying, "You're down here. I know you're down here."

ELEVEN

Louise dug. The sun was setting. Time was measured in Rachael's visits. Since the dig began, Rachael had brought three glasses of water and a turkey sandwich. Louise hated turkey and made that well known. The sandwich was taken away.

Sweat mixed with the light rain that started a few moments ago. Together, the moisture on her skin cooled and chilled her. Soon, Louise's joints would tighten as they always did when it was damp outside. Her chest was already tight. Her face, red. Her hair, frizzing from the weather and work.

You done yet?

"No." She stabbed the shovel into the wet soil. Louise felt the raindrops on her neck as she moved dirt out of her hole. The sweet smell of spring hung heavy in the air and made shoveling easier than usual. But with nightfall came a chill that Louise knew all too well; her thin, old skin was no defense against the icy needles of an approaching storm.

A gentle patting surrounded her. Her shoulders were level to the ground, her ears were above the dirt outside her hole. Like a good gravedigger, she dug down and out in layers. Not straight down.

Simon always said you needed space to dig deep. To have space, you must dig around where you'll be digging.

"What do you think's down there?" Rachael asked on one of her trips. Louise thought it was when she brought the second water, but the exact timing was fuzzy. "There's nothing down there. An old tool shed used to be here. Nothing's down there."

Rachael sounded like she was trying to convince herself more than convince Louise to stop digging. Last time Rachael came out, she took the old water glass and left a full one. Nothing was said.

A tool shed, the voice said. *How would someone be buried under a tool shed?*

"Easy," Louise whispered, remembering her own shed back home. "Keep the floorboards loose. No one would check under 'em."

But the tool shed explains why the wheat's different. Simple answers, obvious answers, but not when you don't want to hear them. The voice in her head sighed as if to say, *That's how it is.* Louise imagined the blurry faced man and his neat little suit plopping down in the gaudy red velvet chair. Men like that always loved gaudy things. Just another way to brag, to rub your face in what they have and you don't. *Like my sanity? I have my sanity and you, well, I mean, it's pretty obvious—*

"My sanity is fine."

As the sun set, it broke through the clouds and gave the tree a golden glow. With the rain's slick sheen, the knotted and gnarled tree looked like it was dripping rainbows. Each rain drop refracted in a colorful glimmer over the tree's surface.

Or you're about to have a stroke. That's not natural, the voice commented on the reflected light. *Or do you think that's ghosts too?*

Louise Cathmun believing in ghosts. That's so ridiculous. You didn't grow all those companies with superstition and paranoia. You did it with your brilliant mind. Logic and reason. The voice chuckled. *And now I'm taking that. You're hoping for something you don't even believe in, all to avoid the logic and reason you've used all your life. I'm real. I'm here. I'm digging into your head while you're digging your grave. So poetic.*

"Shut up. Damn, your mouth runs like a—" The analogy vanished in her mouth. She had it a moment ago, had it while the sentence was being crafted in her mind.

Like a what? He laughed. *Like a, a, a…* His tone dragged out, getting throaty, imitating the slow drawl of the idiots in movies.

Louise replied with another stab in the dirt. Each shovel took her deeper into the mud pit. Each thrust into the ground made her chest pains burrow deeper.

"You're not there, but she is." Louise focused on the ground. The big wheel flashed through her mind.

"Who is?" Rachael said in her annoyed voice that Louise thought was reserved only for annoying customers. "I told you—"

"Yeah. I know you did." Louise winced from the pain in the chest. Her arms were heavier than they had been. Each toss of the muddy slush was a little harder than the last. "But if I'm wrong here, I'm up shit's creek. Rather lay down here than face that bastard. He's not taking me."

"Who?"

Louise shook her head and dug faster.

You'd have found something by now. Just quit. Go back to your room.

Lay down and let me have a little bite. A taste. You'll never miss what I take. Hell, you won't even know it's gone.

The rain intensified. Drenching sheets of frozen water poured on Louise and Rachael. No longer satisfied with raining from above, the storm was pooling in Louise's ditch. Water crept up around her ankles and soaked her socks.

"Stop! Just stop! There's nothing down there!" Rachael screamed over the storm, her taut face going from anger at the stubbornness to pitiful pleading. "Come out of there. There's nothing down there! There can't be!"

"Why!?" Louise screamed back. Her knees buckled at the force it took to get that loud, but she kept to her feet. The ditch was getting smaller around her. "Why can't there be anything down here?!"

"Because Lily's coming back!"

Lightning split the sky, sending an eruption of thunder through the air that echoed Rachael's fury.

"She was taken, and she'll be back! She'll come back here! She knows I'd wait for her! I told her I'd wait in our room while she rode her bike!" Rachael reached for Louise, but Louise didn't stop digging. The old woman knew Rachael wasn't trying to lift her out, but hand her the pain she kept for Lily. Simon would reach for her like this when he tried to remember something, but Louise realized he wasn't trying to take the memory from her. He was trying to hand it to her because he couldn't produce it. He couldn't find it. That bastard took it from him, and that bastard's taking days were over.

"Fine! Die here! You want to die!"

Louise wanted to scream back, "It's better than the alternative," but the words wouldn't come together. All she could think was the echoing of laughter from the blurry faced man. A mouth formed in the blur now. It was thin-lipped, crusted with sores, cracked and bleeding. Dentist scrapers were the man's teeth, all crooked and curled, as needed to dig into the hard-to-reach places like memories of love, joy, life.

Rachael stomped away, the sucking splashing mud trying to hold her back. Another bolt of lightning crashed down, and thunder immediately followed, shaking clumps of mud from the edges of the pit. The clumps splashed up, smearing streaks of dirt on Louise's wrinkled, beaten face.

You are done. You've got nothing. You've got no one.

Louise fell to her knees. The shovel was too heavy to hold in her leaden arms. Now her whole body was in the pit. Water rose to her waist as she leaned down, her heaving breath making ripples in the sludge. She shook her head, exhausted, and plunged her hands into the mud. She scraped it back. Large swaths of liquid earth squirted through her fingers as she kept shaking her head.

You're too late now. I won't get a chance at you.

A bolt of lightning exploded in her chest; not from the heavens, but from her heart. Thunder followed through her body, sending quakes into her guts. Her hands couldn't curl anymore, but she felt the mud wasn't mud anymore. It crackled instead of squished. The pain ripping into her body from her chest stopped. It didn't fade. It didn't settle. It vanished. Her arms were light, her body hardened, as she dug faster. Louise lifted to her feet and paddled between her legs like a dog until her fingers curled into a thick-walled plastic bag.

Wrap your fingers into it, Simon said in her mind. The other voice was gone. It was now Simon. *Rip it out. Like pulling weeds. Grab it good to get the roots.* His voice was kind and loving. He could have been standing right behind her, but Louise didn't look. She did as he said, using both hands to curl into the plastic bag, and ripped it from the earth.

Lightning shot through the sky, illuminating the night and the black trash bag Louise pulled from the mud. She climbed out of the ditch. The bag was light, easy to carry, but she didn't take it far.

"Rachael!" she screamed. "Rachael!"

"What!?" Rachael said from the edge of the wheat. She hadn't gone far since she left.

"I—" The pain in Louise's chest broke open again. Whatever had dammed up the suffering had ruptured. Her legs collapsed; her face hit the muddy earth with a hard splash. "I—"

Rachael ran to her. "Louise!" She stooped and turned Louise out of the mud.

"I found her." Louise pointed to the trash bag beside what she knew now was a grave, but not hers. "Call 911, for shit's sake. Don't just look at me. I'm shittin' dying here."

Rachael snapped out of her stare at the bag and called 911 on her smartphone. The operator answered, and Rachael began doing something over top of Louise, but Louise couldn't see her anymore. Simon was standing over her, smiling. He pointed to a little girl riding a big wheel through the wheat field. Her pigtails flew out behind her as she raced into the sky. The purple sparkly lightning bolts glittered with the stars. The rain stopped. Those lightning bolts flew off into the night as Louise closed her eyes, and the world went black.

TWELVE

White light flashed above her. Louise had heard that this was what the afterlife was like, but didn't expect to see so many people in her face. Never having been a people person, she'd assumed paradise would be less anxiety-inducing than having a bunch of people pressing their mugs so close to yours that you can count every nose hair.

"Bullshit," Louise groaned.

"Mrs. Cathmun?" one of the annoying people said. "Can you hear me? Mrs. Cathmun? Can you—"

"For shit's sake, give me a moment to answer," Louise said.

The faces receded, still hovering, but not so close now.

"Are you Mrs. Louise Cathmun?" a young lady said.

"I answered to it, didn't I?"

"Please answer the question," the young lady persisted, and it pissed Louise off.

"That was an answer. What, they don't teach you conversation anymore? Too busy with your head in those damn phones to talk to real people."

The young lady walked away and muttered under her breath, "Oh yay, personality."

"With good hearing too!" Louise shouted and sat up, but couldn't get too far. Her body cramped with tremors of pain. She stopped trying to fight.

The white light faded into a hospital room. Everything was bleach clean and stank of antiseptic. There were *beeps* and *boops* you'd expect in an intensive care unit. The annoying people summoned a doctor, who explained she'd had a major heart attack. She died in surgery a few times but kept coming back. When the doctor told her she was a tough one, Louise nodded like he said the most obvious thing in the world. He said she'd be staying in the hospital another few days to monitor her health.

After a day of chocolate pudding and yelling at nurses, Louise was allowed to have visitors. Rachael was the first one in the room. She told Louise about what happened after she passed out. The ambulance. The hospital. Then Rachael went back home and called the police about the trash bag. Lily was in the bag. She was murdered. A hint of a smile flicked at Rachael's lips.

"Lily must have sent that guy to the hurt locker before he killed her. Police said they found hair in her fist and skin under her nails and skin in her teeth. They used that to do DNA stuff and found the shitbag. They arrested him and found a bunch of toys in his back yard. Sick shit. He killed kids and kept their toys as trophies."

"I'm sorry about your sister," Louise said. She didn't look at Rachael.

"The police asked me how I found her," Rachael said. "I told them I was burying my dog and just thought he'd like it under the tree."

"You have a dog?"

"No."

"They buy it?" Louise finally looked at her. Rachael was tired, but didn't seem as exhausted as when they first met. Her shoulders weren't as slumped, her face was not as taut. Life had come back to her cheeks and eyes.

"They did when they saw the DNA results."

"How'd they catch him?" Louise shook her head, unable to grasp the last piece of the puzzle.

"He did one of those DNA-disease things where you see if you're susceptible to certain diseases because of your genetics." Rachael shook her head. "Police found a DNA match immediately. What dumbass kills kids and then checks if they're going to die of cancer?"

Dumbass. Louise smiled at the voice. It was hers. *Done in by not wanting to die from some horrible disease.*

"Well, everyone does dumb shit." Louise shook her head. "But I guess dumbasses do dumbass shit. How are you doing?"

Rachael shrugged in a non-committal answer. "Working on it. You?"

"Not dead yet."

"Did Lily tell you she was there?"

Louise returned Rachael's shrug. "I can't think of another reason I'd be out in that field. Can you?"

"Why didn't she come to me? Tell me?" Rachael teared up. Her fists curled in tight, white-knuckled knots.

"Maybe she didn't want you to suffer. Didn't want you to be the one to find her." Louise thought about when Simon died. He had wandered off that morning and was found in the park. He drowned in the pond. The police called Louise. They found her contact information in Simon's fanny pack. She knew he'd wandered off, knowing he was going to die and knowing he didn't want Louise to find him. "She loved you."

Rachael hadn't cried for her sister since Louise found her. The tears came now: hot and pouring, a summer storm of loss, regret, anger. The two women sat there. One crying, one patting her hand as they both processed what had happened.

"You are a good sister. Lily was lucky to have you. I was lucky you didn't give up on me," Louise said, then quickly cleared her throat and added, "Although that would be a total shit thing to do to an old lady."

Rachael chuckled at that and leaned into Louise, who held her while she cried. Louise patted Rachael's head, like she did for Simon when he'd cry. And just like she did for him, Louise stayed quiet and gave Rachael the space to let it all out.

THIRTEEN

(a few weeks later)

"I can't believe you did this so fast." Rachael looked at her new office setup. Everything was in order. Every folder and drawer had a purpose. Even the smell of the office was different. It smelled like work and not a sweaty mess.

"Easy," Louise said as she entered the bills into a new spreadsheet on Rachael's new computer. Louise reconnected with her old management consultant self and brought order to the motel quickly. She applied for a few small business grants, put the gears in motion to turn the motel into a thriving, off-beat attraction. "I've got a few more grant applications to do today, but that shit takes forever. Did you schedule with the bank?"

"Yes," Rachael answered quickly. "I didn't want another 'take my business seriously' lecture."

The two women went about the business of the motel. Louise waited outside the office, checking her watch for the sign repair man to show up. He was already running a few minutes late, and Louise would make sure he knew it when he handed her the bill.

A text message flashed over her phone. It was from the eBay app.

She opened it. Tommy had messaged her again with a picture of a deck of cards—some collector game cards—that he was selling, and wanted to know if she was interested in buying. Louise chuckled and looked up more information about them. They were collector items, and she enjoyed doing business with Tommy. He was a professional. She messaged him back, "Yep, what are you thinking for a price?"

"Pay what you will? My son's done with them."

"That's no way to run a business," she wrote, then continued the message with a long explanation of how he should think about his business. He's professional, but that doesn't mean he's good at business. That's where Louise is going to help him. She helps businesses, and their owners, transform to find success and happiness. She's the best and everyone knows it.

INVENTORY NOTE: 6

Item: 6

Component:

- Haunted Big Wheel Bike

Collection: Public

I acquired this bike from a man who claimed it was haunted. He said the bike took him to some field in the middle of nowhere beside a busted-up motel. I asked him for more information, and he told me he found the bike. He was lying, I could tell, being a person who often deals with liars. When I pressed him further, I discovered he stole it from some guy's back yard.

The original owner had a museum of toys in his back yard, according to the seller. When the seller described the guy's back yard, I knew it was a collection. A collector can recognize another. I doubt the man was collecting things like I collect, but instead, perhaps, collecting trophies. Strange, but that's the vibe I got. The seller didn't want to talk about it. He said the man who owned the bike originally didn't have kids but had more and more toys showing up all the time.

I asked why he stole it and the man said he was dared by a friend to steal it and ride it. One night he got drunk, stole the bike, and then went to ride it at a skateboard park, but instead of crashing and dying on the ramp, the man drove off. When he woke up, he was in the field by the motel. The seller said this happened four nights in a row.

The seller found me by searching online for haunted toys. He just wanted to get rid of it. I bought it for $1. One thing I love about buying from people who messed with the toys: I get them cheap and don't have to trade one of mine for them. Normally people don't want none of this. They'll pay me to take it, but I've found the curse, or haunting (the "Binding," as it is truly called), isn't broken unless money is exchanged. Perhaps that's some kind of spiritual ownership transaction? I guess even the dead recognize the power of capitalism.

I was able to find the original owner through discussion with the seller. When I arrived at the man's house, he was eating dinner. He invited me in; I declined and instead offered to buy the toys in the back yard. He refused to part with them, but recognizing a collector, I offered what all collectors want: curiosity about his collection. I offered to help solve that curiosity by engaging my friends in the police who could help me take these toys off his hands while he considered their origins in a prison cell. Suddenly, he was ready to sell a few.

This is item Six, but only item four in my collection. I've had to trade others to get to this point. At this pace, I will die before I have grown my collection to meet Dodslav's needs. This man, this killer, was manufacturing haunted toys. They were weak, hardly worth Dodslav's notice, but I could use them to trade up. Few in the haunted toy community could judge the potency of their items as I could. And no one cared where the items came from, only that they had a good story and a tragic past. This man harvested sorrow, stitched souls to toys as a gruesome seamster.

I made the deal. Silence for supply.

The latest sacrifice to get what I'm owed.

The killer glared at me when I left. Perhaps I'll find him in my house, among my collection one day, there to reclaim his trophies and ensure my silence forever. May he come prepared, as my collection is hungry and not choosey about whom they devour.

No one is safe from them. No one.

37

ONE

As a kid, this is where Guy Standun dreamed he'd be, on home plate, winding up for a home run. Every moment his mind had to wander put him right here with the bat in his grip, eyes locked on the pitcher as the baseball rocketed toward him. The crowd was cheering as he swung, and that's where his dream died and life began. He struck out.

Laughter erupted in the stands as the crowd celebrated his inevitable loss. What else could happen with two out in the bottom of the ninth? The bases weren't loaded, but a hit would have gotten the guy on third home and tied the game.

Guy wasn't a slugger. Or a fielder. He was a trier. His dream was baseball, and he sucked at it.

"Just one hit," Rodriguez barked as he walked past Guy to the dugout. "Couldn't even get one hit this season?" Before passing him, Rodriguez shoved Guy as he ran by.

"Season isn't over yet," Guy said as he recovered his balance, but he couldn't hide his disappointment. Rodriguez wasn't the problem. It was him. Guy was dragging down the team and killing his dream.

The team didn't look at him as they filed back to the locker room, shoulders slumped at their 99-game losing streak. Guy looked at the massive flood lights painting the field green, showing the celebrating Tigers in their glowing orange and black uniforms. They looked awesome as they ran onto the field and celebrated, breaking their own losing streak. Not nearly as long as Guy's team, the Pirates, who had the longest losing streak in their Minor League division's history. The Tigers' pitcher, Clover "Curveball" Carmichael, was lifted by his teammates as they chanted his name.

"Clover! Clover! Clover!"

And that hurt worse than the loss. Just once, Guy wanted to be the one held up. The one cheered. A winner.

His faded yellow and black uniform looked more like a bee costume than a pirate. It was sad, like everything else about his team. And with that, he went back to the locker room to bear the blame for game 99. Just like he did for 98, 97, 96, 95, and on and on.

He glanced up at the stands, scanning the fleeing audience to see one face. Hope held out, but like every game, that face wasn't there, and hope crumbled to despair. *Who am I kidding?* Guy gently kicked a baseball on the field. *I can't do this.*

"Hey, mister?" A kid in a black hat ran up to Guy. All the other Pirates had gone into the locker room. The girl held out a baseball and a black marker. Her parents were standing by the field's entrance, watching. "Can you sign my ball?"

"Don't you want whoever hit it to sign it?" Guy asked as he kneeled to the kid. There was no way he hit that ball, because his bat hadn't found a ball all season.

"No. I want you to sign it," she said, and glanced back at her parents. They nodded.

"Oh, okay then. Who do I make it out to?" He'd never signed a ball and wasn't sure what to do, so he replayed in his mind the first time he got a ball signed by his favorite player. Guy was nine, and the player was the amazing Dougie Merricko. Everyone called him Merricko the Magician because he could hit any ball out of the park, no matter how bad the pitch. Dougie had every record in his time, and still had a bunch that no one would ever break, according to Guy. But more than that, Dougie was a legend off the field too. He opened his Children's Network to help runaway kids and gave them hope for the future. Just like Dougie, Guy wanted to use baseball as a vehicle to help people in the world, not just play a game.

"Lucy," the little girl said, and handed him the ball and marker.

"Well, Ms. Lucy, you made my day." A tear wanted to slide out, but Guy blinked it back. No need to cry at his first ball-signing. Would anyone blame him? Little Lucy didn't ask anyone else. She asked him, and that was magic. He wrote on the ball the first thing that came to mind:

To Lucy, don't ever give up on your dreams!

Guy "Guillotine" Standun.

No one called him *Guillotine*, but he always hoped they would. He'd send pitchers to the guillotine when he took the batter's box, but that hadn't happened yet. Guy handed the ball and pen back. Little Lucy took them and ran to her parents.

"Have a great night! Safe travels!" Guy called to them. They waved, then turned.

"That was a nice thing to do," the dad whispered, but not too softly for Guy to hear.

"I wanted Clover to sign it," Little Lucy said, not so quietly. Her parents rushed her out.

Guy nodded, sighed, and let the tear he tried to hold come out. It wasn't a happy tear anymore. No point letting failure and pain soak back into his body. He had enough of both.

TWO

"I gotta make a change, Guy." Coach Lieberman shook his head and kept his eyes on the folders scattered over his desk. "The other guys," he motioned out the office door, "they're gonna leave if we don't win soon. No one wants to play on a losing team."

"I'm finding my stride," Guy explained. "I'm going to kill it next game. I know it." He wasn't convincing the coach or himself. They both stared at each other over the chaotic desk. A slow fan whirled above them, making the room chilly for a sweat drenched locker room office. Every surface was industrial metal, from the chairs to the filing cabinets and desk. Their voices bounced off the hard surfaces, creating an echo of echoes in the office.

Outside the wooden door, the other players laughed and shouted about how they'd win the next game after coach dropped *Gutless*. That's what they called Guy when they thought he couldn't hear them, but it turned out Guy's hearing was extremely keen, especially for criticism.

"Look, Guy." Coach shuffled some papers. "We both know you've only made it this long because of your talent," Coach held up his hand, "and that talent ain't ball." He pushed a folder to Guy. "Maybe…" Coach took a deep breath. "I don't want to be rough, kid, but maybe you're dreaming someone else's dream?"

Guy took the folder, opened it, and read the heading. He sighed. "My dream is baseball. Not," he shook the folder, "playing with money."

"Playing with money?" Coach jolted back from the desk. "Guy, what you've done with our investments has been staggering. Our owners love you. You've created so much return that we had to hire a legal team to review what you're doing and make sure we can explain it to the IRS."

As a kid, Guy wouldn't have seen himself growing up to be an investment manager. Does any kid? So what if he's good at it? Who cares that he's made the team rich with retirement funds that will keep their grandkids wealthy? Baseball was his dream. Money didn't matter. The cheers, the crowd, fans loving you, that's what mattered.

"Look, next game's it. You don't get a hit, you're in the office the rest of the season."

Guy nodded. He understood, and he knew he was an anchor on the team. It wasn't fair to them that he was so terrible.

"Maybe go see if you can find what you love about the game, then for god's sake get in a cage and hit some balls," Coach said, and handed Guy another folder. "There's a baseball memorabilia thing going on in town. Maybe check it out before we hit the bus tomorrow?"

Coach would bark at other players. He'd scream, he'd get in their face, but never with Guy. The owners didn't want their cash cow getting abused, but Guy saw that as just another thing missing from his dream. Where was the coach that pushed him? How could he get better if no one cared how bad he was?

But the team cared. And as soon as he left the office, they made sure he knew it. Icy stares. Angry shouting. While he was in the office, they threw his clothes in the shower. The team made it very clear: he was unwelcome. One guy, Peters, grabbed the folders Guy was holding, ripped them from his hands, and was about to throw them in the shower when Coach Lieberman screamed at Peters so loud the room shook.

"Give him those papers right now or you're off the team!"

Peters shook. He was aspiring for AAA, and being cut from AA was career death. "Just screwin' with him." Peters threw the papers at Guy. They scattered over the floor as the team members finished getting changed and left for wherever they were going to forget about the loss. Some went to bars. Some went to strip clubs. Some went to their hotel rooms to pass out, exhausted by another loss. Guy collected the papers, the fund information for the team's retirement accounts, and changed into his wet clothes.

He searched on his phone for the baseball thing Coach talked about and found it. Baseball Memorabilia Madhouse at the Fairgrounds. Open from Noon to Midnight. It was 9:04pm. Plenty of time to get dry clothes from his hotel room and check it out. Perhaps he'd rediscover the magic of baseball and change everything.

THREE

Guy had been to a swap meet many years ago with his dad. That was when he still came to his games. The smell was what he remembered most. It smelled like desperation. This place had the same stench. Everyone was hustling something. Some were trying to cash in their last collectable, others were trying to convince someone their item was the real deal, or mint condition. Everyone here wanted one thing above all: money.

These people were the disciples of baseball heroes like Dougie Merricko. They collected their hero's cards, clothes, cereal boxes, books, posters, baseballs, and anything else that they might have touched.

The Fairgrounds were a campus of large flat buildings that housed everything from animal shows to RV sales. This event, the Baseball Memorabilia Madhouse, was more like a vendor showcase. High ceilings carried every conversation into a booming cacophony that permeated everywhere in the massive open room. Narrow, makeshift halls were made by lining up tables. Each table was selling baseball-related stuff, and some tables were very nice. Some just had a tablecloth, and one didn't even have that. The barren wood table was chipped, with splinters stretching up to snag Guy's wrist. There was a piece of white paper on the table that said Vendor 99. Guy took it as a sign since he just lost his team's 99th game of the season.

"Selling anything?" Guy chuckled as he scanned the empty table.

"Are Gee Toy Hunter?" the man asked. His beard was long, well maintained, but shaped like a trapezoid. Guy wondered if that was intentional. He wore a trucker cap that said *Got Ghosts?* and a red and black flannel shirt that stretched over his sizable gut.

Guy didn't hear the man over all the ambient noise, but didn't want to ask him to repeat, so he nodded. "Yep."

"Trading or buying?" Trapezoid Beard asked.

"Buying, depending on what you have," Guy said.

The man pulled a small box out from under the table and placed it on top. He pulled on two leather gloves and reached into the box. Inside was a very abused baseball. The man held it out like a gem.

"Dougie Merricko's lucky ball." Trapezoid Beard twisted the ball to show all the dirt and beating it had endured.

Guy chuckled. "Yeah, right."

"What do you know about the ball?" the man asked.

"Dougie said it was the secret to his success, but that was a joke. Something he told reporters so they'd stop asking him stupid questions."

"But he wasn't shy about showing it. And what's the thing everyone commented on?"

"How bright the wool was. Everyone said it looked like muscle," Guy answered, but noticed something else about the ball. It had

Dougie's private signature on it. Not the one he used for everything he signed, but the special signature that was only for the most elite—aka valuable—items of his collection. In small letters, Guy saw the letters *DJM*. Incredibly rare. And it was Dougie's handwriting.

To seal the deal, the man pulled back some of the white cowhide where the stitching was frayed, and showed the bloody red wool that did indeed look like pulsing muscle. Guy reached to touch it, but Trapezoid Beard snapped it away.

"Price?" Guy asked.

The man studied him for a moment. "Are you a player?"

Guy nodded. "Trying to be."

"Then I'll give you a deal. I'll give this to you today for $1,000, but you promise to give me season tickets when you are a big-time grand slammer." Trapezoid Beard held out the ball. "Deal?"

"Why?" Guy reached for the ball but hesitated. His gut twisted and Coach's words replayed in his mind. *Are you dreaming someone else's dream?* Should he let this go? Move on? Keep the thousand dollars for something else? But this was Dougie Merricko the Magician's lucky ball, he'd be crazy to let this go. If baseball didn't work, he could sell it for easily three times what it cost, if not more.

"$1,000 is what I need for tonight. I have somewhere to be, and to get in costs $600. The other $400 is to enjoy once in." The man winked and laughed.

Guy assumed that meant a premier strip club and shrugged it away. "Deal." He took the ball and felt a shock dig into his palm. It vibrated up his arm in a quick tremor that jolted down to his heart.

There, it burned a moment and passed. He shook off the sensation, assuming it was the ball just hitting a sensitive nerve.

The money changed hands, and the deal was done. Guy smiled as the fleshy hide baseball settled in his hand. Energy thrummed from it, making Guy think of a heartbeat. He knew this was the moment the old Guy, the one who couldn't help his team on the field, was over. Now was the time for dreaming about baseball, hearing screaming fans, and feeling the solid *thwack* of a baseball finding its target.

FOUR

In his hotel room, Guy put the baseball on the TV stand. It rolled to the side when he let go, so the rip in the covering looked like a smile. A few of the faded red stitches had torn or frayed enough to let the ball's dirty white covering open.

Guy flopped on his queen bed and searched for where he left the TV remote that morning. He found it on the bedside table and clicked on the sports channel to watch baseball. The Astros were playing the Orioles, with both teams still working toward their first run. On his smartphone, Guy turned on the background noise that helped him focus: talking heads discussing today's investment news.

While a bunch of men bickered about tech stocks, Guy analyzed the players on the screen to see how they swung, how they ran, how they caught. Every aspect of their performance was absorbed and emulated as he got up from the bed and went through the motions of playing baseball. Many years ago, one of his coaches encouraged him to imagine playing while he wasn't playing to train his body and mind.

"Anchor your foot more."

Guy straightened up and searched for where the raspy voice came from. His phone was still on the bed, the old men arguing now about commodities pricing and something going on in the Middle East. He must have heard them saying something and translated it to baseball as he watched the game. Not a usual thing, but it could happen.

On the nightstand, Guy had a glass of water and the last bits of his dinner from McDonald's. He grabbed a fry and took a sip of water.

"You are what you eat."

That voice again. But no one was in the room, and the men talking on the phone didn't have thick New York accents.

"Hello?" Guy scanned the room and walked to the door. He listened for someone outside.

"Over here."

Guy pushed off the door. The voice was coming from the TV. He checked if he'd left the volume on. Normally he set the TV to mute while he watched the game to avoid getting distracted by the announcers. These games were for learning, not enjoying.

"Closer." The white covering of the baseball flapped like lips. "Yep, you found me."

Guy jumped back, hitting the bed, then bouncing off and falling to the floor. The baseball laughed as he popped up from beside the bed and stared at the lips. More stitching had popped open as it talked. A wide grin pulled the white hide covering away from the red fleshy wool inside.

"Now you see me?" the ball asked.

Guy didn't answer.

"Let's get past the whole, *oh wow, a talking baseball* thing as quickly as possible," the ball said. "You want to be a ballplayer?"

"How'd you know?" Guy checked the room again, looking for anyone else talking. He picked up his glass of water and examined it for powder on the bottom or something to suggest he'd been drugged. Maybe it was a dream? Did he fall asleep watching the game?

"Normal people don't pretend to play while they watch. You look like you're practicing. I can help you. I helped that other guy, and look at what happened for him."

"Dougie Merricko?" Yes, a dream. Guy knew this was a dream and so went along with it. He'd wake up when things got too weird.

"Yep." The ball chuckled, its lip rippling as the last thread holding it closed snapped. "Good ole' Dougie. He was a trip. Okay, so here's the deal, the same deal he had. I make you good, but you gotta feed me."

Guy glanced at the fries on the nightstand.

"No. Look." The ball opened its lips wide, exposing the pulsing sinew and gore inside. The wool looked like throbbing muscle tissue. "What do you think I eat? It ain't fried crap like that."

"Blood?"

"Ding ding ding! He can be taught," the ball mocked him and laughed. "Yeah, so you give me a few drops and I'll give you two home runs in tomorrow's game."

"How?"

"How to feed me?"

"No, how do you give me two home runs?" Guy sat on the edge of the bed now, leaning toward the ball.

"You are talking to a baseball right now," the ball said, and closed its lips. It waited for that to sink it. "Magic or whatever, look, you want those home runs or what? I'm starving, and this is going to be easier if I just show you."

Knowing this was a dream, Guy shrugged and thought a cut would wake him up. He went to his McDonald's bag and got out the plastic knife. "This probably can't do much." He raised his thumb and pressed the knife teeth to it, but nothing happened. The knife just bent.

"You gotta want it to happen. You don't want to be a baseball star, you don't want fans cheering and loving you, that's fine."

"No." Then the knife snapped, and a shard of plastic stabbed into Guy's palm. Blood erupted in a drooling volcano. "Ah! Damn it!"

"Bring it to me!" the ball shouted, and rocked toward Guy. He held his hand over the lips as they quivered and slurped to catch the beads dripping off his palm.

Why didn't I wake up? Guy looked for any changes in the room, but there were none. Only the loud slurping of the ball sucking the air, catching the crimson stream running from his hand.

"Okay, that's good." The ball swallowed in a popping contraction that made Guy step back. "Clean yourself up and get some rest."

A warm, fuzzy ball grew inside Guy's palm. He could feel it expanding, bursting in a wave of heat that coated him from his hand to his heart. From the inside out. "What?"

"That's your two home runs tomorrow. Swing at anything and it will be a home run. But you only get two. Think of this as your trial run. When it works, we'll talk about what's next." The ball laughed. "Get some rest. That feeling you just had's gotta soak in."

Guy went to the bathroom and cleaned his palm. He wrapped it up, and when he came back out, the baseball was sitting on the TV just like it had been. No lips. Threading was back, stitched loosely, but stitched. It was just a dirty baseball with drips of blood around it.

He felt dizzy. Maybe the cut and the long day had gotten to him, and he'd imagined everything. Guy climbed into bed. A screaming siren snapped him away from sleep as soon as he closed his eyes. He sprung up, saw the siren was the phone ringing, and answered it.

"Where the hell are you!?" Coach Liebermann shouted. "Get your ass on the bus! We've gotta go!"

The curtains were closed, but from under them, Guy saw sunlight. He checked his phone. It was morning. He overslept. The cut on his hand was gone. The baseball sat in front of the TV, smiling at him with those loose stitches and a bit of dark brown smeared around the seam.

FIVE

Guy took the batter's box for the first time in the 3rd inning. All day he couldn't stop shaking, and right now was no different. The bat swirled around him as he approached the box. Energy rattled inside his bones, begging to burst out.

Earlier in the day, Coach noticed something was different and asked what was going on. Guy didn't know. He remembered the weird dream with the baseball, but that wasn't it. He told Coach the trip to the Memorabilia Madhouse was just what he needed.

A fastball launched from the pitcher. Guy didn't even see it, didn't even tell his body to swing, but his bat had no problem finding the ball. Every member of the Pirates collectively gasped, sucking the air out of the field, as Guy sent the baseball out of the park like a missile. No arch, no high drama, just a straight shot beyond the stands and into the parking lot.

No one cheered.

Guy didn't run. He turned to the umpire with a questioning expression. The umpire just stared at him.

The catcher stood and patted Guy on the shoulder. "Nice hit. Take your victory lap."

He did, checking to see if the baseball bounced back, or maybe it didn't go as far as he thought. When that idea hit him, his run turned into a sprint. There was no way he was going to be lazy on his first home run. Guy booked it around first, second, third, his head on a swivel to see if anyone was throwing the ball, but no one was moving. They just watched him run. He hit home plate with a heavy stomp as he panted and caught his breath from his first ever hit out of the park. But it wasn't his last. He did it again when he came back to the plate in the 6th inning.

When he came to the plate in the 8th, he didn't swing at anything and was walked, intentionally, by the pitcher. He stood on 1st base until his teammates struck out.

Pirates lost their 100th game, 15–2. Guy was the only one to score all game. No one talked to him in the locker room. No one looked at him. They kept away and moved to the other side of the room when he got close.

"Standun! Get in here!" Coach barked.

Guy went to his office and shut the door.

"What the hell was that?!"

"I don't know. It just kind of happened."

"That doesn't just happen. It's not like you said, *You know what? Today I'm going to be a slugger.*" Coach pointed out into the locker room. "They're saying you've been faking. Calling it in and not caring until you were about to be cut."

"That's crap!" Guy stared at his teammates. They were watching him now. All their eyes locked on the coach's office to hear what was happening. "I strike out, they hate me. I get runs, they hate me." He threw his hands up in defeat.

"Have you been baggin' it?"

"No!" Guy snapped back, clenching his fists. How dare Coach ask that? He'd been busting his ass for this team, and they should be licking his shoes for all he's done for them. Those ungrateful bastards.

"You okay?" Coach shrank back from Guy and pointed. "Your hand's bleeding."

The rage evaporated out of Guy in a sobering speed. Blood poured from the gash in his palm, the gash that wasn't there when he woke up this morning. Why was he so angry? He never got that angry about anything.

"I'm sorry. I don't know what came over me." Guy's hands shook. His body felt cold, hollow, like sloshing ice water poured into him from some dark place. "I don't know what happened tonight," he lied. "The swings just felt right. Got lucky. That's it."

They wrapped up their discussion shortly after and Guy went to the doctor to get his hand checked. The doctor cleaned it up, bandaged it, and sent him on his way. Back in the locker room, his clothes were a soaked mound in the running shower. Steam filled the air from the hot water.

"Damn." Guy went in to get his clothes and bag. He shed his uniform and went into the open showers. The room was green tile with white grout that looked more like a prison than a locker room. The spouts dangled from flexible metal tubing with the controls at a center column. Guy twisted the knobs to shut off the water and went to his bag.

The dense steam lingered in the room as he opened his bag and saw everything was soaked inside, including the investment paperwork Coach gave him yesterday. Dougie's lucky ball was in his bag too, and it rolled to the bottom where it looked up at Guy and smiled. The stitching was broken, and the fleshy lips pulled back from the crimson wool.

"How'd it feel to hit those home runs?"

"What's it matter?" Guy scooped up his clothes. He was assessing how wet his clothes were and didn't notice the shadow moving outside the shower room.

"Oh, it matters. It matters how you feel. They'll cheer for you," the ball said.

Guy shook his head, wondering why the hell he was talking to a baseball, and left the shower room. Rodriguez was standing there, staring at him.

"Who you talking to, Gutless?" Rodriguez said.

"Leave me alone, Tommy," Guy answered as he dried off. His uniform stank, but it was all he had until he could dry his clothes at the hotel.

"Nah, you talking to your conscience? It giving you shit about being a bagger?"

Guy didn't answer. Just shook his head and got changed.

"I'm talkin' to you!" Rodriguez pushed Guy as he was putting on his shoes. They sloshed as he squished into them. The push sent him tumbling over a bench. "We all knew you were a piece of shit. Phonin' it in while we all bust our asses."

The locker room was empty. Only the two of them. Guy wondered where everyone else was.

"Just got lucky," Guy said as he stood, grabbed his bag, and headed to the door.

"That luck gonna get your ass kicked!" Rodriguez shouted after him as Guy left.

In the empty hallway leading to the exit, the baseball chuckled. "You know what I eat. You'll win tomorrow's game if you just feed me. But I need more than you can give. I need it all."

Guy stopped in the hallway by a large steel rack of baseball bats. He grabbed it to keep his balance as what the baseball was saying snapped together. It could make him great if he fed it people.

"Is that?" Guy looked into his bag. The ball was on top of his clothes, even though he knew he buried it. "That's not right." He shook his head, denying the idea that was forming. It couldn't be.

"Yeah!" Rodriguez shoved him into the rack of baseball bats. "It's not right! It ain't right to be ridin' your team!" One of the bats hit the concrete floor with an echoing clatter. Guy fell, the edge of the metal rack slicing his forehead in a gusher. Blood coated his face immediately, blinding him as Rodriguez reached down and ripped him up like a rag doll. Guy had heard other teammates saying Rodriguez was juicing, but now he knew for sure. The man was powerful, and so angry Guy could feel the heat beating off him.

"No! It's not what you think!" Guy said as he was yanked close to Rodriguez's face. The man's breath smelled like whiskey, and he had a bloody nose. Who knows what he was putting into his body, but Guy was going to endure his wrath for some perceived slight.

Rodriguez slapped him. Blood splattered on the wall behind the bat rack.

Where is everyone else? Guy tried to look around, but Rodriguez grabbed his face, squeezed his cheeks so hard his teeth sliced them open, and then threw Guy to the other wall. He hit it with a crack as his head smashed into the floor.

Rodriguez lunged toward him, but Guy kicked his knee—his bad knee—with everything he had. A loud pop echoed down the hall, and Rodriguez screamed as he slipped on Guy's blood and fell back-first into the bat rack. Another thunderous crack echoed through the hall, but it wasn't his head, it was his neck.

"Oh my God!" Guy staggered to his feet. "Oh my God!" He stumbled over to Rodriguez and reached for him. "I killed him!"

But the other man was too drunk and high to die. His body didn't move, but his head lolled at an unnatural angle over the baseball bat rack's bottom. Raspy breaths were sucked through a gaping mouth.

"What'd you do?" Rodriguez moaned. "What'd you do?"

"I'm sorry! You attacked me—"

"You tried to kill me!" Rodriguez screamed. His chest rose in frantic breaths. "I can't feel anything. You tried to kill me! Help! He's trying to kill me!"

Guy stood back and shook his head. Rodriguez was trying to kill *him*, not the other way around. Guy just defended himself, and the dumbass slipped on the blood *he* made Guy bleed.

"I can clean this up?" the baseball said. "You don't even have to ask, just gotta want me to."

Guy looked at his bag. The baseball had rolled out and was looking at him expectantly with its eyeless stare and wide smile. Guy looked at Rodriguez, listened to his screaming about how Guy

was trying to kill him, and behind those screams, he remembered
all the verbal jabs, the shoving, the wet clothes, the comments from
this jerk even after Guy made him rich enough to never work again
after baseball. Then hundreds of thin red threads bolted out of the
baseball's gaping mouth. They wrapped around Rodriguez's arms,
legs, torso, and squeezed. The ensnared man screamed again, but
all the breath was compressed out of him as the threads dug deeper
into his skin. More threads shot out of the baseball and wrapped
Rodriguez in a cocoon of blood-slicked crimson string. A quick pop
and grinding gravel sound followed as the strings crushed Rodriguez
into a clump of flesh and then tightened more and more, with bone
grinding bone down to dust. The threads dragged the bleeding
mass to the baseball's mouth and then swallowed Rodriguez whole.
Serpentine threads then slid out of the mouth and mopped up the
bodily fluids that leaked out during the devouring like an efficient
cleaning crew making short work of the horrible mess.

The baseball drew in the last threads and smacked its lips in a
comical, exaggerated satisfaction. "Well, that worked out," it said, and
smiled at Guy. "You need to get cleaned up."

"What?" Guy said, unable to process what was happening.
Rodriguez was gone. Any sign of him, gone.

"Go back, take a shower. Put on your wet clothes and go to the
hotel to clean up your uniform for tomorrow's game. You're going to
crush it tomorrow!" The ball laughed. "I just know it."

Expressionless, thoughtless, Guy pushed the ball back into his bag
and returned to the locker room for a shower.

SIX

Coach was looking for Rodriguez before the game started, but let it go when it was time to take the field. No one suspected Guy killed him; who would suspect someone they nicknamed *Gutless* to do anything to the biggest, baddest man on the team?

Guy had that warm, unstoppable feeling coursing through him again. It was just like yesterday, but more intense, and he could see others were feeling it too. Their faces were brighter, more intense. They twitched with the energy ready to explode out of them.

Before taking the field, Guy told the team, "Let's go break this streak." But they laughed him away, and when the first guy struck out, Guy wasn't sure if he'd just imagined what happened last night. But then the next guy got on base, and the next, and the next, then he was up to bat. He hit a grand slam. The crowd erupted in cheers. Everyone likes a grand slam, no matter who hits it.

After an inning of no hits for either team, the Pirates repeated the grand slam, with Guy driving everyone home. The crowd cheered again, and this time, Guy heard it was for him. When he hit home plate, his teammates gave him high-fives and a slap on the butt. Coach nodded approval, and when Guy came to him, he said, "I've been working hard, Coach. I just needed to find my stride."

"Apparently." Coach nodded and smiled.

In the dugout, Guy went to his bag and pulled out his lucky ball and felt the stitching that had closed back up where the mouth was. His thumb rubbed the ball mindlessly as he saw other players getting hits, getting runs, getting the win.

On his final trip to the plate, the pitcher threw so wide that the catcher had to get up and stretch to catch the ball, but Guy had no problem finding it with his bat. The high, wide ball was turned into a home run, ending the game 14-7, Pirates win.

After 100 games, they had won. The crowd screamed as Guy ran around the bases. He heard their adoration, and it brought tears to his eyes. He checked the stands for his dad, but he wasn't there, even if Guy swore he heard him. The only time he ever saw his dad was when he'd cheer in the stands, and Guy wished he could see him now.

In the locker room, everyone celebrated. Coach ordered some champagne and sprayed it around the room. Tonight, everyone's clothes were getting soaked; not from the showers, from the win. They shared stories of their hits, how they didn't think they'd get the ball, but somehow it was like magic. They talked about how the other team fumbled the ball when trying to get them and how everything just seemed to go the Pirates' way tonight.

Guy didn't cheer. He stood in the shower holding his lucky ball and wondering what the price of tomorrow's game would be.

"Yo! Guy!" Davis came into the shower and twisted on steaming hot water. "What's gotten into you, man? You like the home run king now?"

"Just been practicing." Guy squeezed the ball. He wondered if

Davis would slip in the shower, bust his head open and ensure the next game for the team.

"Well, whatever it is, keep doing it." Davis scrubbed his armpits and butt. "And, man, I'm sorry I was such a dick. Throwing your shit in here and stuff. I'm sorry, man."

Guy wanted to turn and throw the baseball through Davis' face. He wanted the ball to devour the bastard. What, now Guy's useful, so Davis is sorry? If he weren't cranking balls out the park, Davis would still throw his clothes in the shower and treat him like crap. A stitch broke on the baseball, the lips coming out, and Guy shook away the thoughts.

"Yeah, man, we all make mistakes." Guy took a calming breath and finished in the shower as another stitch snapped open on the ball. It was feeding time, and Guy didn't know how long he could hold his wants at bay. He'd feed his entire team to this beast for what they've done to him after all he did for them. They were no different from Rodriguez. Some just hid it better.

A moment later, Guy left for his hotel room, walking out into the hallway from last night. No blood, no sign of a struggle. The ball had cleaned the scene thoroughly. Another stitch popped in his bag, this one ripping in a loud zipper sound.

"Do we understand each other?" the ball asked.

"If you eat the team, we won't be able to play. Too few players on the field and all."

"Then find someone not on the team. Don't let logistics impede your dreams, Guy. You're the Guillotine, now act like it."

Guy thought about all the people who he should target. Bad

people. People abusing their wives or kids, drug dealers making money at the expense of people's future, the list could go on…but how would he find those people?

"Is this how it worked for everyone?" Guy was afraid of the answer. His hero, Dougie Merricko, Merricko the Magician, was he feeding this thing? Is that how he became Guy's hero?

"Yes." The baseball laughed. "Why? You want to know what the other's did?"

Guy nodded as he got in his car, a modest Honda. "Yeah, that would probably help."

"You're still warming up, so we'll keep it easy," the ball said. "You know any bad parts of town?"

SEVEN

Guy did what he discussed with the ball. He drove around town until he saw what he assumed were gang members hanging out in front of a 24-hour Speedyshop. He watched them from across the street as they threatened people coming out of the store. These punks were making life harder for hard-working people leaving a late shift. They pushed one guy and took his wallet, then chased him off while waving a gun around.

The guy with the gun walked away from the group and into the shadows behind the Speedyshop.

"There's your guy." The ball chuckled, dry and eager.

"I don't know if I can do this." Guy's guts locked up inside him. Defending himself was one thing. Seeking someone to kill was another. "Yeah, he's a jerk, but he hasn't done anything other than be an asshole." Guy thought of all the assholes in his life. His stepdad. All his teammates. His college baseball coach that told him he'd never be anything. But being an asshole wasn't a death sentence.

"Up to you," the ball said, unbothered by the idea of going a night without a meal.

"Really?" This didn't add up for Guy. He'd never imagined a man-eating baseball would be so easy to give up its murderous ways.

"Yes. It's up to you. You can go back to how things were, and I can just be a baseball. Except now people will wonder why you're not hitting like you were. They'll be wondering what happened, and they'll never stop asking. You'll be the guy who was good for two games and then never again."

Guy remembered a period in Dougie's career when he had a slump. Right before Dougie started his children's charities. Everyone said the charities were just to distract people from him being washed up. But maybe it was something else. He tried to stop feeding the ball, and the ball stopped giving him whatever it gave him? Eventually, the slump ended when Dougie gave in to the ball. The charities were probably his way of balancing the scales, doing good while doing wrong.

"But I can just find someone that's a bad person and feed you every once in a while."

"Sure, but you're assuming one person will do it. If I don't eat, I need to make up for lost meals. Now it's just a person a day, but you skip some meals and…" The ball laughed. "I mean, I gotta eat. You know what I mean, Guy?"

Guy did. Once the ball started, it couldn't stop. Of course, that wasn't shared when the ball took the first taste of Guy's blood. When this all started. Only the upside was talked about, never the down.

"How about this… Tomorrow, the crowd will chant your name. Your team will win, you'll hear your name, and we'll work out a deal to carry you through the rest of the season. You guys will win every game and you won't have to feed me as much. How's that sound?"

Guy should have asked for the catch, but the ball had him at the crowd chanting his name. He'd never had that. Only his dad ever cheered for him, ever called him out by name. It'd be just like those games when he was a kid. When his dad still came to the games. No one else would get the attention, only him. That never happened for Guy. He was the invisible one, except on Saturdays when his dad would come to the games and cheer for him.

Before he knew it, Guy was out of the car with the baseball in hand. He went around the other side of Speedyshop and saw the guy with the gun standing by a dumpster, pissing. He wore an oversized yellow jacket that might have started life as a firefighter's coat, but looked more like a clown's outfit on the scrawny guy. Black glossy boots were pointing toward the dumpster, and his jeans were bunched up under his butt. The guy didn't have any hair. Guy thought it was from shaving a balding head versus choosing to be bald.

Behind the store was dark without the streetlights and only a sliver of moon to show anything. There were three dumpsters. Two had trash spilling out of them, with bulging black bags dangling from open lids. The other was crammed with cardboard boxes. Even in the faint light, Guy could see all the graffiti covering the walls around him. The street was wide enough for one large delivery truck, but nothing else.

When the sound of pissing stopped, Guy could hear the gravel crunching under his feet. His focus was on what was about to happen. He hadn't noticed he was off the blacktop pavement and on loose gravel stones. The pisser turned and saw Guy as he hitched up his pants up. He smiled, half-lit by the streetlight closest to them.

"What you—" the pisser started, but Guy held out the baseball, palm-up, like he was giving it to the man. The pisser smirked and would have screamed when the threads ensnared him if it all didn't happen so fast. Guy turned away, not wanting to look, but he felt the vibrations of the cracking bone, the squishing flesh, and worst of all, the quivering satisfaction of the ball as it swallowed the man whole. It licked up the leavings, keeping clear of where the pisser relieved himself. Guy assumed that was one bodily fluid it did not prefer.

"And now we're done. Let's get out of here. You need a drink from the store before we go?" the ball asked.

The cut on his palm burned as the familiar fuzzy feeling returned and gushed through him. Guy squeezed the ball, feeling the energy super-charging him for tomorrow's game.

"Maybe a burrito or something?" the ball asked.

"I'm not hungry." Guy grabbed his knees at the surging energy running through him. He stood there for a moment, catching his breath, and then drove back to the hotel.

EIGHT

That night, Guy couldn't sleep. He kept wondering how many people Dougie killed to be the greatest. What was the body count that led to his home run record? Or his World Series dynasty? The media always said he was a private person. Now Guy knew why. There's not a lot to talk about when all you do is stalk the night and kill people.

The ball sat on the TV stand. All the stitches were closed. It had been fed and was done for the night.

Guy turned on the financial talk shows he liked and listened to the hosts bicker about where to invest. Soon, he couldn't take laying in bed anymore. Guy went down to the hotel bar for a nightcap. It didn't close for another hour.

The hotel bar wasn't fancy, but it was nice. There were couches with small TVs in them for you to watch whatever you liked while enjoying a quiet drink. All the other players had gone out or to bed by now, and the bar was empty. Guy sat on a stool at the wooden bar and the bartender came to him quickly.

"How can I help you?" the bartender asked. He was a short man, dressed in the hotel's red vest, white shirt, and black pants uniform.

"Decaf hot tea?" Guy asked.

"Anything in it?" The bartender smiled.

"No thanks. I've gotta get up early."

The bartender nodded and went to his console to enter the order. "Anything to eat? You want to get to sleep? Our nachos will knock you comatose. They're super heavy. Put you right out."

Guy tapped the bar with nervous fingers. The ball had just had a heavy meal and now it was sleeping well. He wanted the same. "That sounds good."

After a bit of silence, broken only by people coming in from drinking elsewhere and going straight to their rooms, Guy's food and drinks arrived. The nachos were on a plate the size of his torso piled high. Gooey cheese drooled from the chips and mixed with chorizo, ground beef, jalapenos, black olives, and some kind of green leafy decoration. He didn't realize how hungry he was until he took his first bite. It was bliss.

"That good?" a woman asked as she sat at the bar. "Lenny, hit me."

The bartender moved quickly, gathering the components for a drink in a martini glass. She reached over and took a chip overloaded with cheese and toppings, crunched it, and nodded in delight.

"Yeah, that is good." She was tall, muscular, with sharp brown eyes that sliced through any objection Guy had to her taking his food. Her dress was dark green with white and yellow flowers that looked frilly compared to her makeup-free face and frizzy hair. "Don't mind me."

"No," Guy stammered. "Please, help yourself. I'm not going to eat all this." But he had already finished half the plate. "I'm Guy."

"Guy? Like, that's your name?" She laughed a high-pitched, airy laugh that instantly infected Guy. He smiled and held his own laugh back. "Your parents did you dirty there."

Guy looked at her, wondering where her filter was. Had she been drinking already? The bartender set a pink drink with an umbrella in front of her. She stole another chip and took a sip.

"Nice work, Lenny," she cheered him.

"Thank you, Ms. Georgia."

"Georgia?" Guy asked. "Like, the state?"

"Nope." She took another chip. "Like Daniella Georgia. Friends and hot guys call me Dani, so you can stick with Ms. Georgia."

Guy laughed, but he wasn't sure why.

"So, long night or early morning?" Daniella started, and they talked until the bar closed. But they didn't leave.

Guy hadn't had a conversation like this ever. It flowed naturally from topic to topic. He told her he couldn't sleep. She told him she had just flown in from a delayed flight. He told her about his love of finance. She told him about her passion for human rights. He told her about his parents' divorce. She told him about her mom's overdose. By sunrise, Guy hadn't laughed so much ever in his life, and he'd never felt the heat that was building inside him. It wasn't whatever the ball did to make him a talented baseball player, but that was there too. This new feeling burned with the need to feel it again. It was being with someone who wanted to be with him.

"Are you leaving town today?" Guy asked, afraid of the answer.

"No. You?" Daniella said.

Guy shook his head. "Can I take you to dinner tomorrow?" He smiled, looked at his watch. "Sorry, tonight?"

"Nope. I have plans, but how about some ice cream afterward?"

"Well, Ms. Georgia, I need to get a quick sleep before heading off to my game today." Guy slid his room number to her. "Call me when you'd like to get ice cream with some Guy." He winked.

"Game?" she asked.

"Yeah, I play baseball. Got a game this afternoon."

She nodded and took the number. The nachos were long gone, but a smear of cheese was on the note.

"I'll be in touch, and we can discuss a less generic name for you." Daniella stood as Guy left.

In his bed, Guy couldn't sleep. He was too busy replaying the night with Ms. Georgia in his head. The baseball sat by the TV, quietly digesting the night's meal. What did it mean by, *You won't have to feed me as much*? Guy replayed the conversation with the ball in his mind, letting it stomp out the pleasant thoughts of nachos and the coming ice cream, replacing them with the macabre habits success was requiring him to develop. There was always a price for your dreams, and Guy was about to receive the bill.

NINE

Guy was cheered when he arrived in the locker room. The team was exuberant. Energy thrummed through the room, and Guy knew it was coming from him. He was the battery bringing this team to life, and his lucky ball was the charging station.

"Ready for another win?" Guy asked, and raised his hands like he was unsure of tonight's outcome. The locker room roared with laughter. Everyone felt certain losing was impossible.

"Davis said you's was just gettin' warmed up all season," Peters, the shortstop, said. "Next season, how's bout getting warm a bit faster?" They all laughed. Guy joined them.

"Can't rush," Guy said and shrugged.

"Standun! Get in here!" Coach barked.

"Uh oh!" Davis said quietly, and the rest of the team *ooohhh'd* and waggled their fingers at Guy.

Inside the office, Coach's desk was its normal chaotic mess. The older man motioned for Guy to sit, and he did.

"Finance dweebs told me you didn't make the changes I gave you a few nights ago?" Coach said.

Guy nodded slowly, remembering the paperwork he was supposed to do but didn't when the baseball started talking. Then, the next night, Rodriguez threw the papers and his bag into the shower, ruining the paperwork. He hadn't thought about it since then.

"Someone on the team threw my bag in the shower," Guy said. He didn't want to mention Rodriguez and remind anyone of the missing man. "The paperwork got ruined."

"Why didn't you say something?" Coach flung his hands in the air. "Finance said those changes had major returns, well, would have had major returns if they were done."

Guy shrugged. "Guess my stuff shouldn't have gotten thrown in the shower."

Coach bristled at that. "Or you should have told me the paperwork was ruined and get you another copy."

"Wasn't thinking about it." That was the truth. After Rodriguez died, Guy wasn't thinking about anything but getting clean, getting out of there, and hoping it was all a nightmare. But after yesterday's game, he knew it wasn't a nightmare. It was a dream. One he could live in for as long as he did what was necessary.

"Look, you got a few hits, but that ain't carrying your spot on this team. Your other skills are what the owners care about."

"So, being a good ballplayer don't matter to them?" Guy stood up and motioned to the papers on the desk. "It's just the money." He thought the owners should be the next meal for the ball. They're what's wrong with the game. They're chasing money when they should chase the greatness of the game. "Well, I'll make sure they're getting their money and carry the team too. Is there anything else I can do?" Guy smirked as he snatched up some papers from the desk. "They want me to get them coffee too?!"

"Standun!" Coach shouted. "Get a grip! You mouth off in here and that's fine, but talk like that will get you shit-canned faster than you can say *sorry.*" The two men stood leaning over the metal desk to scream in each other's faces. "Take this." Coach shoved a folder in Guy's chest. "Go for a walk, cool down, and after the game, take care of this." Coach stabbed the folder with an arthritic finger. "And for shit's sake, take care of that hand or I'm pulling you out the game!"

Guy felt the fiery blood slipping down his arm then. It was the cut on his palm again; it was steadily leaking. He must have ripped it open when he grabbed the papers, or so he thought. The blood was black and thick, not the deep red of the initial cut. He nodded to Coach and went out the office door. The team stared as he came out of the office holding the folder. Guy rolled his eyes and smiled. His teammates quickly chuckled and went about their preparations for tonight's game.

TEN

At the bottom of the ninth, Guy crushed his fifth home run of the night. The bases were loaded, and the pitcher tried his best to hit Guy with the ball to walk him, but Guy twisted and swung with a thunderous pop that sent the ball out of the park.

Fans screamed his name as he jogged around the bases. The surprise of his hit was shocking to everyone but him, and his smirk told everyone he never had a doubt. He waved and raised a fist to the crowd, accepting their adoration.

"Standun! Standun! Standun!"

As he came home, making the final score 20-5, Pirates win, his team rushed the field and hoisted him up. They carried him as they shouted his name from below, the fans in the stands screamed his name from above, and Guy looked in the crowd to see his father somewhere in the sea of people cheering, but he wasn't there. Ms. Georgia was there, clapping a quiet golf-clap and nodding when their eyes met. Guy kept looking for his dad as the team carried him to the locker room hallway. The hallway where Rodriguez died.

Celebrations continued in the locker room. Guy was invited to drinks and strippers, but he declined, saying he had to get ready for tomorrow's game. Really, what he needed to do was to talk to the ball and find tonight's victim to ensure tomorrow's victory. Would Guy return to the Speedyshop tonight? Was that hunting ground spent? Where else could he go?

Guy looked at the folder in his bag and remembered all the things he had to do tonight. Make the investments. Kill someone. Take Ms. Georgia out to dessert. It was going to be a busy night with no time for celebrations.

ELEVEN

The investments were taken care of first while Guy ate a grilled chicken breast and baked potato from room service. Investments were quick and calming. The numbers, the patterns, the analyst's interpretations of the future all invited him to keep reading, keep learning. As he checked the current markets, Guy saw some interesting opportunities, and diverted some of the money toward them. The owners gave him permission to do such things when the mood struck because he'd yet to be wrong. Guy's hunches often led to triple, even quintuple, returns and were all part of the fun. Sure, he'd lost money before, but it was never for long, and never for someone else. He always tested the waters with his money before putting someone else at risk. Guy couldn't stand the idea of someone being mad at him because of a risk, or anything else.

Time slipped as he shifted funds from here to there and researched three potential investments. Dinner was over. Dessert was coming quickly, and Ms. Georgia should be calling any time. That's when the stitches on the baseball popped and the lips smacked loud with a sucking sound like it was trying to get peanut butter off the roof of its mouth.

"Well, are we going out or eating in tonight?" the ball asked.

"I'm meeting someone. Then we'll go."

"Or you could bring that person here?" The ball's lips spread with a hopeful smile, exposing the viscous red threads under the white covering. Its insides pulsed and wriggled like a growling stomach.

"No!" Guy said. "No. We won't be doing that. We're going back to Speedyshop."

"Yes, yes, we could do that." The ball paused for a long moment, then smacked its lips again. "But see, there's a funny thing about what you're doing." It smiled.

"What's that?" Guy kept his eyes on his laptop as he completed the investments that needed to be done.

"It's never enough."

"I just want to be good at baseball. We're doing it. That's all I need."

The ball laughed loud and throaty as it rolled onto its side. "That's a good one. Yeah, this is all about baseball. Let's pretend that."

"It is." Guy closed his laptop and looked at the ball. His face was stern, jaw clenched, eyes intense.

"Sure. Sure. Whatever you say."

Wanting to change the topic, Guy stood up to get changed for his date with Ms. Georgia. He wasn't sure it was a date, but hoped it was. "You said something about a deal last night? So we don't have to go out and feed you so much?" He stumbled on the word *feed*, as it felt uncomfortable in his mouth. Let's call it what it was, killing people. Murder.

"Yeah, well, see, like I was saying, what you want is never enough. Tomorrow night the cheers won't be as loud, even if they are audibly louder. The victory will sour even though it is just as sweet," the ball said, and rolled back to its upright position, where the popped stitches made a smiling mouth. "But we can fix that. I just need to change my diet. People don't have all the, we'll call it, *nutrition* that I need."

"Then what?" Guy laughed. "You need to eat cats or something?" He wondered why they couldn't have just started there. It wouldn't have been nearly as conflicting for Guy.

"Children." The ball smiled wide and joyful. "They just, mmm! So good!"

Guy choked on vomit. He staggered back to the bed and sat before his knees gave out. The room spun, going dark, lightheaded. "Children? Why?"

"They're delicious."

"But they're so small?" And innocent. And…

"Their body is small, but I don't just eat flesh and bone. Their spiritual energies are so much bigger than adults'. They're like sushi. The rice on the outside is fine, but the bits within, that's where the magic happens!"

Guy picked up the trash can. Chicken, potato, and stomach acid poured out of his mouth. His stomach clenched; another volley of dinner came up. It was bad enough to see the ball eat an adult, but thinking about it eating a kid? Eating their spirit and their body? It was too much, but his retching stopped as another thought hit him hard. Tears burst as the realization formed.

"Dougie Merricko's Children's Network?" Guy thought about it. That started after his slump. That's how Dougie got back on top. He started his home for at-risk youth. There were a lot of kids that *ran away*, but now Guy knew they probably didn't. The trashcan fell from his hands. Puke spilled on his bed, dripping to the floor. His hero did what the ball was asking Guy to do now.

"Look, it's quick, and I can be quieter. You won't even hear them break or crush down. Their bones are a lot softer."

Guy moaned and rolled away from the ball, covering his head with a pillow. He couldn't do this. He wouldn't. How could his hero? How could Dougie Merricko kill the kids he was trying to help? Unless it was never about helping the kids; it was just a farm with easy answers when a trouble kid disappeared.

"Okay, okay. I see this isn't going well. Let's just go get some guy tonight and you'll see what I mean tomorrow. We can revisit this topic. Not like I'm going anywhere."

"What do you mean?" Guy was thinking at that moment of throwing the ball out the window and being done with it. His hand, the one with the cut, itched at the thought.

"When you touched me, we became bonded. We're together until you either get someone else to use me or, well, the other option is really unpleasant."

"What is it?" Guy sat up and stared at the baseball. It wasn't smiling anymore. The idea of leaving Guy was as unpleasant to the ball as killing children was to him.

"We have a bond. It happened as soon as you touched me. That's how I send you the power. If that breaks, then I can't send you anything anymore." The ball sighed long and sad. "But the bond is more than the flesh, just like everything else in my world."

Guy looked at the cut on his hand. The ball nodded.

"Don't lose the bond or all this is lost."

The phone rang, waking Guy to the world outside him and the ball. It was Ms. Georgia; she was ready for dessert now. After asking Guy if he was okay a few times, they agreed to meet at the bar.

"Don't be too late. We have work to do tonight," the ball said as Guy left the room. He nodded and closed the door. Outside, he took a deep breath and tried to leave all the truth of that conversation behind. His palm itched, and he knew wanting to stop wasn't going to be enough. The bond was spirit and flesh, like all things in the baseball's world. Spirit and flesh.

TWELVE

"So, you're some baseball superstar?" Daniella asked.

She and Guy sat in a small restaurant near the hotel. It reminded Guy of a nicer version of California Pizza Kitchen. Their table had a little candle on it that glowed a soft golden light, as the rest of the tables around them were dark. No one was around this late. It would have been romantic if Guy wasn't thinking about killing children. They shared a chocolate pizza, which was a large chocolate cookie with ice cream and hot fudge sauce.

"No. I just got lucky." Guy dismissed the idea. "But you, you're a human rights lawyer? That's amazing." He picked at the piece of the cookie he'd been picking at all night.

"No pivoting," Daniella said. "I saw you today. That didn't look like luck. I'm not a *sportsball* person, but it looked like you are really talented."

Guy shook his head and forced a smile.

"Well, something's bothering me about your baseball abilities… Why didn't you talk more about it last night?" she asked. "You talked a lot about finance, and I thought that's what you did for work. You mentioned, briefly, baseball, and I went to the game. So, who is this *Guy?*" She chuckled and playfully punched his arm.

"Yeah, I'm not sure about a future in baseball." Guy shook his head and smiled.

"You keep hitting like you were tonight and you'll be a major leaguer in no time. If that's what you want?"

Guy didn't know if that was what he wanted. If you would have asked him a few days ago, he would have said yes, no hesitation. Today, he's not sure he's willing to do what it would take. Would being in the majors get his dad to a game? His mom? His head knew the answer, but his heart held out for another outcome.

"I'm not sure what I want anymore," Guy said, and put his fork down. "Excuse me for a moment."

He got up and went to the bathroom. In the mirror, he saw the bags under his eyes puffed up from a pallid face. He wasn't tired from what he'd done today, but from what was to come tonight. The slump proved Dougie tried to stop, tried to let go of what he was building, but couldn't. Could Guy? Could he go back to being hated by his team? Ignored by the fans? Worse, pitied by them so much, they singled him out for an act of kindness. Little Lucy sprang to mind, and how she asked about her ball. Would he have turned on her, have his lucky ball devour her for another grand slam? And how would he explain the sudden surge in ability and the immediate disappearance of the same?

His right palm itched. He pulled back the bandage and saw the scar. It was weeping brown fluid. Black tendrils spidered from the central scar like an infection spreading over his hand. Guy closed the bandage and nodded acceptance.

"Spirit and flesh," he sighed, and returned to the table.

"I'm sorry, Ms. Georgia, but I'm not feeling well. Could we possibly reconnect tomorrow?"

A worried look dug into her sharp features. "We can. I'm sorry if I said something out of turn."

"Oh, no. That's not it. You're not the problem." Guy chuckled. He reached for her hand but pulled back, not wanting to infect her with whatever had him. "I'm just exhausted and still have to run to the store tonight." The image of Speedyshop appeared in his mind, along with the target for tonight's meal. It was the guy who pushed down an old man trying to get gas. The old man stumbled back and fell over the hose connecting his car to the pump. "Seriously, I am sorry and really would like to see you again."

"You've graduated to Daniella." She nodded solemnly and smiled. "And I'd like to see you again too. How about dinner tomorrow night at the hotel? It can't be too late. I have a flight in the morning."

The game tomorrow was early, so this was perfect. They finalized plans, and Guy went back to his room to get the ball. He left for Speedyshop immediately after.

THIRTEEN

Speedyshop was empty. The gang had dispersed without the pisser, who Guy assumed had been their brave leader.

This city had some nice parts, but the seedy places were easy to find. A few streets down from Speedyshop, Guy found a corner with a man leaning against the wall while two women leaned into car windows talking to the drivers. The man watched the women closely with disgust and hunger in his eyes. Guy knew he'd found tonight's meal. In his mind, Guy named the target the Pimp.

The corner was split in two areas by a sharp slice of streetlight. One side, where the Pimp stood, was near a dark alley. The other edge of the corner was the street where two drivers were seeking some company for the night. A few streetlights illuminated the women, but the alley was dark enough to disappear if needed.

"That's your meal." Guy motioned to the pimp watching the women.

"You sure you want to do this?" the ball asked.

"I thought you said we had to."

"I mean, you want to stick with adults? There's—"

"Stop. Yes. We're not doing that." Guy's voice was firm and clear. "That's your dinner."

He got out of the car and held the baseball as he crossed the street. One of the cars drove away as the woman yelled something. The pimp strutted up to her and pulled her back into the alley's shadows. A loud smack came from the darkness, and Guy knew he picked the right person.

The woman ran out of the shadows holding her cheek as Guy passed her. When he crossed out of the streetlight, he felt a sudden cold around him. The night had gone chilly as his eyes adjusted to the dark. Inside, the coldness settled and grew. It numbed Guy's heart and mind. But not his hand; it itched, readying to receive tonight's energy. The man was counting money, his eyes already adjusted to the dark.

Guy looked back. Saw the women were talking, the one comforting the other. He held out the baseball. Before his arm stretched fully, the threads exploded out and broke the man down into the grinding bone-on-bone sounds Guy knew all too well. The meal was quick this time, or perhaps it had always been quick. When it was over, Guy walked out of the shadows, tossing the ball up into the air and catching it as he whistled, "Take Me Out to the Ball Game."

The women watched him go to his car and drive away, still whistling and smiling.

FOURTEEN

The game was early, and fast, and drab. Guy was the same rockstar he had been for the past three games, but the ball was right. It wasn't enough. The crowd chanted his name, but it didn't vibrate in him like it had yesterday. His teammates lifted him up, but not as high as yesterday. In the locker room, everyone cheered, but not as long, not as loud. And Guy's heart sank.

Davis and Peters talked to him about going out partying tonight, but Guy was too busy thinking about the ball to hear them. When he got back to the hotel, the ball would ask for a meal, and if it was like the night before, tomorrow's game would be like today's. *How long until this isn't enough?* One day, only one day, and he could feel the difference.

Back in the hotel room, he looked at the ball. The stitches had popped; the lips were ready to talk. Guy sat on the bed and peeked under the bandage on his hand again. The black lines had stretched a little further, reaching to his fingers and wrapping his thumb. Soon he'd have to bandage the back of his hand too.

"How was the game?" the ball asked, but Guy knew it wanted to laugh. It wanted to prance around and screech: *I told you so!*

Guy didn't answer.

"I know you're conflicted. I get it. Nobody wants to be, you know, doing what you're doing, but I can make it easier for you. Normally, I can't do this kind of thing, but to help you get over the hump, I'll make you a special deal." The ball rolled to the edge of the TV stand to get closer. Guy stayed seated on the edge of the bed.

"Tomorrow, I'll give you a normal game like you've been having, but I'll make sure there are major league recruiters in the audience to see your skills. They'll snap you up so fast you'll forget all about this unpleasantness." The ball nodded, as if agreeing to the terms. "I will need a lot of energy to make that happen, which means…"

"Wait. You can," Guy searched for the word, "*summon* people to the games?" He stood. "Like, you could make someone attend the game?"

"Takes a lot of energy, but yes. I can do that." The ball rolled back. "This can't be an everyday thing though. Like, I don't think you realize how much energy we're talking here, and it's going to put me in a bad way tomorrow, so I might need to eat twice. But yeah, I can bring scouts to the game."

"What about someone who isn't a scout?"

The ball chuckled with a low grumble. "Like I said, I can. If a scout isn't who you want, then who? Just tell me. Let's get dinner and I'll make it happen."

Guy knew who he wanted, but dinnertime had come, and it wasn't for the ball. It was time to meet Daniella.

FIFTEEN

Dinner was silent. Daniella tried to start conversation a few times, but Guy only grunted and shrugged. This date was the pits for both of them, but for different reasons.

"Do you want to just skip dinner?" Daniella asked before their food was ordered. They were on their first glass of wine and Guy hadn't said more than three words to her.

Guy sighed. "Something's on my mind and I'm sucking right now." He shook his head and pushed the menu to the side. "Can I ask you something? And it's probably going to kill dinner, but I don't know."

"Yeah, what's up?" Daniella was happy for anything other than grunting.

"Did you play sports as a kid?"

"Debate team count?" She smiled. That made Guy laugh.

"Yeah, it works for this."

"Okay, yeah. I was on the debate team. You're the Home Run King, I was the Queen of Questions." She laughed again.

"That's just it. I was never the Home Run King. I was okay, but people would never say, *Yeah, that's Guy and he's going pro.*" Guy picked the menu back up, not looking at it, just feeling where the plastic and faux leather edges met. "But my dad always came to my games. And he was so sure I'd be a pro. That's all he ever talked about." Guy shrugged. "When he talked to me."

"My parents came to my debates before my mom died. After that, my dad wasn't much for being out with other people." She shrugged. "It didn't bother me or anything. I get it. There's only so many times you can hear how sorry people are."

"But you went pro." Guy pointed his menu at Daniella. "You are a pro debater. So, did you feel like your parents cared?"

"No." Daniella shook her head. "I was clean and in school. That's what my dad wanted for me. He wouldn't care if I were a janitor at Burger Boi as long as I didn't follow my mom's path."

"I only ever saw my dad at the baseball games. My stepdad never came. I never wanted him around anyway, and my mom did whatever he wanted. They never came to my games. Always went to my stepbrother's games, but never mine."

"Why?"

Guy put the menu down again, held the stem of his wineglass and shrugged. "I asked my dad to stop coming so mom could come, thinking that's what was going on, but she still never came. And after that, my dad stopped coming. I thought if I just played a little better, one of them would want to see me." Guy shook his head.

"Parents suck." She raised her wineglass and clinked it against Guy's. She took a long swig of the white wine and put her glass down. "But look at you now. You're not going to be in the minors for much longer. Someone's going to notice."

"Yeah, someone." Guy took a drink of his wine. Would they notice the late-night drives to the bad parts of town? Would they assume he's just an addict or John and not think of all the people missing whenever he's in town?

The waiter eyed them to see if they were ready to order, but Daniella shook her head slightly, waving him off. She picked up her own menu, pretended to read it and said, "Guy, you're a pretty interesting person. You're more than someone waiting to be seen. Now, we can eat dinner and talk, or I can give you my number and you call me when you're ready to talk." Daniella knew which answer Guy was going to give and began writing her number on a piece of paper.

"If I didn't make it to the Majors, would you still want me to call?"

She slid the note to him. "Of course. Baseball isn't who you are. It's part of you, but not all of you." Daniella got up, kissed Guy on the cheek as he turned the folded note over in his hands. "Talk soon." She walked away and got the bill as she did. Guy turned. He wanted to stop her, wanted her to come back, have dinner, laugh, smile, enjoy life. But he couldn't. Not tonight. His mind was mired in what the baseball said. A decision waited to be made. His dreams for a kid's life, or stay how things are until the hunger for more forced him right back to this place, this decision.

He unfolded the note. It had her email and phone number on it. She signed it, *Dani.*

Guy folded it closed and went back to his room to feed the beast.

SIXTEEN

He didn't talk to the ball as they drove back out to the corner from last night. The ball kept asking him who he'd want to come to the game, but Guy didn't answer.

The night was young. No one was out yet, so Guy went somewhere to take his mind off the questions bubbling there.

On the first night in this town, the bus drove by a gaming center with mini-golf, arcade, and batting cages. He figured the batting cage would be just what he needed to get his mind clear. Just him, a bat, and a ball. No powers. No feeding the lucky ball. At least, not yet.

A glowing blue neon sign flashed *Kirly's Funland* as Guy pulled in the parking lot. White flood lights covered every corner of Funland, turning night into day. Families were playing mini-golf while moody tweens slumped around, pretending not to have fun. Outside the arcade, a cluster of girls were gossiping while a group of boys stood tentatively across the walkway, trying to figure out who would grow the nerve to approach them. Guy stared at the lucky ball as it smiled back at him, patiently waiting for what it knew would happen. He huffed, "Fine." And grabbed the ball as he got out of his car.

At the entrance, he asked for a ticket to the batting cages and the guy behind the counter's face lit up.

"You're Guy the Guillotine!" He smiled. "I saw your game last night!"

"Thanks. Just Guy, please." Guy smiled and shook away the gushing fan's adoration. He pulled out his wallet to get a ticket.

"No, man! I saw you hittin' last night, and it was like, *BAM*!" The cashier pretended to smash a home run, then watch it soar out of the park. "Man! So awesome!"

"Can I just get a batting cage ticket?" Guy pulled out some cash.

"Yeah, man. Can I get a selfie?" The cashier pulled out his phone. "Whoa! Is that your lucky ball or something?"

Guy didn't realize he was holding the ball. The stitches were popped, but the lips hadn't come out. For a moment, Guy wondered if this guy, probably no more than 20, would count as a kid. His hand itched, telling him the answer. *No.*

"Yeah." Guy leaned in.

"Can your ball be in it too?"

"Sure." Guy held up the ball and the guy snapped the picture.

Finally, Guy got his ticket and went to a batting cage at the end of the row. The three batting cages beside him were empty. He didn't want a repeat of the ticket counter. Thinking heavy thoughts required isolation, focus, and being this far away from everyone brought both. Guy didn't notice someone had already noticed him, recognized him, a few batting cages down. The kid smirked as Guy passed, quietly scoffing the Home Run King away.

Helmets hung on the outside of the cage. Guy grabbed the right size for him, grabbed a bat, and went into the cage. The pitching machine was old, with two wheels that spun fast, and a ball loaded from a shoot and fired out based on the speed you set the machine. Guy cranked the machine all the way up.

Squaring up to the plate in the cage, the first ball fired, he swung, he missed. Next ball: same. The next: same. Each ball whiffed into the net behind Guy. Using the last batting cage in the row, with no one else around or watching, was a blessing right now. What would people say if they saw him crush home runs earlier today and now couldn't even hit a straight throw from a pitching machine?

He set the machine's speed to half. But the results were the same. He couldn't hit the ball, and when he did, it was a slight clip, barely enough for a foul ball. Who was he kidding? This was the real Guy Standun. Who would want to see this loser? Not Dani. Not a scout. Not his dad.

"I thought you were good?" the kid who saw him yelled from behind Guy. "Need me to show you how it's done?" The boy was no more than twelve, with the ego of twenty-one. Everything from the kid's clothes to haircut screamed privilege and smug. "I saw your game earlier. Thought you could hit. Guess not." The kid walked into the cage and swaggered up to the plate, shooing Guy away.

The ball chuckled, hungry and happy in Guy's pocket. But it wasn't in his pocket. He was already holding it. Tossing it up and down in his scarred hand. The bandage had fallen off. Black lines wrapped between his fingers and burned in anticipation of this brat as its next meal. Guy knew this kid would grow up to be another Rodriguez, maybe another Peters or Davis. A jerk who made other people's lives suck.

"Go on up there and crank it up!" The boy didn't wear a helmet. He swung his bat and pointed to the pitching machine.

Guy felt his lucky ball quiver, eager to taste the sweetness of youth. He walked to the pitching machine and thought about his dad and all the questions Guy would ask him. Why did he leave? Why didn't he ever come back? What held him away? How did he not know that Guy needed him? But now, Guy was good at baseball. The only thing his dad cared about. The only thing his dad ever talked to him about. He never asked about math, or business school, or any of the million other things Guy had tried in life to find something he was good at. Only baseball mattered. And if he was good, Dad was there. If not, he wasn't.

"Who do you want to be there?" the ball asked when they were out of the brat's earshot. "Just put me in the shooter thing and I'll be done before I hit the net." The ball laughed. "Swagger gives them spice."

"I want to see my dad," Guy said as he held out the ball to the machine. And Guy did want to see him, wanted to see him badly, but one question screamed in his mind as he held out the ball to load into the machine: Why didn't his dad want to see him? Guy made it easy. Every game, tickets were put aside for his dad. He emailed and left voice messages about the game schedule for his dad. Guy offered to pay for plane tickets, hotel rooms, rental cars, anything just for him to come and see a game. Would he ever be good enough for his dad to want to see him?

"But he isn't going to come," Guy said dreamily, staring at the boy. His hand still held the ball.

"No, he will. I'll make him," the ball said, calm and reassuring.

"And that's the problem." Guy turned the wheels up to full speed, the equivalent of a 90-mile-per-hour pitch. "I'll never be good enough for him to want to come." Guy shoved his hand into the spinning wheels, and flesh vomited out of the ball cannon, spraying the brat with the thick black sludge that Guy's blood had become. His bones crunched in the wheels; the lucky ball rolled out of the launcher when Guy's hand couldn't hold it any longer. The pain didn't hit Guy immediately. His body went into shock and collapsed but his hand was still in the wheels, holding him up as they smoked and torqued in jerky motions. A snap twanged in Guy's chest, but he knew it wasn't a muscle, it was the tether that held the ball to him. The ball rolled back to him, resting on his leg. He picked it up with his other hand and stuffed it in his pocket.

"Why?" it asked, broken and confused by its lonely state. "Why did you leave me?"

The feeling came back to Guy's fingers. They burned with the pain radiating up to his forearm and elbow. He didn't want to scream. Instead, his voice grew faint as he answered the ball. "You're right. It'd never be enough. Now I don't have to try. Baseball was never my dream."

Paramedics rushed to the scene as the brat screamed his high-pitched wail. Guy passed out, smiling at the song of that brat's misery. The ball was silent.

SEVENTEEN

"Why are you here?" Guy asked, trying not to sound too rude through the groggy drugs in his system.

"They called me," Dani said. "Found my number in your pocket and didn't have any other contacts."

"Sorry."

"Really? That's what you have? I think me being here clearly tells you a *sorry* isn't necessary. Unless you did this on purpose?" Her question wasn't serious, but was left open for an answer.

"I didn't mean to. Just an accident." He tried to sit up, but only one arm was working. "How bad?"

"You won't be playing baseball anymore," Dani said. "Probably not typing with two hands, either. Your hand is…" Dani took a deep breath. "The doctors said it was beyond repair."

Guy smiled. "Well, that sucks." His expression and tone didn't match his words. "Guess I'll have to find something else."

"Guess so." Dani studied him, wanting to ask questions but leaving it for now. There'd be time. She canceled her flight and was staying in town for a few more days.

"How are the markets?" Guy asked, and looked at the lucky ball sitting in the plastic bag of his belongings on the chair beside him. The stitches were complete except one, which was popped. The lip curled up, and the ball shifted in the bag to nod. Guy nodded back. "Are you going to steal my pudding?" He looked at the cup of chocolate pudding on his tray; it was open with a spoonful missing.

"Didn't think you'd mind." Dani smirked.

"We can share." Guy pushed up again, finding the strength to sit a little taller. Dani handed him a spoon, and they both took a scoop. She told him about the latest market movements and how the three companies he mentioned a few nights ago were bullish. He nodded and savored the pudding, the conversation, the company.

INVENTORY NOTE: 37

Item: 37

Component:

- Dougie Merricko's Lucky Ball

Collection: Private

This baseball supposedly belonged to the legend Dougie Merricko. It clearly has a spirit bound to it, but I do not think it is Dougie's and neither did the previous owner.

I purchased this item from Guy Standun, who used to play AA Minor League Baseball. He purchased this ball at a swap meet. Sounds like he got it from Almun, that jerk, based on the description. Guy sold it to me for $3,000. He stated he wanted it out of the house before his wife had their first child. Baseballs were too tempting for kids to touch, and Guy was right. What kid doesn't want to play with his dad's collectibles? Especially when one of them is a famous baseball.

For me, this item is a perfect addition to my private collection. Guy described how it worked, that it fed on flesh and spiritual energies but granted you the ability to achieve your goals. While I've been mounting an arsenal for the day when I take Drew from Dodslav's realm, I recognize that my skills as a warrior are lacking. With this item, I can change those tides. Yes, it will take a life to do so, and possibly a child's life at that, but have I not done worse in this quest to reunite my family? What is one more life on the ash mound of my sins?

I have the doorway to Dodslav's realm (18). I have the prison for him (29). I have the weapon that can be his undoing (2), and finally I have the ability to accomplish my goals (37). But before storming his gates and taking what I am owed, I will complete our bargain. I am almost there. I can feel it. My collection is almost of the level that Dodslav required.

Mr. Dream, my old acquaintance, told me to escape this world after Drew was claimed by it. Perhaps Dream was right. I have a hard time believing one as foul as he, but Dream never led me astray. In all his sins, he never tried to poison me with his drugs, or his beliefs. After talking to Guy, hearing Dougie Merricko's story and how Guy walked away from it all, I questioned whether I should do the same.

After so many years of preparing, it is impossible to walk away now. I cannot stray. The toys are coming to me easier now. They feel the gravitational pull of my collection and are coming to me. Dodslav will come soon. I need to prepare. A few more toys will do it.

For now, I will prepare this baseball for my collection and seek Mr. Dream for a soul to sacrifice when it is time. We all make choices. We all can be heroes or monsters. I'm not sure which I am anymore.

EPILOGUE

CORNER'S NOTES

Subject, Mr. Neil Lessman, age 52, died of cardiac arrest in his home. EMTs responded to a 911 call in the early morning. Mr. Lessman was in his recliner, hands in his pockets, leaning back relaxed. No sign of struggle. He seemingly died while sleeping in his recliner. Not a bad way to go.

He had a steak dinner with what looked like mashed potatoes in his stomach at his time of death. A good last meal.

Police did not note what he was watching on TV, if anything, in his living room.

The contents of his pockets were standard with one peculiar exception. A small figure made from twisted wire was in his hand at the time of death. I had to pry his hand open to reveal the small orange wire figure. Mr. Lessman squeezed it so hard, the figure's wire ends had punctured his palm. The figure had a tag hanging from it with the number 13 written on it.

My assistant laughed at the site of the figure once it was pulled from Mr. Lessman's hand. He explained the figure was a "Worry Person," and how ironic it was that a Worry Person be in the hand of someone who died of a cardiac arrest. My assistant explained that Worry People are supposed to think about your worries for you while you sleep so that you can awake the next day without those worries. A cute idea, but clearly not functional for someone in Mr. Lessman's health.

In another pocket, we found a note that requested the Worry Person be delivered to DiCoro's Steakhouse if anything were to happen to Mr. Lessman. The card explained they were to be returned to Mr. Lessman's sister, Wendy. We did not have a next of kin on record and will return the Worry Person to Mr. Lessman's sister promptly. On a personal level, I hope his sister Wendy takes the news well. Often family that are estranged can take the news of loss the hardest. Thoughts of what could have been different, what should have been done, lead to heavy guilt and irrational behavior.

We will return the Worry Person right away and then, perhaps, Mr. Lessman can be at peace.

INVENTORY NOTE: 13

Item: 13

Components:

- 1 Worry Person

Collection: Private

Ah, a real treasure! And perhaps right in time, as I can feel Dodslav's eye upon me. I obtained this Worry Person from a mystic in New Orleans by trading that old baseball I had. I've never been sporty, and that baseball wasn't specifically potent, so this trade was perfectly in my favor.

According to the mystic, these Worry People could do a lot more than worry about your problems. They could be containers for your spiritual energy and, if properly treated, your physical body. The mystic said a few drops of blood would do it and gave me the motions and incantation to do the transfer.

This might be just what I need as I prepare to face Dodslav. I don't know how that encounter will go, but too much time has passed. I can't wait any longer. Drew has suffered enough. He needs to be free.

And so do I.

These things in my basement, they eat at me. I feel it. Every day, I'm less. Wearing thin. And nothing is enough. I've collected the worst things, and they eat me while Dodslav watches and waits and laughs at my stupidity. Is he trying to wait until I'm so poisoned that Drew looks like a choir boy?

Mr. Dream was right. I've fallen in with a bad crowd. I keep falling. How much further can I fall? How much further is there?

END NOTE

I cannot express how much fun I had with this collection. What began from a single sign grew into a world that I love and cannot wait to explore further.

We will see Lucy, Nadia, Neil, Dodslav, and many others again, but for now, they need to brew. Their world is still cooking in my mind and needs time to simmer. Fear not, their cook time is low and their strange world is opening further and further in my mind.

I hope you enjoyed *Life Changing Yard Sale*.

Thank you for reading it.

Tim Kulp

7/2/2023

ACKNOWLEDGEMENTS

As always, thank you to Maria for your support, inspiration, and tolerance for the insanity that comes along with "Artist Tim."

Eve, thanks for your constant support and certainty in the path I've chosen. You are the Doubt Slayer, the Eradicator of Negative Self-Talk, and I hope you have an equally amazing cheer squad for your own creative journey.

Thank you Victor for your laughter and frequent reminders that it is important to step away and play. Also, thank you for letting me borrow your toys and I hope you found their condition upon return acceptable. While my stories dwell in dark matters, you always bring the light.

Thanks to Chris and Linda for going on this creative journey with me. I appreciate your listening ear and encouraging words.

Thanks to Sean for the excellent editing work and, most importantly, helping me navigate the sportsball stuff I didn't know.

Thank you to my Early Reader team who provided support and guidance through the early phases of these stories. Your kind words and focused direction helped me unearth the stories I knew were there to be told.

Finally, thank you reader for your time and interest in taking this journey with me. I hope you found it time well spent.

OTHER BOOKS FROM T. KULP

BLOTS

[dis]connection

Library of Lessons & Lies

Early Birds Pay Double

OTHER BOOKS FROM CY BORGMYN

The Light of Enki

Trial of Mirror Mountain

Treasure of Crumbling Cavern

NEWSLETTER SIGNUP

First, I want to express a heartfelt thank you for completing *Life Changing Yard Sale*. I hope you enjoyed the journey as much as I enjoyed crafting it.

I'd love to keep sharing my writing journey with you. If you're interested, I have a newsletter where I share updates about my work, snippets of upcoming stories, and other literary musings.

As a token of appreciation, I'd like to offer you a free story -

Early Birds Pay Double

It's a little something extra just for you.

Sign up for my newsletter at

https://timkulp.com/newsletter-signup.

Thanks again for your support and see you in the next story!

Tim